Praise for *The Shore*

"Runde is an expert at the fastball to the heart. . . . *The Shore* is never sentimental; it is absorbing, lucid, and true. Anyone who has lost someone by inches will recognize the struggle to push through despair and affirm the dogged endurance of love."

—*The New York Times Book Review*

"An emotional family drama that's both devastating and a little bit hilarious, and Runde pulls it off beautifully, with endearing characters and deep insights."

—*Glamour*

"Filled with lovable characters and heart-wrenching moments . . . A powerful story of a family coming together to find comfort in the midst of crisis."

—*Woman's World*

"One of the best beach reads of all time . . . Touching and gripping and life-affirming."

—*Today.com*

"An engrossing escape . . . Runde weaves poetry and poignant questions into her debut. It's an empathy-fueled exploration of caretaking and coming-of-age struggles."

—*NJ Monthly*

"A love story and valentine to the workers who keep the Jersey Shore going."

—The Star-Ledger (Newark)

"The Shore is not read but breathed, as life-affirming, natural, and beautifully flawed as the world and emotions it embodies. Runde is a powerful, masterfully restrained writer, a keen interpreter of the human psyche. . . . A perfect comp for readers who enjoy—and have had their hearts broken and repaired by—Mary Beth Keane, Cara Wall, and Ann Napolitano."

—Bookreporter

"A comforting debut on family and finding resilience in the face of sorrow."

—Booklist

"A heartbreaking family journey; a summer read that is at once sad, hopeful, and ultimately uplifting."

—Library Journal

"Vivid . . . Runde's evocative descriptions conjure the salty humidity of the Jersey Shore. . . . This transportive work successfully captures the dissonance and resilience of family."

—Publishers Weekly

"A heartfelt family drama saturated with a sense of place and the passage of time."

—BookPage

"A sympathetic portrait of a family in crisis . . . Sweet, sad, and surprising."
—*Kirkus Reviews*

"Locals and longtimers are forced to reckon with their families, choices, and secrets."
—*The Millions*

"A novel about how a family contends with hardship and the ways we often flee from the people who know us best, *The Shore* is an emotional and authentic read."
—*Shondaland*

"*The Shore* is a sharp and affecting novel, a wholly original exploration of what it means to love and lose set against a fabulously vibrant backdrop. Runde's writing is both deeply felt and deeply funny—often in the same breath."
—Claire Lombardo, author of *The Most Fun We Ever Had*

"An intimate, tender story about love and loss and moving on. The beautifully flawed, funny, complex Dunne family will stay with you long after the book is finished."
—Tracey Lange, author of *We Are the Brennans*

"*The Shore* was a joy to read. I loved the Dunnes from page one, and Katie Runde has so much to say about love and grief and growing up and the way we sometimes manage to learn who we are when we're in the midst of losing the person we love most."
—Rachel Beanland, author of *Florence Adler Swims Forever*

"How can a novel be simultaneously a delicious page-turner that transports the reader to warm seaside days while also being a deft, deep meditation on illness, grief, and loss? *The Shore* is both, and I wept over this tender family story of mother, father, [and] daughters interwoven with fine renderings of a summer town, a summer economy, and the people who make it go and who still call it home when the tourists leave. This is a lovely, expansive look at the hard work of caregiving, saying good-bye, and keeping on."

—Lydia Kiesling, author of
The Golden State

"A stunning anatomy of the varieties of sorrow and consolation, with a brilliant understanding of the ways different generations find unexpected common ground. *The Shore* takes a place bursting with colorful characters and its own idiosyncratic anthropology and makes it intimately familiar. Runde perfectly captures the fraught expressions of feeling between parents and children on the raucous eve of their independence, and she nails the way everyday longings, fears, and joys don't always scurry from life's stage when the monster of grief descends from the rafters. The reader, under the spell of Runde's superb storytelling, never wants to leave this family behind."

—Matthew Thomas, author of
We Are Not Ourselves

"Runde's gift is a poetry of things: coffee cups and casseroles rush in to break your heart, expressing the truths about the anguish of love and loss that would melt like cotton candy into cliche if you tried to say them directly. *The Shore* is about the ugly, hard parts of loving someone, about the vacation town once the vacation is over, the awkwardness of growing up and the un-fun wisdom you learn to hold onto instead of push away. Tender, heartfelt, and infinitely readable."

—Rufi Thorpe, author of *The Knockout Queen*

"*The Shore* is everything I crave in a novel: characters who become like family, gorgeous prose, and a setting so vivid, you can almost smell the ocean and hear the boardwalk games. Katie Runde is a gifted writer and shows us how to bear the unimaginable in these pages. Readers will hate to leave Seaside behind."

—Ethan Joella, author of *A Little Hope*

THE
SHORE

— A Novel —

Katie Runde

Scribner

New York   London   Toronto   Sydney   New Delhi

Scribner
An Imprint of Simon & Schuster, Inc.
1230 Avenue of the Americas
New York, NY 10020

First Scribner trade paperback edition May 2023

For information about special discounts for bulk purchases, please contact Simon & Schuster Special Sales at 1-866-506-1949 or business@simonandschuster.com.

The Simon & Schuster Speakers Bureau can bring authors to your live event. For more information or to book an event, contact the Simon & Schuster Speakers Bureau at 1-866-248-3049 or visit our website at www.simonspeakers.com.

Interior design by Wendy Blum

Manufactured in the United States of America

1 3 5 7 9 10 8 6 4 2

Library of Congress Cataloging-in-Publication Data has been applied for.

ISBN 978-1-9821-8017-1
ISBN 978-1-9821-8018-8 (pbk)
ISBN 978-1-9821-8019-5 (ebook)

For my mom and my sister

Your blessings and your curses often come in the same package.

—Bruce Springsteen, "Born to Run"

THE
SHORE

Brian

He writes one word on each Post-it: *ember, embark, embolize, embarrass, empathy*. With each scribble, he tries to explain the vague feeling that something is not the same. He thinks he's translating; he thinks he's making it easier this way. The scribbled words come in a series like this, or scattered, but always one at a time.

He hides some, and hands others to his wife, Margot. When he *talks* to Margot, and to his daughters, the sentences are still whole ideas, complete structures of subjects and verbs, but they come out silly, mean, or wild. He can never say why he loves them or tell a story about a day they drove to the inlet together; he can only demand, decimate, and declare. He can tell them in a hundred ways, *NOW*, or *NO*, or *NEVER*, but he can't explain his fear or his gratitude, or ask if they're okay.

There's another voice, somewhere: a silent, buried layer, apart from the chaos and compulsion. This other voice would say so much, if it had a way through.

Part I

CHAPTER ONE

Liz

Gabe appeared as Liz was zipping her backpack to leave, as he had every evening this week on his way home. She heaved the last umbrella into the box at Sun and Shade Rentals and snapped the combination lock shut. Gabe set a greasy pizza box down on a towel and passed Liz a thermos. She took a long pull and tasted the familiar sourness of lemonade with the surprise bitterness of gin.

"Cheers, boss," he said, folding a slice and filling his mouth, grease dripping onto the towel. "Oh, and can I have next week off?" Carl had just promoted her to assistant manager, which meant an extra dollar an hour.

"Can I fire you now? I think I can fire you," she said, taking her own slice from the box. "Except you brought me boozy lemonade and pizza, so I won't. And thanks." Gabe was nineteen, a year and a half older than Liz, though his fake ID said he was twenty-three. She couldn't believe that thing worked; the guy in the ID picture had a man bun and sunken gray eyes, and looked nothing like Gabe with his short, salt-dried curls and sunburn.

Liz knew what the routine would be at home: another casserole dropped off by one of her mom Margot's friends. Margot accepted their casseroles but ignored their texts and invitations to come to book club or yoga class. She hurried by them in the grocery store and declined their phone calls. They always lingered on the porch, reminded Margot of the particular date of an event she was welcome to join, and sighed before taking their clean dishes back and climbing into their minivans.

Liz and her younger sister, Evy, called the zitis and taco bakes they ate the Inevitable Death Casseroles, or IDCs, but only to each other. In front of their mother, they agreed they were tasty, and they scribbled thank-you notes for even the blandest cream-of-chicken-doused things. Their dad had been dying for eight months, of a brain tumor that turned him obsessive, insistent, or infantile from one moment to the next. They didn't know if he'd act like this for another few weeks or a few months before the tumor spread, but they knew they had enough IDCs to get them through the end of July, maybe all the way through August.

Liz, Evy, and their mom took turns with him now, not at a bedside yet but out in the world where all the same rules of how to behave still applied, even if he couldn't follow them anymore. For Liz, tonight felt stolen, and as necessary as a fresh gulp of air.

She texted Evy three pizza emojis and told her she would be late and to enjoy the IDC without her. Evy would get to stay out with her friends tomorrow, she would get her own stolen summer night while Liz took a turn at home. Evy texted three middle fingers back, then a thumbs-up and a heart.

Margot

You needed every minute before check-in time on Saturdays to get all the grime and stray hairs out of the bathroom drains, to stock the towels and wipe down the countertops, to transform each rental property from cluttered and messy to tidy and welcoming. All the E&E Rentals houses were fully booked this month, and today Margot had bleached the bathrooms, changed the sheets, and swept up the sand in four of their beach cottages. Her cleaning staff was scattered across town doing the same, texting her last-minute questions about loose screws and leaky faucets.

Margot mouthed, *Thank you, Jimmy,* when he dropped Brian at the house after bringing him along to Home Depot so she could clean without interruption. Jimmy was Brian's old surfing buddy. He always disappeared for somewhere warmer in the off-season for weeks at a time, then returned for as many hours of work as he wanted. He had a shaved head and the lined, weather-worn skin of a man in his forties who'd spent decades in the sun, but the bright eyes of someone unencumbered by any real responsibility.

When Jimmy had left for Rincón last fall, Brian was fine; when Jimmy came back in April for preseason maintenance, Brian had called him a *goddamn pussy piece of shit* before Margot had a chance to tell him about the tumor disrupting Brian's language, his judgment, his sense of what was okay to say out loud. That day, Jimmy's face had fallen flat; he'd slow-nodded and made sense of it, worked fifty hours for them on a deck project, and then drove across the country again back to Santa Cruz. When Margot didn't hear from him, she figured he was gone for good, until his truck rattled into their driveway again in May.

"Life moves pretty fast sometimes, so look around the bend before it turns," Brian said now as they entered the rental, half-remembering the *Ferris Bueller* quote before he wandered away from Margot and Jimmy.

"Right, sure does," Margot said. Brian sat down at the kitchen table with his back to them.

"He was into a lot of *Karate Kid*, little *Point Break* today," Jimmy said. He quoted old movies to distract Brian and keep him calm, though that never worked when Margot tried it. Maybe Brian got a contact high from the seeped-in weed smell of Jimmy's van.

"Okay, well, *vaya con Dios*, Marg."

"Is that—um?"

"Johnny Utah?" He slapped his forehead with the palm of his hand, like, *who doesn't know every word of a nearly thirty-year-old surfer movie, unbelievable!*

"Oh, riiight," Margot said. She handed him three Coronas the renters had left in the fridge. "Well, really. Thank you."

"Take it easy, man," Jimmy said to Brian as he headed out the door. "You're one radical son-of-a-bitch!" He looked at Margot, like, *how about that one?* But she was already starting to work through her to-do list. She hid ant traps in the corners and set the thermostats, then packed up the laundry, the dirty mop, the half-full bottles of sunblock, the paperbacks, the Soft Scrub, the screwdrivers.

She tossed an *In Touch* magazine into the tote bag for Liz and Evy, who had stared at her in wide-eyed worry when they realized they'd both been scheduled for their other boardwalk jobs during the week's busy turnover time. Margot had demanded, "How did this happen?" as they walked out the door this morning.

She knew she snapped at them too much, and before they rolled their eyes and *whatevered* her, she could tell it stung. She knew she should take a beat before criticizing them, resist the easy, stream-of-consciousness rants her own mother had always defaulted to. She knew yelling at them was lazy and obvious and the opposite of what she intended. Snapping was something that mean, manipulative moms did to their daughters, not her. When had she given in to this way of mothering? How many times could you hiss, "How did this happen?" to your daughters before you did permanent damage?

Margot and her girls used to play Scrabble together some Saturday nights, for Christ's sake, before Brian got sick. She would study her tiles and listen to the girls' gossip and to their silence. She would pay attention when their sarcasm turned softer and when they trailed off, naming their worries and their wins. What another nasty trick of this tumor, to change *her* as much as it had changed Brian.

"Hey, if you'd rather go make the taffy at Sal's, I'll stay with Dad," Evy had joked once on her way to work, but the truth was, Margot thought the idea of being by herself for a few hours, tying little white paper bags with neat bows to display in the candy shop window, sounded pretty great.

The front door slammed and Margot froze.

Brian went outside.

Her body responded the way it always did now whenever she had to chase him, find him, argue with him, or drag him away from chaos he'd caused. She ran after him, breathing heavily in the humid July air.

"Hey!" she shouted. "We have the car, right there. Come back, we have to get all this stuff home." But he didn't stop or turn around. He never did. She smelled the bleach and sweat on herself and said again weakly, "Come back, Brian."

He turned toward her momentarily, but then ran back toward the street, where he squeezed between two parked cars and stuck his arm straight ahead, as if that would stop a distracted driver from hitting him. He paused in the center of the street with his arm out, like a Heisman Trophy statue, like a lunatic. His whole body had changed, from athletic and agile, strong from working and running and surfing, into someone hunched, swollen, and clumsy. As if in response to his body going softer, her own body had switched into survival mode, become leaner, always ready. When her dark, gray-streaked hair thinned, she got a quick, blunt bob at the Supercuts before she grocery-shopped, not even bothering to have them blow it dry. Today she'd tied it up and let it down again, all unkempt and wild.

A van slammed on its brakes and then gunned it around Brian, as he strode back to the sidewalk, where his shoulder grazed a splintered telephone pole. Margot noticed he was wearing an old ripped T-shirt from the New Year's Eve 5K, when they'd all layered up and run together wearing glow necklaces. Their friend Robbie had handed out cheap champagne to the runners outside the Buccaneer bar, as the fireworks exploded at midnight above the winter-darkened pier. Brian had lost a bet with Robbie when he didn't run a personal best, and plunged into the frigid ocean after the race, while the girls shrieked on the cold beach and the Boulevard dance clubs shot spotlights into the sky.

Margot still couldn't convince him to get in the car. She gave up and said, "Fine, you want to walk, we'll walk," as he spat on a parked car's windshield. Ten minutes later they were standing on their own front step, but she remembered her keys were still in the ignition four blocks away and had to drag him back there again.

Evy

Evy twisted a hundred saltwater taffies closed. Then she upsold a family a half dozen caramel apples, and stood outside Sal's Sweets with the sample tray for two hours before she took her break. She sat on a box in the storage room, sipped a warm LaCroix, and checked each of her social media accounts, posting one of the thirty shots she'd taken of the new color she'd dyed her hair, a more-dramatic mahogany red, and the time-lapse makeup video she'd made where she did her eyes in shimmery-rose-gold shadow and black eyeliner. She posted one more selfie from work, with her hair under the pink Sal's Sweets baseball cap, and captioned it CAN-DYLAND. Then she went to a site called GBM Wives, "*a supportive forum for spouses of glioblastoma multiforme patients.*"

Evy had discovered that her mom had an account on this site one day last fall, when she was looking to intercept an email from her tenth-grade history teacher, early on in her dad's diagnosis. Here in the GBM Wives forum, her mom wasn't afraid of real talk. She was still funny and gave her full attention; here she didn't zone out or get distracted or snap or run down to-do lists instead of asking if her daughters were okay.

When Evy finally joined in the discussion, she chose the username Pamplemousse7, after her favorite LaCroix flavor. She gave vague details about her made-up self and her situation, saying she lived "in the suburbs," and had "a few kids."

It wasn't her first time adopting an online persona. At sixteen, she'd had years of practice making fake accounts; she and her friends messed around with dating app profiles, swapping in different stock photos to see what would happen. She had two Reddit usernames, one to talk back to some QAnon maniacs, and another to ask some stuff about sex after her friend Hailey showed them all a Pornhub video that evoked follow-up questions she had been too embarrassed to ask anyone she knew.

At first Pamplemousse7 posted links to articles and said some generic encouraging words to the other ladies like, *Everything will be ok, xoxo!* But then she became braver, feeling that these women were the same as her. They really *got* all the stories of her "husband's" temper tantrums and fist-flailing tirades in the middle of the Wawa coffee station. When she tried to tell most of her real friends about those, they blank-stared back at her until she changed the subject.

Why spy on her mom this way, why sneak into an online support group and invent a username to talk to her and to strangers twenty-five years older than Evy? Maybe it was because between the screen and the keys, she got brave, she got an extra second to think, she could say what she needed to say. Maybe it was because it felt cruel to call her mom out in real time when Margot forgot what she was saying midsentence, or because the week in October her dad got sick, her mom had stopped wearing makeup or remembering to turn off the TV when she left the house. Maybe it was because her mom's temper was impossible to figure out. She would ignore six missed curfews in a row or weeks of unfolded laundry without so much as an annoyed reminder, and then let loose with shrill, wall-vibrating bouts of accusations and catalogues of Evy's wrongs when she walked in three minutes late.

It wasn't just her temper. When she sat on the couch, Margot never sank all the way into the cushions, leaning her spine ten degrees forward and holding her breath, and then letting it out like she was blowing through a straw.

In almost every tragic story Evy had been told as a child, *both* parents died before the movie or book even started, leaving their children orphans in Depression-era New York City to beg on street corners or to sing and dance about the hard-knock life. She had no buried back catalogue of big-budget musical lessons to tell her how to deal with two parents who were technically *still here* but definitely not themselves. In the GBM Wives forum, Evy tried to gather evidence that the mom she missed might still be in there somewhere.

When she wrote her posts, Evy's fingers flew across the keys, and she felt a frenzied need to get it all out. She wrote in rules or rants, lists or warnings; she wrote long, angry, disguised stories and one-line questions. When she posted as Pamplemousse7, Evy felt a lightening in her shoulders and a loosening of the muscles that wrapped around her spine.

Almost every day before her shift at Sal's Sweets, Evy wrote or responded to posts by women wondering whether it was too late to trade in their husband's brain tumor for some malady that made him shit himself or weakened his heart instead.

She often thought back to those first few weeks her dad was not himself. She was sure it would have helped if someone had given them all a heads-up. There were things she would have wanted to know, things she'd already figured out:

If you're new to this group and you want to know how it's gonna be, I'll tell you. I'm not being mean, I'm being real. Honestly I wish someone had told me all this.

If you don't want to know then skip this post and go on Pinterest instead, look at macramé wall hangings or muffins! Still here? Then you must want to know:

Everything he does from now on goes into these four categories: Toddler, Zombie, Jerk, Rain Man. He's these people now.

Go ahead and get your Googling out of the way: glioblastoma multiforme brain tumor. Click click, scroll scroll, go ahead: weedy tentacles are gonna keep growing in his brain, even after they cut out the big pieces and poison and radiate the rest. They're dulling and then obliterating, in our case, the quote-unquote social and emotional function, which means everything important about him, all the humor and patience and normalness. Byeeee! Yours might be different though—depends where the thing decides to burrow in—yours might be quote-unquote motor skills, speech, anything a brain does!

Whatever you do to try to stop it is just the medical version of cheering for the band at the end of a concert, stomping your feet, screaming and yelling for another encore.

Ugh, right?

It's worth it, isn't it, to buy a few more months even if he isn't himself, even if he can only see in tunnels and splotches? But IS it all worth it, if Toddler Zombie Jerk Rain Man mind-fucks everyone around him by forcing them to try to guess what kind of person will show up each day? If it's a person parading around who looks like your husband but who's acting like an agitated stranger you wouldn't want to sit next to on a bus? If it means taking care of a person who is not a person you know? Even then?

Done Googling? Good.

Evy felt a little psychic and a little wild when she typed as Pamplemousse7, but she also felt free and wise, relieved and connected to these women. Margot responded to all the other Wives' posts, and today she responded to Pamplemousse7 with this message:

Thank you for sharing this—maybe it's ok to think of him as all these different people. You have to make categories, don't you, make some order out of the chaos, wake up to a stranger and say to yourself, I don't know what to do, so I put his medals from all the 5Ks and marathons in a bin in the garage.

Liz

"Rough crowd today," Liz told Gabe, taking another sip. "But I still love this job."

She'd applied for a job at Sun and Shade because it was outside, because you worked mostly alone, and because the shifts didn't go until after midnight like they did at the soft-serve stands and arcades; Liz and Evy still worked a lot of mornings at E&E Rentals, helping their mom with turnovers, but Sun and Shade's hours were more regular, and the pay was better. Her parents swore they put half the girls' E&E wages into a college fund, but she knew from what she overheard that they had a lot of debt, and that renovations on the rental houses were expensive. She wanted to make some more money of her own.

"What's your favorite thing about Sun and Shade?" Gabe asked. He'd started there the same week she did. After they'd worked together at Sumner Avenue on Fourth of July, he started bringing her coconut iced coffees and waiting around for her after their shifts. He had brought her boozy lemonade after work once before, but she'd had to go home after a few sips to help her mom. "You like it more when creeps hit on you, or when a seagull takes a big crap on an umbrella and you have to clean it up?"

She recognized this sarcasm, this dismissive teasing, this addicting, frenetic attention, because she had studied the patterns of how straight boys did this to girls day after day at school. You couldn't escape it in the fluorescent-lit hallways or on the bleachers at assemblies, the way the girls responded with high-pitched airy *come ons* and *shut uuuups*.

"Yeah, I know, it's so crazy," Liz said, "how those guys know yelling down at me from the boardwalk that they like my ass is exactly the way to get a date with me."

"Is that all a guy has to do?" Gabe asked, fake-serious, typing into his phone. "Cool, yeah, I'm noting that here. Okay."

She reached over and tried to swat his phone out of his hand; then he flipped his screen around and showed her what he'd typed, gibberish he read out loud: "YELL. ABOUT. ASS. Got it," he said, and Liz laughed.

She was starting to understand that life was too short to be a tiny, tight-lipped version of yourself. But the rules the *shut uuuuup* girls followed were still the ones she knew best, even if she hated them; you had to rearrange the pieces of what you already knew before you went inventing new ones for yourself.

"Don't stop there," Liz said. "There are sooooo many things you can yell across the boardwalk to make girls fall in love with you."

All summer she'd teased him back, for arriving late to work, for living with his mom in a town a few miles over the bridge. She accused him of pretending he'd made up all the cool Brooklyn stories about his band and suggested he wasn't really going back there in the fall, and she made jokes about him mooching off his aunt, who let him stay for free in her Seaside house whenever she didn't have any renters.

"You want to add that hot tip to your notes too?" she asked. "I'll wait."

He took a long drink from the thermos, then passed it to Liz. Her friend Sonia thought for a while that Liz had made Gabe up. **Sure, tattooed Brooklyn band guy shows up right when I leave**, Sonia had texted. **Oh yeah, there's one of those guys here too, he's my grandma's neighbor, we hang out all the time.** Sonia was at her grandmother's house in Florida until August, forced into playing bridge on Beverley's screen porch instead of Cloud Campaign II on Xbox or Frisbee on the beach with Liz. It wasn't the same, texting Sonia with ten exclamation points the first time Gabe brought her coffee, or texting **my dad was so tough** today almost every day, as it would have been flinging herself onto Sonia's bed and telling her everything, but it was their only option.

"You know what else works great?" Gabe asked. "You find some girls minding their own business, and you tell those girls to *smile*."

Liz was used to ignoring those creepy *smile* guys on the boardwalk. She was used to the constant carnival in this town from May through September, to hearing the sounds of smashing bottles and exploding fireworks through her bedroom window. She knew the deep, tired quiet that descended after Labor Day, the way a town could be two different kinds of places.

"Yes, we *act* like we hate it," Liz said. "But we love random men telling us to smile, we're always forgetting what to do with our faces. Shhh, don't tell any other girls I said that."

"Too late, I already texted all of them."

In Gabe's social media posts, there were pictures of girls from his other life, hauling amps onto stages, standing in front of paintings in museums, balancing a round of beers in their hands, staring out the windows on long train rides. She didn't know if they were his friends, or if they'd been more than friends. She wondered what simple, generous gestures he had made for them, like he had for her.

"Hey, come here," he said, angling his phone to get both their faces, and the lit-up rides on the pier behind them, into the frame for a selfie. He would post it later, along with a photo of a new tattoo he'd gotten this summer on his forearm, of Odysseus tied to his mast. "Okay," he said, "now make whatever kind of face you want."

Margot

While the casserole cooked, Margot poured a glass of wine and worked through the payroll, the insurance, the cleaning crew's schedule, the emails; she set up some Google ads and cross-listed the open August dates on Airbnb; she assured a fancy family that their rental was in the town NEXT to the one where *Jersey Shore* had been filmed and that the wildest thing on their street would be the ding of a bicycle bell. She replied-all to a group of construction guys from Bayonne and said their condo WAS in wilder Seaside Heights, right next to the clubs, a perfect location for them. She read posts from the GBM Wives forum before returning to her inbox full of E&E renters' constant questions.

She did not return texts from the Seaside moms' group chat about the next book club or to individual messages from any of them (*thinking of you, are you around tomorrow for me to drop off a lasagna?*). She had returned texts and attended book club through December, when the women had all complained about the Christmas gifts their husbands had bought them, between talking about *The Five Love Languages*. "Brian is such a words-of-affirmation," she said, "and I'm definitely an acts-of-service," because everyone else had explained what their love language was and looked at her expectantly. "He's doing really, really well," she assured them. The head nods and silence lingered until she realized it was her job to change the subject, because it would be rude if any of them did.

Brian was in the shower, one activity he would consistently agree to without a fight. Tom Petty singing *it's good to be king* echoed in the bathroom on repeat, so Margot knew he would be in there awhile. She felt the light shift to the sunset glow-up and closed her laptop, slipping outside with her wine.

A small crowd gathered along the edge of the bay to wait for the late-evening sun to slip below the bridge, ready for the shared ritual, staring west until the last sliver of red disappeared and left the sky bereft. Margot let herself remember her life with Brian, before, but only in controlled doses, testing out her tolerance for the ache each time.

Last summer, Brian had been here with her, absorbing every subtle shift in the warm bleeding-out light, saying, *They all have to go home and we get to stay right here.*

They'd grown up in neighboring towns beyond that bridge, though they hadn't met until they got jobs after their high school graduations at the Cranky Crab, a fish restaurant here on the barrier island with nets and rusty traps decorating the walls. Their hometowns were close enough that a ten-mile drive to the restaurant was worth it for the summer-crowd tips, but far enough away that a lot of people who lived there went years without seeing the ocean.

A fleet of Sunfish traced paths along the water's surface, their sails against the airbrushed sky. The breeze shifted, and the wind chimes outside the garage apartment behind their house played their metallic, dissonant song. They used that apartment now as an office for E&E Rentals, but it had been their very first rental property. Brian taught high school economics and history then, and Margot taught fourth grade; their salaries and their second jobs at the Buccaneer paid the mortgage on their own bungalow but didn't leave any extra, so they spent two hundred dollars on a gallon of seafoam-blue paint, a white duvet, fresh towels, a yard sale watercolor of waves, and secondhand brass lamps they scrubbed clean. Then they listed the apartment. If it hadn't rented, they would have had to move to one of the anonymous 1960s split-levels on the other side of the bridge, or keep working every weekend and summer at the Buccaneer forever.

They were trying for their first baby then, and they hoped income from the rental would help money feel less tight. One winter morning in her first trimester, Margot had miscarried, the red-black clot sliding out of her in a faculty lounge bathroom stall, her back and belly aching in its absence. When Brian arrived home that evening, he sat on the edge of their bed. He brought her a lemon tea and her softest pajamas and turned on a *Friends* rerun, clenching his eyes shut until she melted into him and wept. Margot sweated and cried and slept the next day; when she awoke, she craved some distraction, some temporary focus on an ambition that did not have to do with her body or its failure or the bright-cheeked children she would return to teach. She thought she could distract herself with lesson plans, but her notes blurred and smudged as she stared at the same page for fifteen minutes. Her tea went cold. When her friend Deborah Ellsworth called, Margot was digging her dull pencil into the cardboard cover of her plan book.

Deborah wasn't the kind of friend Margot would tell about a miscarriage. She was a real estate agent in town who had referred a few renters to them. "When I heard about this, I immediately thought of you," she said. "How would you and Brian feel about being property managers?" Deborah's client Carol wanted to rent out her oceanfront Victorian for a few seasons before she sold it. She told Margot how much Carol was offering to pay. "And there's a bonus if you rent it the whole season."

"Definitely, yes," Margot answered, knocking her tea over onto her lesson plans. The idea of spending time in that house and finding people to stay there wouldn't feel like work in the same way Buccaneer bar shifts did. She got excited imagining the geraniums and impatiens she would plant in pots on the Victorian's front steps, imagining a family arriving and reading the welcome note she'd leave them.

Managing the Victorian, they had learned to anticipate the whims and demands of wealthier clients, to respond to their expectations for convenience and attention. They provided French-roasted coffee and fresh flowers, a pitcher of premixed cocktails made with high-end gin, and a hand-drawn map of their favorite spots for fish tacos and pizza and the only fancy restaurant on the island. They made themselves exactly as available as each family's subtle cues told them was necessary. The renters called them with small questions, like where to make a dinner reservation or sign up for a surf lesson, and for strange requests, like whether they knew a place for a secret girlfriend to stay nearby (their garage apartment rental, on a rare vacant night!) or for help finding a lost antique bracelet in the sand.

They'd built their bungalow empire one fixer-upper at a time, one signed sheaf of mortgage papers at a time, one magic-sounding listing and booked-up summer at a time, until they owned dozens of properties. They'd had Elizabeth, then Evelyn eighteen months later. They named the company E&E, LLC, one E for each of their girls, and their red signs appeared all over two towns until they were successful enough to quit their teaching jobs.

Whenever Margot had said it was too much, whenever she was overwhelmed by in-progress projects or unbooked dates, Brian would slow her down and pick one thing they could do right away, to kickstart the momentum that any project took on once it was begun. When a problem seemed too big or complicated, his shorthand for reminding her was to say *garage apartment*.

They were finally back in the black, after Hurricane Sandy's destruction seven years before had drowned everything in foamy brackish water. E&E Rentals had been featured on cable news on the two-year anniversary of the storm. The producers had juxtaposed the footage of Margot and Brian showing off their raised and renovated properties with clips of the sunken Star Jet roller coaster. The reporter had to talk to them separately because of how often they interrupted each other's versions of their rebuilding story.

The music in the bathroom shut off, and then there was Brian, standing on the porch with a dish towel half covering his penis. He sat down on a deck chair and said, "There's bird shit on the pergola," handing Margot another Post-it with the word *embark* scribbled on it. This was the third penis thing this week. And he was obsessed with writing words that started with *em* on his Post-its: *ember, embark, embolize, embarrass, empathy.* She found them everywhere: in his pockets, stuck to the TV screen, inside paperbacks. This morning, she'd found one that said *empty* staring back at her from the bathroom mirror.

"Somebody ought to do something about that bird shit," Margot said. Running E&E alone was unsustainable. Everything they had built together didn't feel like a proud fought-for empire anymore but a crumbling, unwieldy thing. The renovations, the repairs, the mortgage payments, the money hemorrhaging then accumulating again, the marketing, and the maintaining were drowning her.

E&E had been a shared dream, a long conversation, an idea borne of necessity and naïveté. Before they were old enough to buy beer, Brian had asked her to move to the shore with him, in an email from a thousand miles away. He'd bought her an emerald engagement ring years before he gave it to her. Then Brian had strapped their babies to his chest and hummed *you are my sunshine* while he replaced faucets and rusty screws.

E&E, and her life with Brian, was inseparable from Seaside. Carrying the half-formed grief for the versions of him who had already Irish-exited had changed her, stolen her heart and grit, transformed the pride and hustle she used to feel running E&E into dread and an attempt at good enough.

Coexisting with a stranger was not possible without imagining escape. When he died, she would sell off every bungalow, and she would take the girls to live somewhere the sun set below a mountain instead of a bridge, somewhere safe from offshore storms, somewhere every wind shift, every gull caw, every bright-red E&E sign, would not remind her of what she'd lost, again and again.

CHAPTER TWO

Evy

Evy had fifteen minutes left in her shift at Sal's when Hailey called in sick. There was always a little lull around dinnertime, and the place was a wreck from the last rush, the counters covered in sugar, the floor in need of a sweep, all the rainbow candy displays depleted.

"Evy, can you stay an extra hour while I call around?" her manager, Irene, asked, disappearing into the back room to call in someone else for Hailey's shift. "And tell your friend if she pulls this shit again, she's fired."

Irene popped her head back out to hand Evy her own cell phone, usually relegated to a box in the back unless you were on break. "Here, I don't care if you text between customers, since you're staying late. Don't get used to it. Sweep the floor, but don't worry about restocking."

Evy texted her mom to say she'd be another hour, then scrolled through the GBM Wives forum updates since her last break, glancing up whenever a customer appeared at the register. She finished the post she'd started, laying out the rules for the uninitiated GBM Wives:

> *Rain Man is all about patterns and routines. He likes to repeat motions, words, ideas, and phrases. He doesn't like when you*

make him change what he's doing, even if he's been walking laps around the block for forever, or reciting the "measured out his life with coffee spoons" poem he memorized thirty years ago so loud while you go and return something to Kohl's.

When he paces, rants, mutters, fidgets, counts? Go along with it, count with him, nod like you understand his plans, listen and try to be patient, keep an eye on it so it doesn't get out of hand.

Toddler is trickier: there will be tantrums, sudden eruptions, and moods that swing from contentment to wild-eyed anger over tiny things that don't matter. Bouts of weeping take over his sarcastic, stoic toughness. To get through to Toddler, use bribes, use a stern voice. That voice will feel like it doesn't belong to you, but just do it anyway.

Just do it anyway is a good rule in general, actually. Put that in your notes app or something so you don't forget it. Toddler is impulsive but not quite in the way a drunk adult is. You'll need to summon some toughness, convince yourself you mean business, take your best guess at when to give in.

You'll need to get over caring about anyone staring at you in public, get used to changing plans really quick, and pick either a reassuring mantra or a curse that's not a curse that sounds funny, like "crap on a cracker!" to get you through. Don't start sentences with "don't" . . . he will do whatever he wants, whenever he wants.

Jerk has a look in his eye, or actually something missing when you look in his eye, an absence that is alarming, a vacant dullness that makes you want to look away. You won't be able to unhear the things that come out of Jerk's mouth the way you can't unspill red wine from a white rug. Jerk has no filter, no conscience—it all comes out.

*He breaks the rules that even terrible regular people follow.
He's horny, hungry, and angry. All at once. It's not like when you
have a virus you can't get another virus at the same time. He
can Jerk multitask. Impulse hijacks the system. Nasty one-liners
you'd be shocked to hear from a drunken sociopath will replace
his encouraging, curious way of talking. He's the center of a
universe conspiring against him. His insults are immature, like
attempts at connection, but they're all wrong, backward, upside
down, in a language no one understands.*

*Jerk will be the hardest to forget, impossible to forgive even
if you watch a lot of old Oprah videos saying that thing she says
about how not forgiving is drinking your own poison. Jerk can
obliterate the places you were trying so hard to keep safe and
protected. If you let him. Don't let him.*

*Zombie happens in the few minutes after he drinks a couple
beers when he's also taking meds that aren't technically supposed
to go with alcohol (but also, who gives a fuck, see: cheering on
the band) and before he goes off to bed. Also, if it's been a long
day and he's cycled through Toddler Rain Man Jerk so many
times he got himself a little frozen.*

*Eventually, Toddler, Rain Man, Jerk, and Zombie will be
gone, and the tumor will infiltrate the other gray matter on its
way to choking off the blood and air supply from the rest of him.
When? We don't know. A week, a month, another YEAR? Anyway, one day, probably before you even have time to say good-bye.*

Going back and forth between her friends' social media posts and
group texts and the GBM Wives, where she pretended to be a middle-
aged mom, Evy felt that she wasn't any particular age anymore. It was
getting harder and harder to act interested in her friends' gossip about

who got so high they fell asleep hugging a bag of Cheetos or whose parents would be dumb enough to let them throw a party next weekend. It was getting harder to pretend she cared about most of her friends' dumb not-problems. At parties, she always got drunk enough not to care that Hailey might literally melt into a pile of goo if she didn't get to have her hair cut in a fancy all-organic salon forty-five minutes away, or that Cameron went into a monthlong depression when his ancient golden retriever died.

Evy's only friend who had *already* been through something hard was Olivia. Her parents had split, but not in that we-still-love-you-pick-out-a-bunk-bed-for-Dad's/get-extra-gifts-at-Christmas way. They split in a Mom-spends-a-week-in-inpatient-psych way, in a Dad-lives-in-another-time-zone-with-a-massage-therapist-now way.

When her family imploded, Olivia got a job at the vintage store and signed up for community college classes to learn to code. She cut four inches off her long hair and stopped wearing thick black eyeliner, bought herself a huge tan leather purse, slid heavy silver rings onto her fingers, and lacquered her nails glossy deep gray. She seemed to sit up straighter, even when everyone else was slumped down for the third day of a boring history documentary. Evy thought it was a beautiful and enigmatic transformation, and she wished she could handle the heartbreak her own family's chaos had wrought by suddenly becoming a more-adult version of herself the way Olivia had.

Evy longed to ask Olivia whether she ever missed the version of herself she had been last year, when she wore messy braids and frayed sweatshirts and stayed late at school making pottery and eating candy in the hallway. But whenever Evy texted her, Olivia's cool, busy life interrupted them and the conversation ended; whenever they were alone for a moment among their group of friends, Olivia had to leave for her coding class or a shift at the store.

Evy was in love with Olivia, and studied the way she had forged her own path through her parents' wreckage toward something all hers. She wanted to imitate it, understand it, and channel it. She envied it and absorbed it.

Other crushes had captured Evy's attention before. She had felt her pulse flutter for K-pop boy band singers, for indie-film actresses, and for a cashier at Sal's Sweets last summer named Hannah who'd left for college in August and posted about beach volleyball all year.

There had been Sam Ellis from her art class last year, who wore braided bracelets up their wrist and traced patterns in ink onto their skin and tapped their foot when they were nervous, who sent her a sweet message when they noticed Evy had finally added *bi* to all her social media profiles, who always shared their vending machine Sour Patch Kids with Evy before the bell rang.

Evy had liked her lab partner, Jordan, who started varsity soccer and turned red when he heard his name on announcements for scoring goals, who brought her little gifts he made in wood shop, like her name carved onto a keychain, and asked her to the winter dance with a text full of snowflake emojis.

She wished Olivia would one day break open with the whole story Evy had only overheard the short version of, about the time she had to call 911 when her mom freaked out. She wanted Olivia to text her late-night assurances that she had gotten through her parents' drama and disappearances, and Evy could get through her dad's next outburst too. Most of all, Evy wanted to get in trouble for staying out late with Olivia, standing with her at the edge of the black pulsing waves, shivering with their skin touching even if the night was ninety degrees.

But wishing and wanting didn't make people become who you needed them to be. Evy couldn't word-vomit ten texts about her feelings to Olivia, not yet. But she could say, "Hey, cool ring" to her at parties, and, "We should hang out sometime when you're not busy!" and then say it again, whenever they hung out in a group. She could send Olivia links to stories about women with million-dollar app ideas and tell her that would be her soon, and she could hope the emojis Olivia sent back would one day say more.

Evy couldn't make Margot say, "No kid should have to do this and I'm here for you if you need to curse or cry," when her dad called her a disgusting wasted little weed after she told him to stop cutting up all the lemons in the bowl for no reason. She couldn't make her say, "You must be so tired, I've been having such a terrible time too." When Evy tried to talk to her mom about hard things, Margot's default was some-thing generic, like "Quite the roller coaster," and then a long pause.

Little rebellions like missed curfews or low grades got Margot's attention, but even then, she said, "The last thing I need is to worry about where you are all night. Get home on time or get used to your room for two weeks."

In the GBM Wives forum, though, Evy found the kind of mom who could offer straight-up support and empathy, without always defaulting to discipline and distance. In the GBM Wives forum she found the kind of person her mother used to be. In the forum, Evy also unfortunately discovered the R-rated details of her parents' sex life before Brian got sick, and Margot's account of the last times they did it. She found out her grandparents had been paying for their health in-surance for years, no matter what happened with her parents' business, and that her dad's treatment would have bankrupted them without it. In the forum, Evy noticed how often her mom used the word *despair*.

Evy hadn't told Liz about the GBM Wives because she could already hear what her sister would say, some sensible, grown-up thing like *You really shouldn't be doing this. Respect Mom's privacy. Blah blah blah.*

She used to assume Liz's way of moving through the world came easy. Every teacher, every year, read Evelyn Dunne's name off the roster and then sighed in contented awe as if *Elizabeth* Dunne had opened the door to Narnia with her essays or algebra equations.

At first, Liz had even been more patient with Brian's chaos, keeping her face set in her I-got-this way while he smashed a wineglass or made everyone pray at McDonald's, while Evy yanked Brian away and cried, while Margot said, "Jesus fucking Christ" under her breath.

Liz always listened: to Evy's hiccup-crying stories about her friends and to her half-assed questions about what grades you *really* needed if you wanted to go to college. Liz had a way of sighing and slowing down her words when Evy asked for advice, which sometimes made her feel silly and small. Evy needed her sister for so much, but she didn't need to tell her about this.

Margot

Brian leaned on the kitchen counter, casual, the dish towel still barely covering him. She asked, demanded, then finally gave up on getting him into pants. He stood up and sat down, readjusting himself, and she turned away from him each time. She finished the sunset wine, the last of a bottle she'd opened yesterday, but held off on opening another bottle until dinner. Evy's text had said she would be home any minute.

She'd replenished the wine rack earlier that day, when she realized they were out of both coffee *and* cabernet. Margot refused to get groceries delivered ever since the shopper brought her decaf coffee once by accident. Why the Casserole Bitches never thought to drop *that* stuff off, Margot would never know; so after the house turnovers were finished, she'd brought Brian to Acme and then to Spirits. She always tried to get in and out of the store without him wandering away or yelling at an old lady shaking the cantaloupes, to obtain the bare minimum of calories, caffeine, and cabernet to get her through another few days and get the hell out of there.

Then she'd dragged Brian around town, fixing little problems at the rentals: missing keys, two Wi-Fi resets, a clogged toilet, and a complaint about the wind, the actual wind, was she supposed to be a goddamn wizard? The wind person had complained for half an hour; she should have slipped one of Brian's Xanax into their coffee and been on her way.

Margot saw on Instagram that the Casserole Bitches had been on J Street beach all afternoon, their chairs in a semicircle while they gossiped, the low tide rolling in calm and perfect over their pedicured toes. Before Brian was sick, she would have joined them, listening to the inside info on where the retinol cream they all used would go on sale, while Brian handled any texts or problems from the renters—while he handled *the wind*. Then she would have met him for what they called their BYOBB, a bike ride with a beer, and ended up at Park Seafood for steamers before they grilled a late dinner. They would have caught some off-key Jimmy Buffett cover band at Klee's and sung along to "Changes in Latitudes" too loud, but everyone would be loud by then; they would have held their hands up for two drinks at the bar without having to say what they were having. Brian would have brought her coffee and a buttered roll the next morning. Already back from surfing an early set, he would have smelled like the beach and the bakery.

It had been a good life with him, for a while.

Just before Evy got home, Margot hit send on a GBM Wives post she'd been writing all day, between interruptions:

> *I met up with friends at the beach once this summer, and I'd rather shove my face eyes-open into the sand than do it again.*

Have these women collectively made a pact to only speak in low-mumbled clichés whenever I'm around, and after he's dead will they be worse?

If I could, I'd fly you all here for the afternoon, we could wear all-black swimsuits, light a pile of dead seagrass on fire to make everyone think we're casting spells so they'll leave us alone. I need at least five of you to drop your PTA meetings and mortgages and move to this island with me, I'd put you in five adjacent adorable rentals.

I already decided what I am doing when he dies: I'm leaving. I'm selling all the houses and taking the girls with me somewhere else.

Unless you consider my offer. The sunsets? The sparkly magic black and blue ocean? The everybody-knows-your-name places where they sell pints of beer or clams drowned in butter? The houses?? Oh, you mean the ones we transformed, the ones we got lucky on, the ones we made beautiful every week after goddamn week together? THOSE? ·

Everyone here is old enough to have used a real film camera, right, where you got strips of negatives in the envelope, those smaller, backward, brown shadow-versions of the photos? The idea of staying here is like that: all the same, but backward and small, all dark on dark.

I know I'll get some replies sending me real estate listings in your towns and some with reasons why you would stay if you were me—god knows I've sent plenty of my own opinions on what you all should do. But I'm not looking for your common-sense reasons to stay. I'm not looking for compromise.

Yes, I know I could sell the E&E houses and still live here. Yes, I know there are plenty of towns within ten miles where I could move, pretend the landmarks aren't almost the same. Yes, I have thought about my daughters.

No, they will not understand.

No, it's not fair; no, it's not what's "best" for them, but, come on, "best"? We're so far past best. Here's what's WORST: they get to go to their senior proms with their friends, but I fade, and I rage, and I stagnate, and I fake it, and I never reinvent myself because I'm only a shadow puppet, I'm only a carbon copy of a carbon copy.

In fact, I have thought only of my daughters, and weighed their inevitable hate against what it would do to me to stay.

Evy

"Dad, you gonna put pants or shorts on or something . . . ?" Evy asked. He was standing at their kitchen counter with a dish towel barely covering his private parts, but his butt was still exposed, while her mom set an IDC on the table and said, "I've asked *several* times," on her way to pull forks out of the dishwasher.

The first time this happened a few months ago, Evy had screamed, "Dad, that's disgusting! Mom, why are you just standing there, he's frigging naked!" and run to the other room so she wouldn't have to see it, so gray and hairy and out there. Some buried voice still screamed, *This is messed up!!!* inside her, but all she could muster outwardly now was a sigh.

It was after seven, and Evy had hoped her late departure from Sal's would at least earn her a dinner alone in front of the TV; but here her parents were, still getting ready for another casserole together in crazytown.

Often she skipped dinner altogether and grabbed pizza before she met her friends. If she showed up two or three times a week for family dinner, that seemed enough to keep the peace. Before making evening plans, she and Liz always checked to see if the other person would be home to handle this batshit improv show.

She tried to resist distracting Liz in the middle of her night with the band guy she'd been whispering about, but she couldn't help it. She sent Liz a **GET IT** text with three flames and a kissy face.

"I've been telling your mother about the *constrictions* in them, the ways the cycles on the laundry spinner are causing too much elastic, as well as the negative scents," Brian said, pointing at Margot like *her, she did it, the pants problems are all her fault.* "Obviously," he said, "she's oblivious."

"Right," Evy said. It was always so confusing to drop into the middle of one of these wacko arguments, when her mom was already pissed off and her dad was so worked up that little spit droplets formed at the edges of his mouth, when things had escalated to dish towels on dicks and whatever pants-injustice feelings were happening inside her dad's head while her mom made creases in the napkins.

The dad-dick towel shifted, and Evy looked down at the floor and held her hand in front of her face so she wouldn't see what was behind it, as if the sight of an actual uncovered dad penis would damage her retinas and psyche for life, because honestly it might. She looked at her mom to see if she was going to try to do anything about getting her dad into pants, but Margot was uncorking a bottle of red wine and really concentrating on that. So Evy said, "Well, uh, maybe there's some other pants or shorts that didn't go through the dryer?"

The cork popped; Margot poured a glass and drank a third of it, glaring at Brian and Evy. Evy couldn't tell if her mom was also mad at *her* for being late (even though the lateness wasn't her fault for once), or for some other reason, or in fact not mad at her at all, but glaring in her direction with quiet rage simply because she was *there*. Margot disappeared into the bedroom, emerged with an armful of shorts, and dropped them on the couch. "Here," she said, leaving Evy and Brian with the pile while she sat down at the table. She plopped servings of casserole and salad onto all three plates, gulping wine in between. Brian sat on the couch with the dish towel still on his lap, grabbing a pair of pants and smelling them.

"So they feel tight *and* they stink?" Evy asked.

"She exposes them constantly to terrible products, and they evoke a certain odor, and the heat? Unimaginable," he said. He then smelled the crotch of the next pair, which he declared, "Useless. Disgusting." He repeated this six more times.

Margot shoveled silent forkfuls of casserole into her mouth. Evy grabbed another pair of shorts and held them up. "What about these?" she asked, but Brian shook his head.

"Evy, just come eat," Margot said. "You eat such junk when you're at work, you need some protein."

"I ate a hot dog for lunch, that *has* protein," Evy said. "And I put ketchup on it, so, vegetable." She actually ate very healthy, except for some boardwalk food here and there. She made sure to drink a lot of water and take a vitamin after she drank too much with her friends. She'd also made a green smoothie before work and eaten peaches she'd packed herself for a snack. She could tell her mom all that and explain how she read online that green smoothies are good for cell regeneration and even anxiety, but all Margot would hear was *hot dog*.

In real life they debated hot dog protein, while in the GBM Wives forum they debated what counted as a meaningful end of a life and whether they might be better off if they secretly swapped out the experimental drugs for useless sugar pills.

Evy left her dad on the couch with all his unacceptable attire and sat at the table, taking a bite of the gray chicken and soggy rice. Brian pulled a pair of paint-stained cargo shorts from the bottom of the pile and said, "Well, she's swooped these away quite a few times, just a bitch better left untrusted, but here we are again." When he said *bitch* Margot recoiled like it stung, even though Evy had heard him call her that several times this week. Brian stood in front of the open window and dropped the dish towel while he pulled on the stained shorts. "They still don't allow the inches within the fabric I need," he said, stomping his foot before finally sitting down at his place at the table.

"Wild Saturday night around here, huh?" Evy said, turning to her mom, who raised her eyebrows and sighed. Later with the GBM Wives, Margot would explain how Brian had escaped from the house they were cleaning that day and wandered into the street. Later Liz would come home and tell Evy whether she GOT IT with the band guy on the beach, and they would work out their who's-home-when schedule for the next no-pants-casserole night, and the next.

The white blob dotted with flecks of broccoli went cold in front of Evy. She shook red pepper onto her plate.

"It needs more than that," Margot said, sliding salt across the table. "And it's overdone, it was in the oven when I got your text so I left it in there a little longer."

"I told you, Hailey didn't show up, so—" Evy started to explain again, but Brian interrupted her, his jaw clenched in frustration: "You know Robbie will need me to handle *all evolving problems* with the ice machine."

Robbie was another old friend of Brian's, and now he was part owner of the Buccaneer. Since Brian got sick, Robbie had let him pretend to help out up there when it was slow. Brian always bragged about how much Robbie needed him.

"I'll call to arrange a meeting," Brian said, grabbing Evy's phone, squinting at the screen and breathing in and out with a guttural growl.

Margot said, "Brian, come on, Robbie's *busy*, it's a Saturday night in July." Evy tried to snatch the phone back, but Brian held it away from her, jabbing at passcode numbers again and again until it locked. He swept his arm across the table and hit two glasses, spilling water and red wine everywhere as one shattered on the floor. Then he flung his hand backward through his casserole, covering his arm with gooey cheese and rice. Evy grabbed her phone and ran to towel it off, while Margot stacked up the wet plates covered with ruined food, the red-stained napkins she'd creased, the inedible soaked bowl of salad. She did it all in an over-it, unhurried way.

Brian sprang up, his shirt spattered with red wine and bits of chicken and broccoli he probably couldn't see because of his radiated optic nerve, his neck reddening as he hissed at Margot, "I have known you to be a succubus from the very start!"

"Dad, don't," Evy said. She could say, *Dad, don't talk like that to Mom, don't get all upset, don't be like this, don't say the mean crazy stuff your brain tells you to say,* but it wouldn't matter. All of it was useless void-shouting. Back in October, she would have raged and ranted right back at him, reasoned and pleaded, cried and created a scene on top of a scene. But chaos always reigned; there was nothing you could say to tame it.

There must have been one last, normal family dinner, when her dad told her to put her phone away and her mom laughed at his dad jokes about nacho cheese (*get it, Ev, what do you call it when it's someone else's cheese?*) and both her parents geeked out about their real estate spreadsheets while she finished the guacamole before Liz could. Or it could have been spaghetti. It could have been chicken cutlets. There was no announcement, no one remembered, and then there was never another like that.

Brian stormed away and slammed the bedroom door, and Evy and her mom waited to hear if he would wreck something in there or pass out in his paint-shorts and casserole-wine shirt. It stayed quiet, and Margot gave the kitchen mess her full attention, moving quicker and with more intention now that Brian was gone.

"This Robbie stuff again, he's so obsessed," Evy said, loading the dishwasher while Margot attacked the stains with a foaming spray, swept away broken glass, and dumped the casserole directly into the trash.

"I'm not saving this," she announced.

Brian fell asleep, and Margot disappeared to the screen porch to read. Evy's phone worked again, so she caught up on a long group text from her friends. Hailey and Cameron were going to a party; Olivia was skipping it to finish her coding homework.

Evvvvvvvy, come with us! Cameron texted. Evy pictured the scene of the party, at the house where all the foreign students here on summer work visas lived: Cameron flirting with Declan, a guy from Dublin who worked at the Tilt-A-Whirl; Hailey all over the boy she'd made out with at the last party. At that house there was always too much warm vodka and too much yelling.

Hailey texted: **Kelsey and Alex might come tonight . . . they're just doing set construction stuff this week.** Their friends who did drama camp instead of boardwalk jobs had disappeared for weeks, for their intense all-day rehearsals. Evy didn't even know what musical they were doing this year; she hadn't seen Kelsey and Alex, or any of their drama friends, since they went to Pride in Asbury together in June.

Cameron sent the group a picture of Declan on the beach in Wayfarer sunglasses, an explosion of emojis, and a countdown clock with the number of days until Declan had to go home to Dublin.

GET IT, Evy texted. She actually didn't even know whether Cameron and Declan had hooked up or if Cameron was still hoping to, and she felt guilty for forgetting to ask him about it. Was everyone else

GETTING IT, or trying to, tonight? She was GETTING so tired her eyes stung staring at her phone, and her head ached. The intense dinner drama with her dad had drained her more than she'd realized.

I'm staying in tonight,, Evy texted the group. **Next time tho!**

Hailey texted **boooooo**, Cameron said **k**, and Olivia sent a stressed-out cartoon-face version of herself to the group, but then sent two memes from *The Office* to Evy individually.

Evy read Margot's most recent post while she sat on her bedroom floor, pausing after each sentence in her laptop's glow, expecting a whole block of text at the end to explain that of course this selling-everything-and-moving idea wasn't real, it was a new thing Margot was trying: fiction! What the actual fuck was this *Yes, I have thought about my daughters* shit, this *dark on dark* emo-mom nonsense?

She wrote a draft of a response:

Yeah, great plan, Margot, really on your parenting-teens-with-an-almost-dead-parent A-game. Brilliant, you should go on a podcast, you should go get your PhD in fuck off. While you're at it, why don't you move some certified child molesters into this new house in this magical undisclosed future mystery location, where you will not have to deal with the horrible horrible fate of having nice ladies bring you dinner or deal with walking past a bar you used to work at for a few summers—oh no, how would anyone survive that, yep, you better drag us all somewhere random you find on a Google search for "not here."

Oh, and another hot tip, surprised you didn't think of it, maybe a couple of meth addicts can share my—I mean, your DAUGHTER'S room, your daughter who is definitely not me. That will also provide a wonderful distraction from being SAD, all the molesting and meth-doing.

You are gonna beat the system!!! You will discover the secret to fineness, you will Zumba-dance your ass right around all the shitty shitty shitty feelings literally everyone else since the beginning of human life has experienced by MOVING. Cool.

Evy hovered her finger over the POST button and then moved it away. In the absence of a specific plan, Evy did not imagine that—if her mom forced them to leave Seaside—Margot would bring them somewhere cool, like to an apartment in Paris where she would let them smoke cigarettes and drink wine on the balcony, or to a Hollywood Hills house where a movie star used to live, where they could lounge by the pool and recreate *Vanity Fair* photo spreads from the eighties. She did not imagine Margot's post meant she wanted glamour or adventure. She imagined the worst: an anonymous beige house in a big development, near some strip of Toyota dealerships and Targets and T-Mobile stores that could be anywhere.

Her mother did not sound like the person who had been posting on the forum for months, the woman who worked through her shit, sure, in her thousands of words threaded through with plenty of worry, but who always managed to reassure herself and the other women, who noticed when she was getting melodramatic or self-pitying or tired and signed off. She did not sound like the mother who'd given Evy the sex talk when she was ten by following a binder of curriculum she'd borrowed from her health teacher friend. She did not sound like the mother who had picked up enough of Evy's signals to ask, with a warm-nervous casualness while she unpacked the groceries, if there were any boys *or* girls she was hoping might ask her to go to the winter dance.

This post sounded like giving up; it sounded like a desperate, imaginary whim Margot would pretend was real right up until she had the keys to a new terrible house in some place half a day's drive from the shore.

Evy Googled "laws for teenagers living alone"; she looked up her closest relatives and aerial shots of their houses; she logged into her own bank account and saw three hundred dollars in there; she drafted a text to Olivia asking for help but didn't send it; then she read the other women's responses to Margot about leaving—half for it, half against it.

She walked up the street to the ocean. At night, the waves crashed in white and rushed out deep, dark blue marbled with shadow. Margot was wrong: it was never black on black at night, but little silver shreds of light sparkling on the surface.

CHAPTER THREE

Liz

Liz stood up, and the blood rushed from her head. She felt the slow warmth of the gin take hold. She and Gabe wandered into the blur of colored lights on the boardwalk, finding their way past the dangling pink cotton candy, the swirls of giant rainbow lollipops, the smoke from the Italian sausages.

Everywhere people tried to win the games, drawn in by the violent pop of the shoot-out-the-star, the tick and whir of the spinning wheels, the metallic thunk of rubber against the too-small basketball hoops. Liz and Gabe knew better, joked about what a waste of a dollar the games were while voices shouted: *One-win choice! Come on down! Give it a try!* Kids pulled on their parents' arms and rubbed their eyes, wanting hermit crabs, temporary tattoos, stuffed tigers, glow-in-the-dark necklaces, wanting to be picked up or put down, wanting one more ride or one more minute to decide which color Italian ice to order.

"Should I try to win you a stuffed bear? Those guys are all trying to win stuffed bears," Gabe said. Liz's face flushed: that uncomfortable, uncontrollable giveaway. He passed her the thermos, and she took another drink; it was the contrast she liked the most, between the pulsing

43

entropy of the crowd and the muted calm that built with every sip. She knew what it felt like to drink a few warm, watery beers in someone's basement, to choke down a swig of Hot Damn before passing it along to the next person. She drank just enough at high school parties to tolerate listening to student council girls talk about Instagram filters while Sonia made out with some linebacker doofus on a beanbag chair.

This kind of drinking, though, this unhurried shared secret, this cold bitter lemonade that muted every worry into a background blur, was new and nice. It made the ugly parts of the boardwalk fade even as they were right in her face: the people who swore in front of their kids, the heaps of trash you had to step around when the cans overflowed, the shrill, nasty things people shouted at each other or at no one in particular.

She gauged the building buzz carefully, pausing long enough between sips to scan her body's response; it was always Liz who helped Evy through her late nights of crying and puking after she got wasted, who watched her little sister's weekend mornings lost to miserable hangovers. Every time Evy swore she hadn't meant to get that way; it was so easy for her to give in to carelessness.

Gabe told her he had dropped out of college and bought a bus ticket to New York to rejoin his bandmates because of some music-fueled wanderlust. "I bet you'll go to someplace with buildings named after billionaires and hang up that Audrey Hepburn poster in your dorm room," he said.

"I'll write my college essay on what umbrellas mean to me," Liz said. She'd already written drafts of all the standard admissions-essay topics; she wasn't worried about getting into college or embarrassed that her grades were good enough that she might go to a famous one with billionaires' kids. But she didn't really want to talk about college with Gabe.

She wanted to hear his striving-rock-star-college-dropout stories. She wanted to imagine herself as the kind of girl who went to bars and shows and Brooklyn parties, who carefully chose her bra before she went out, knowing someone might see it. Almost all her undies were pastel, solid-color and soft from too many washings, and no one had ever seen them.

"Skee-Ball is the only game I like," Liz said. "It's way in the back and no one stands there staring at you while you play."

"Well, challenge accepted," Gabe said, steering them through the arcade's maze of screens and Whac-A-Moles until they were standing, barely touching, crouching and ready with sweaty quarters in their hands. Liz zeroed in, the smooth, heavy weight of the ball getting the right spin and speed and flying into the hole with a solid thud. She beat Gabe by a hundred points, their tickets snaked out onto the floor, and they left them for someone else as he pulled her back into the boardwalk crowd, then onto the beach, where they left their shoes under a bench.

"I've seen this move, you know," she said. They were in the shadow of the thrum and glow of the rides on the pier, closer to the ocean. "The take-her-down-to-the-beach move? You think it'll work on me?"

She had kissed exactly one person before, a track team sophomore named Jesse who had rolled toward her on a couch with his eyes closed and put his dry lips against hers for a few seconds before rolling back off her and then emptying a bag full of Dorito crumbs into his mouth. Never mind Dorito-breath Jesse, and never mind the vestiges of self-consciousness she was shedding, layer by layer.

"You seemed okay with the see-if-she-wants-to-drink-a-bunch-of-boozy-lemonade move and the let-her-win-at-Skee-Ball move," he said, shrugging, "so I thought I would at least try it."

He leaned down to kiss her, and a cold wave rushed over their feet. The lemon and gin taste, the callused guitar-player hands pressed against her back, and the insistent warmth of him as the wind shifted and blew in cooler off the ocean—these were the special effects, a movie scene merged with reality.

Margot

Margot slid into her bed early, alone. Liz was still out, and Evy had retreated to her room. Brian slept in the guest room; his last night in their bed had been months ago, when he started snoring with an intensity and volume she could not tolerate and churning the covers into a sweaty mess, when he reached for her with a string of strange hissed-whispers that made her cringe.

She opened her copy of *The Girl with the Long Shadow*, a book she'd reread so often the pages were buttery and soft, the spine fragile and cracked. The book always helped her settle down. It was a fantasy, and the main character Nora's courage as she travels through time and then returns to her reality never failed to immerse and distract Margot.

When Nora time-travels, a glittering, warm highway of light carries her. The wiser women who have slipped away from their own impossible present-tenses advise Nora on how to steel herself for the body-numbing second when her heart stops on either end. They tell her how to train her subconscious to record and how to forget, when necessary.

Nora only stays a short while in each time period before the loosened fabric of space and time tightens. She's sent back to the present, where she has to readjust to moving slowly forward, where she's navigating an ordinary crumbling marriage. She comes back each time feeling powerful and resilient with her secret magic, and less patient with the relentless expectations of domestic life.

The book had been marketed to women: on the cover was a pink and teal graphic of an hourglass. The particulars of Nora's journey were as elaborate and technical as any of the sci-fi or fantasy books about imagined galaxies that Brian used to read. Brian had loved *The Girl with the Long Shadow* as much as Margot did. He'd bought the book for her as a Christmas gift when she was a new mom, but his inscription reminded her of the real gift, which was taking baby Lizzie for three days and two nights to his sister Eileen's for a visit, so Margot could be alone for the first time in months. In the blessed silence she hadn't even had to ask for, she'd slept for sixteen hours, read hundreds of pages at a time without anyone shrieking or needing her, giving in to her body's insistence on rest, waking up and sinking deep into the imagined world of the novel. She'd pumped eight bottles of milk for her baby to drink when she came home. She'd held up a onesie from the hamper and inhaled the baby powder and milk smell. She'd wept after she got off the phone with Brian, when he told her about a walk around a lake near Eileen's, knowing he had probably slept less than four hours trying to get Lizzie to sleep in a Pack 'n Play.

In *The Girl with the Long Shadow,* it was so easy to see how one decision was dependent on another, the ways that the choices were and were not ours, what we needed to get through the messes we make.

Where would Margot go right now, if she had Nora's power to transport backward or forward? To last fall, to the last time Brian brewed coffee and brought it to her in bed? To their first night together in this bungalow he'd renovated for her? To the moments eighteen months apart when Brian held her hand and whispered each daughter's name in a brightly lit delivery room? To the day they finally finished rebuilding everything after the destruction of Hurricane Sandy? To the day in the near future when she would leave Seaside, ready to begin a story in a new place?

So now we start again, uncertain and untethered, weary was Margot's favorite line from the book. She would tattoo it on her arm if she had the guts, but she was not Nora, and memory did not always infuse her with strength but sometimes sapped the small reserves she had, disoriented and distracted her from the focus she needed to make it through the day, the week, the month, the end, whenever that was.

Liz

Liz arrived early to work at Sun and Shade the next morning. The sand was still cool, the boardwalk quiet except for some plodding-along joggers. She spent the fifteen minutes before she officially opened deleting five versions of a text to Gabe before settling on **Hey**

As in, Hey, thank you for the neon-lights kiss and the gin-induced spinniness, and hey, let me keep a little of that spinniness and a little of that neon light under my skin, jack up the warm-buzz, the kick-drum pulse, and the soft-focus lens, let the flashbulb-feeling settle a little and let me blink blink and see that ocean sparkle extra special, hey, let me have all that, okay? That's mine. To keep forever.

As in, Hey, I know you hook up with hipster groupies, and hey, I don't know what your deal is and whether you're secretly a scumbag whose game is so good you knew how to press every single effing button or whether you're a kid like me who wants adventure and an interesting life, who loves it here and can't wait to leave and love it more, who doesn't want to be disappointed.

As in, Hey, just text me back. Just hang around these few weeks, because distraction is medicine. Hey, just keep bringing me dinner because boardwalk pizza's buttery crust fills a hole in my soul that no IDC ever could. Hey, you really have no idea how much the attention on a warm night and the way you look at me makes me stand up taller, fills me with something bright and certain, whispers to me that this is the teeniest part of what's ahead—the corners of the world full of kind oddballs, brilliant fuckups, intense introverts, wild old souls out there that I have yet to meet.

Hey, I've seen all the movies, and I know how this ends, I know, I know, I know: waving at the beat-up car driving away with the Labor Day traffic. It's what I'm signing up for, so sign me up for all of it, I get it.

Hey, text me back, and then take me out anywhere late.

Hey, want my virginity? Please, please, say you do, because I don't want it. Once is seven hundred universes away from never, and I want once before I go back to those basement parties with the Jesses and then to freshman orientation with slurry frat guys, before Never Have I Ever with roommates from a different state, before I spend my summer-job money on new black flats that will give me blisters from standing too long at my dad's funeral. Hey, take that virginity, it's yours, because it doesn't feel like some special gift but an awkward burden. Hey, let me through that grown-up gate! Hey, take this now, hey, check, check, next!

Hey, have you ever had to take care of someone, like really take care of them?

Hey, what have you already lost? Is there a way you get used to it, because every new thing that's gone feels like an infected wound exposed to the wind, chafing and blistering and refusing to scab over.

Hey, maybe I'll keep that to myself.

Maybe that will always be the question I ask about anyone, from now on: What have you already lost?

She took a sparkly sun-on-the-ocean picture and posted it in black-and-white, no caption. She watched for the three dots below her

Hey to see if he was texting back, but saw nothing and forced herself to put her phone away.

She turned the combination lock on the big wooden storage box and felt the smooth release when it opened on the last number. She collected the trash: a broken sandcastle mold, greasy paper plates, a straw, a plastic spider ring, and four empty beer cans. Then she stacked the beach chairs into two rows, planted six display umbrellas, hauled out her signs, and counted out her bank. Ready for another day.

Only later, gulping ice water on her break, would she see the text Gabe had sent when he woke up:

hey, this is the day I'm supposed to send you one-word texts back, right? like yeah hey hey I'm distracted and busy, hey u, way too busy to text even though I somehow got a day off on a Sunday what is that about, maybe I'm about to get fired.

hey this is the day I'm supposed to act like I don't care if we hang out again, whatever, wait a couple hours and make you think maybe I forgot all about last night and I don't care?

nah, if you need me I'll be here playing cover songs all day about girls named Mary and Bobby Jean because someone's said all this better than me before, if you need me I'll be waiting, boss, I'll be hitting that little blue arrow right away without reading it over to see if what I said made sense or if I said too much

hey, I want to hang out again, and hey, no, I'm not busy and I'm not cool.

CHAPTER FOUR

Margot

The stained-glass window of St. Agnes cast a fading rainbow glow over Evy and Liz fanning themselves with bulletins, and over Brian, gazing at the crucifix and projecting his *AMENS* too loud at the Sunday evening mass.

"And also with you . . . spirit," Margot said, screwing up the call and response.

"SPIRIT WITH YOUR SPIRIT," Brian hissed, as if Margot had committed a mortal sin. The "with your spirit" wording the church had switched to a decade ago had never stuck in Margot's long-term memory. They had been lapsed Catholics for years, until Brian got sick and decided to hold everyone's hands to pray before meals, until he started making the sign of the cross in the air in the middle of a conversation.

Margot had given in to his demand to drag them all back to church, hoping this fixation might distract him from his trickier ones, like forcing her to Google the members of his grade-school baseball team so he could call them all up. Going to mass usually settled Brian as much as any anxiety drug, and tired him out enough to give them another two hours of peace afterward. In church he existed in a state of something close to calm. They slipped in during the opening hymn and left as soon as the priest sat down after communion, avoiding eye contact with the Catholic Casserole Bitches who sometimes referenced God when they dropped off their lasagnas.

After his loud *AMEN* and hissing at Margot, the family across the aisle all stared at Brian. If this were a place Margot actually prayed, she would say a silent one for patience and grace for herself, and another for that family to hit every red light on their way home and shrink their favorite pants in the dryer. But she didn't actually pray here. How could she, in a place that had hidden such dark secrets, in a place that might let one of her daughters get married and not the other? She wasn't here for the prayers. She was here for the quiet music and echoing voices that calmed Brian down.

Evy and Liz giggled, and Margot shot them a glare. She feared any disruption could trigger Brian; the ritual was everything, and if he got distracted, they might never get him back. But of course the girls rolled their eyes. Evy had called her and Brian out years ago on all the things they didn't actually believe about being Catholic. She'd convinced them that this formal, ancient place that dismissed so many as unholy was not for them anymore.

"Dad said I could decide for myself, and I'm deciding," Evy had said, when Margot insisted she join them again at mass after Brian got sick. "You act so woke but then you're gonna make me go fake-pray there? Why?"

"It's not about—" Margot stopped, too tired to explain to Evy, because she couldn't really explain all the contradictions and compartmentalization to herself either. "You can decide for yourself again after he's dead." Evy had cried, but climbed into the van anyway. Margot felt nauseated that whole mass.

A few days after snapping at Evy, Margot had written in the GBM Wives forum: *I was mean to my daughter, how could I have said that? I will never make her set foot in there again after he's gone, and I might not either. But after that mass Brian said he felt the bells in his bones and heard a God-whisper. I want us to be together when everything is calm.*

Pamplemousse7 responded: *Do you think your daughter would probably understand if you explained it to her that way?*

Margot wrote back: *I should tell them that this is one of the only ways left to connect. I'll try to say that.* Then she had tried, but what she'd actually said out loud to Evy? Not that.

From then on they went to mass together every week. Evy sat on the edge of the pew, looking as if she might bolt at any moment but still standing and bowing her head when she was supposed to. She skipped communion, kneeling alone as she waited for her family to return. She listened to the nonsense homily from the eighty-six-year-old priest, or she listened to music on an earbud she sneaked into her left ear and thought Margot couldn't see.

Of course the girls giggled. And she shushed them, because where could she even start, in the middle of the profession of faith, explaining how any one of these masses could be the last time their family stood calm and together in one place? She would never say *Decide for yourself after he's dead* again, but she would also never say *It's a language your dad still understands and it's one thing that still feels familiar for him.*

She would try to tell the girls in other ways what it meant to her that they showed up. She would make breakfast for dinner whenever they asked; she would cut tiger lilies and put them in a jar on their nightstands as a little surprise.

Liz

"Evy's doing a turnover at the house on C Street; she'll be back around noon so you can go to work; I'll be at the J Street house all day with the contractors; you said you're in at one today, right?" Margot monologued to Liz, moving from room to room.

Liz's last layers of sleep were evaporating, but she had a fragile power to reenter her dreams if she ignored Margot. "Storm's supposed to roll in, so let me know if Carl calls you out, okay? We can have that leftover ziti for dinner—I guess—and don't forget we have *Penn tomorrow*—love you."

Liz sat upright in bed and mumbled a groggy, "Got it," as the screen door slammed behind Margot. She would be alone with her dad for hours. She needed coffee. Without her contacts in, the room was blurry. She wanted to close her eyes again and boomerang back to the boardwalk lights of her Saturday night with Gabe, to linger for hours on those islands of memory.

Liz pressed her contacts into her eyes and blinked, then peed dehydrated dark yellow. *Penn tomorrow* meant they would all drive two hours to see Brian's doctors at the University of Pennsylvania hospital, and the day before was always the hardest balancing act of what-ifs and dread, bracing for the news that either a) they were leveling up for a few more months in this glitch-ridden game they were stuck in, or b) the screen would go blank any minute and the power would go out on the whole system.

Before Sonia left to visit her grandma in Florida, she and Liz had gotten almost halfway through their Cloud Campaign II video game, but still they only knew a fraction of the landscape. When they played, they would pause and watch walk-through videos that showed them how to open doors they hadn't seen, but still there were infinite unopened ones.

Liz often hit pause on her real life now; it was the only workaround she knew, her only trick, so she did it over and over. She pressed pause when she thought about Gabe and the next time she might see him, and she pressed pause when she was at Sun and Shade, planting umbrellas and giving herself over to the chaos and sweat, ignoring the *hey honeys* from the dirtbags on the boardwalk. She pressed pause when she scrolled through photos and videos of friends in all her social media feeds and tapped the red hearts over and over.

She hovered her hand above the PLAY button on this game she was supposed to be figuring out. She didn't know the next right move after her mom said *Penn tomorrow*, so here she was back in bed for another five minutes, paused, her avatar pixelating and freezing, a glitch within a glitch, a line of broken-girl code.

She shuffled to the kitchen and poured a sludgy, hours-old cup of coffee. Brian stood next to her with his hands folded across his belly. He wore Margot's red-framed sunglasses, a tight, ratty T-shirt, and a floppy paint-stained hat. How did he find something with a paint stain nearly every day? Liz didn't think the outfits were kooky or funny. The clothes were an unspoken stand Brian took after ignoring the normal golf shirt and khakis Margot put out for him.

"Two miles sound good today, Brian?" Liz asked. She and Evy had started calling their parents by their first names a lot of the time.

Last night at church he had said the wrong prayers. Today they would go for a walk to get through the morning. She slathered sunscreen on both herself and her dad, the way she would a small child, then dumped sugar in the tepid coffee, stirred, and chugged half of it down. She turned her attention away from Brian pacing and back to the memory of the sweat and salt in Gabe's T-shirt, feeling the reverberations of the kiss, the night, the guy, the buzz, the secret, hoping they would carry her through.

If Gabe were off this morning, Liz would have made Brian walk along the bay so they wouldn't run into him. But by now Gabe would be opening the Sumner Avenue umbrella stand, a half mile past their turnaround point on the boardwalk.

She didn't want to give Gabe the weak little speech where she summarized the GBM WebMD page and her thanks-for-asking-thanks-for-caring SparkNotes. That always felt icky to her, watching the baffled, trapped expressions descend on people's faces.

She held Brian's hand at the intersections, but once they were on the boardwalk she let him go, and he swung his arms wide. His strides were erratic and exaggerated.

He used to be a runner, covering this same route in the early morning, alone or with Liz, his gait powerful and even. Before his phone could measure distance for him, he drove out to the inlet with Liz and Evy in the backseat, to see how many miles it was. He pushed them in a double jogging stroller when they were little, stopping to stretch at the playground when they needed a break. He'd run the Jersey Shore Marathon or Philadelphia Marathon every year, sometimes fast, sometimes slow, depending whether he'd followed a training plan or not. He'd made the girls pose with him on the Philly art museum steps like Rocky, he high-fived them as he passed them cheering, he always made a friend during the race who ran a better time because Brian both distracted them and made them pick up the pace.

When Liz started winning races, Brian had asked about her favorite parts of the courses and what she thought of her new running shoes, he'd brought her Gatorades at meets, and he'd cheered for her and all her teammates until he wore out his voice, but he never told her how fast he thought she should go, or when she ought to try to pass the fastest girl from the other team. Liz knew she was lucky he had been like this; she'd watched other girls' parents before races waving around stopwatches and sticking their heads into the team huddles, while her dad grinned at her from the concession stand, giving her a thumbs-up while he ate a hot dog.

On their boardwalk route now, Brian recited all the landmarks.

He called out, "Gazebo one! Gazebo two! Busted water fountain one! Good water fountain two!"

Whenever anyone passed them, Brian said, "Pick 'em up, kid!" and the runners stared at him in his hobo hat and cheap women's glasses, probably wondering who this weirdo was.

To distract him from cheering on strangers, Liz asked her dad about the stocks he followed; he'd been interested in the market since he'd taught his econ students about it, back before he gave up teaching to run E&E Rentals full-time. Since he got sick, he'd become obsessed, badgering Margot to let him buy and sell shares several times a day, memorizing facts about capital gains taxes and dividends. It was a safe topic because stocks were not social or emotional, and Brian felt like an expert. He forgot you weren't supposed to call your daughters whores when they wore bikinis, but he remembered all the board members of PepsiCo perfectly.

Hardly any of Liz's friends besides Sonia asked her about Brian, but when they did, the word *weird* was her substitute for loneliness, dread, and fear. *Weird* was a weak emotional label, and addicting if you relied on it too heavily. But just like the late-afternoon coconut iced coffees she'd gotten used to drinking, you could get dependent on *weird* if you used it enough. And Liz used it all the time.

She kept the conversation with Brian going in a saccharine-bright voice that felt fake, fake, fake. Before he got weird-sick, her dad used to answer her no matter what she asked. *What about the companies that spilled oil, do you own any stocks in those? Why? What if a company doesn't treat its workers well? What happens if everyone panics and sells off all their stocks at once?* He'd listen first, let her tell him what she'd already figured out on her own before he asked her, *Well, have you thought about it this way, well, what if this were true too?*

She would never in her life be able to stand men who assumed she knew nothing, who bloviated or condescended, because of Brian. He had always been willing to change his mind, and she wouldn't realize for a long time how rare that was.

When he asked if they could stop at the Buccaneer to help Robbie out, her heart sank. Robbie was so patient with her dad, but she knew it was getting harder to have Brian around at the bar, to find jobs he believed were important that wouldn't mess anything up. Liz didn't want to show up unannounced when Robbie was probably in the middle of something, or not there, or tired from the weekend. This was all beyond what Brian could understand about another person now.

"You want to go to the Buccaneer?" she asked. "Now? Why don't we just turn around up here and go home?"

"Well, Mondays are important for Robbie," Brian said. "And he always says beer flows best between friends." She could remind her dad about the last three times he'd said Robbie would be there and then he wasn't, but it wouldn't matter. When normal limits were imposed, when common sense was explained, when a whim or want was denied, you had to drag or cajole, apologize or lie, insist or give in. Would Brian drink a late-morning beer and then refuse to wipe foam off his upper lip, would he wander into the kitchen instead of the bathroom and stay there for forty-five minutes, or would he stand next to a normal family eating pizza and insist on ordering them hot wings they didn't want? All the *if-thens* could end in disaster.

"I'll have him pour it light," Brian said. "With no foam." He was always taking a stand now for silly ideas; he never ever changed his mind when it was set.

"You and Mom can go to the Buccaneer some other time."

"Oh, she's quite the obliterator," he said. "Plus, she thinks Robbie is a dirtbag."

"Yeah, well, what if we just, uh, go home and you can have a beer there maybe? How about if we do that? I think there's beers in the fridge."

"I need to ask Robbie about if he's all set for next weekend with his inventory."

This was a glitch, and he thought it was the game.

"Robbie's not even usually there, Dad, this time of day?"

"We have to push past this little group of swim protectors," he said, pointing at four lifeguards ahead of them. Liz let him surge ahead. The lifeguards stared at him, then at her. One of them had been in her chemistry class, but she pretended she didn't recognize him.

They walked into the Buccaneer together, and the few people there looked Brian up and down in his silly hat and tight T-shirt as he took huge marching steps toward the bar. Robbie was not there.

"Vinnie, my man," Brian said to the bartender. Vinnie was a Jersey bro who always played EDM and hated the slow weekday shifts. He usually ignored Brian and leaned on the bar, looking at his own biceps.

Brian drank his first Coors Light (with a normal amount of foam, whatever that meant). Liz ordered herself a water, and Vinnie said she better tip him as much as if she was ordering beers. SportsCenter baseball recaps played on the TV, but Vinnie changed the channel to MMA fighting. Liz's pulse spiked: Brian liked baseball better. She inhaled an invisible straw full of air and held her breath.

"What's this kung fu shit, Vinnie?" Brian asked. Vinnie shrugged. Brian scratched his own back and moaned a little bit when he got an itchy spot.

"Can you stop, like, making that noise?" Liz whispered, and Brian ignored her.

Liz asked Vinnie how he got into MMA, and he explained the difference between the jujitsu and kickboxing components, the importance of his nutrition and training regimens, and the social media followings of the biggest MMA fighters.

Liz used to roll her eyes and say, "Daaaad, do you have to talk to literally everyone, all the time?" But she'd learned a lot, listening to him trade stories with people. She'd learned how many cities flight attendants traveled to every week, how the manager at the grocery store predicted how much candy to stock before Halloween, and where her track teammate Ximena's mom lived before New Jersey (Tucson and then Tampa).

"What do you say, you about ready then?" Liz asked Brian. Vinnie was finally helping someone else, and she didn't want her dad to order another beer.

Brian ignored her and asked Vinnie again, "Where's Robbie?" Liz said sorry to Vinnie as Brian slid off the barstool and wove through the empty tables toward the back steps. "I'll bet he's in the office."

"Okay! We're going upstairs," Liz said over her shoulder to Vinnie. She didn't ask, *Can we go upstairs?* She didn't bother with all that anymore.

"He's not—uh," Vinnie said.

"Yep! Thanks!" Liz said. She found Brian in a supply room, between boxes of plastic cups and napkins. He was hugging a clipboard to his chest.

"Robbie needs these out for next weekend," Brian said, counting boxes of plastic cups. "Friday night they'll need all these—I'll get two or three sleeves ready."

She said sure, fine. Stern and consistent: all business. It did absolutely no good for her to lose it.

When he stared at the Dunkin' Donuts cashier's chest, or decided to help the kid at the grocery store put away carts in the pouring rain, her heart didn't race like it used to, her eyes didn't dart around anymore.

Before Brian got weird-sick, Liz would turn red if her mom called her name from across the Kohl's and held up a shirt, or she would slam the car door without saying good-bye if her dad dropped her off right in front of the movie theater. No one had really been looking at her then. Now everyone *actually was*, all the time.

If Margot thought Brian should only be allowed to put away five shopping carts in the pouring rain, she would ask Liz, "Why did you let him do ten?" And there was no answer to why five or ten or any, or to why they left the house with him at all.

She would understand what this time with her dad had both taught and taken from her when she had her own children and heard herself repeating the phrases she'd used so often with him: *We'll have to see about that, do you think that's a good idea?* And she would understand, during the times of her life when she didn't feel useful, why her dad had invented jobs for himself right up until the tumor made him sleep all the time.

"I'll need an hour here at least," Brian said. It was hot and smelled like sauerkraut in the storage room.

"Okay, well, I'll be downstairs," Liz said. For pain, you could offer medicine. For this? Today you tipped five bucks for a water and stood in a dusty supply room, then left him alone with his dumb pretend clipboard.

Liz sat on a bench in front of the Buccaneer, waiting to see if the fog would lift or linger. Later she would go to work with Gabe at Sumner Ave, for a slow afternoon. Carl would assign them two hours of cleaning and sorting. Along with the trash and broken umbrellas, they would find someone's car keys under the boardwalk and make it their mission to find the people who'd lost them, getting the lifeguards to announce the lost keys over their speaker and posting on social media. They would deliver the keys to a panicked family behind the water park, then celebrate their good deed and spend their ten-dollar reward on pizza and kiss before Liz walked home, past this same bench in front of the Buccaneer.

Robbie's pickup truck pulled up in back, and he gave Liz a weary wave before he headed upstairs. Brian followed Robbie in and out of the back doors of the bar three or four times, bringing a box every time.

"We got 'em all loaded up," Brian told Liz, wiping sweat off his forehead with a napkin.

"Saved me a few trips," Robbie said. He always seemed so sad, like he missed his old friend as much as Liz missed her old dad. He would probably have to put all those boxes in his truck back in the supply room after they left. "Glad you came by, man," Robbie said, giving Brian that guy-friend-slap on the back. Robbie asked Liz how Margot was doing, the how's-your-mom Jersey code for really giving a shit about someone, for acknowledging you went way back, and Liz asked about Robbie's mom too, who was fine and lived in Florida.

The whole way home Brian talked about Robbie's Sysco order, about the dimensions of his supply room, and how lucky they were the boxes fit in the back of his truck. The guilt of the lie Liz and Robbie were in on tightened around her like a too-snug life jacket.

Even though Liz now recited all the prayers in church again, they felt so formal, and she doubted they'd ever worked. Another kind of praying, where you beg God in quick bursts, had found her. *When it's my turn, not this,* she thought, and whether it was heard or echoed into the ether, she would never know.

Liz took her dad home.

CHAPTER FIVE

Margot

In a few hours, a doctor at Penn would tell them if Brian's tumor was growing and how aggressively, or he would give them what he called *good news*, which meant another three months stuck in the orbit of this person she used to love, who now scared her, defeated her, and pissed her off.

She didn't wish for either outcome; she wished for the entire day at Penn to proceed as if it were an entity apart from her, she wished for the gauzy protection of magical thinking to descend upon her when she pulled into the Penn parking garage, she wished for an impossible and unlikely peace to carry her from the beginning of this day to its bitter end. But before they left for Penn, they had a house turnover to do.

Evy

I'm always up by four in the morning the days we go to Penn, Margot had written to the Wives. Evy figured this was why her mom had scheduled the two of them to do a turnover before they drove to Philadelphia, instead of the cleaning crew. When she and Evy took care of houses together, Margot gave orders, but not in that exasperated, already-over-it way she did at home, and she also made jokes.

Her mom said both in the GBM Wives forum and in real life how she felt about the girls helping with the houses. "You guys were champs today, total champs," she would say to them after a fast turnover. *They work so hard, and I'm so proud of them*, she told the Wives. There was no dissonance between *those* two versions of her, nothing to figure out in between.

Margot unlocked the door to the rental. "Partiers," she said, as if affirming something she'd suspected, like on *Law and Order* when the cop said, "The warehouse," and then went to find the murderer there chilling *at the warehouse*.

Solo cups and beer cans covered every surface. The area rugs smelled of spilled beer. A bowl of squashed limes was sprinkled with ash. The kitchen tile was splotched with syrupy brown, the shelf of board games tipped over into a pile of Monopoly money and Jenga blocks. Every dish was piled into the sink, streaked with congealed nacho cheese sauce (*what do you call cheese that's not your cheese?*).

"You take the bathrooms, I'll start on the kitchen," Margot said, already in motion. She put Dolly Parton on the speaker, her favorite I-mean-business music.

Since she'd read her mom's post about moving, Evy had written five drafts in response and deleted all of them. She'd stared at her mom until Margot said, "What, honey? What's up? You okay?" then immediately left the room before telling her what was *up*. She'd seen more recent posts by Margot, advising other women about brain tumor drugs and surgeries, and those sounded much more like her and not like a liar lady who might set fire to all their possessions and move them to a yurt in Pennsatucky.

She'd read her mom's original post over and over; how could those lines *I rage and I stagnate, I'm not looking for compromise* have been typed by that woman downstairs who had made a calm plan to deal with this disaster?

Evy could just see the bitches who had rented the house and left it like this, weaving in and out of Parkway traffic, hungover, never imagining real humans with other shit to worry about would have to spend extra time cleaning up their mess.

"Hey, Chloe," Evy said under her breath as she sprinkled Comet into the bathtub and yanked a wet gunky blob of hair out of the drain, "hope you had a fun party, oh, you're getting a mani-pedi today? I'm going to a tumor hospital that smells like death, except the parts that smell like ass, and this is exactly what I wanted to be doing first, cleaning up your puke before I drive all the way out there, and I don't hope you die, but I do hope you get many, many herpes."

Growing up cleaning strangers' messes, you learned what people wasted, what they hid in the bottoms of trash bins, what particular things they forgot and called you about, frantic to get back, the day after they left. Turnovers taught you to focus—if you got distracted, you'd never finish in time; if you neglected a single chore, a renter would find a hairball or a poop ring in the toilet and it would ruin their day.

Evy lit a candle in the bathroom to get rid of the lingering smell. When she thought about it, she didn't want her mom to have to keep scrubbing toilets or worry anymore about whether some Airbnb person was a lunatic. She wanted her to have a job where she wasn't alone or overwhelmed, where someone was telling *her* every day she was a champ, or whatever adult bosses said to people who worked hard, like, "Exemplary spreadsheet, excellent meeting!"

Evy remembered going to her parents' classrooms, back before they did E&E full-time. Her mom's was bright and organized, with plants and posters, learning stations and a color-coded library, shelves of games and a huge bulletin board about the solar system.

Her dad's classroom had blank walls and piles of ungraded papers on every surface, but one time when she was there with him, he'd stopped what he was doing to talk to three different students about which colleges they should apply to, whether one was still playing wide receiver, and when another was taking her driving test. When he left teaching, her dad had dumped all but one of his cardboard boxes full of plans and tests and lessons in the trash and come home with only his Wildcats coffee mug. Her mom still had all her teaching supplies in the garage, in labeled bins; she could have a classroom set up again in an hour if she needed to.

Imagining the red E&E signs around town gone, Evy felt a stab of sadness. But she could see a certain logic in her mom not wanting to run the rental business without her dad, in wanting to go back to a job she had loved and left when she was getting really good at it.

It was the moving, and the way her mom had talked herself into it. It was *I have thought only of my daughters, and weighed their inevitable hate against what it would do to me to stay* that still made Evy feel so heavy that she lowered herself onto the tile floor and locked the bathroom door. Any idea that started with *I have thought only of my daughters* should end with them staying in Seaside, together.

Evy texted Olivia a picture of the spotless bathroom and the candle and wrote, **this was covered in a stranger's puke before, please clap**, and Olivia sent her a clapping hands emoji and texted: **wow, sounds like there's more to that story??**

When she blew out the candle and went back to the kitchen, Evy knew she would find her mom puttering at the sink, adjusting the blinds, writing a welcome note for the next renters in her prettiest cursive, being a good hostess and keeping them on schedule. She wondered if Margot was thinking at that very moment: *I'm not looking for compromise.*

Evy texted back to Olivia: **You have no idea.**

They finished with time to spare and went home for showers before heading to Penn; they would be halfway to Philadelphia by the time the new renters arrived for their week of rest and relaxation.

Margot

On the drive to Penn, they played *The Rocky Mountain Murders*, and the podcast narrator explained where each of the dead bodies was found: in a shed, behind a gas station, and in a basement. Margot and the girls hung on every word of the awful crime story, but the narrator's velvet-edged voice put Brian to sleep. This was one reason they always did these drives together: so they could zone out to stories about murder. The one time Uncle Pete had driven them to Brian's appointment, Pete had asked questions the whole way about tumors and real estate and talked to Brian about baseball, and Margot had wanted to murder *him* for not taking the hint when she turned up the volume on the podcast. Their ritual was important.

Brian had been sleeping more every day, waking up disoriented and detached each time. His obstinate impatience when he was awake seemed to wear him out now.

Since October, Margot had binged so many podcasts and documentaries about serial killers, psychopaths, and British lady-assassins. She stayed up too late and terrified herself, she blasted them on full volume while she tidied the house. The girls got into the murder stories too, watching and listening with Margot to women crying about finding a loved one's dismembered body in a blood-soaked bedroom. If someone skipped an episode or left for a second and missed something, they recapped updates to each other with single words: *The SHACK! The TRUNK! The BASEMENT!*

On *The Rocky Mountain Murders*, the killer explained from a prison pay phone how he had chosen his victims, where he bought the ropes and knives, how long he watched certain girls (they were always girls) before he made his move.

"Tell us about the hotel room!" Evy hissed from the backseat.

Margot and the girls wanted to hear about the darkness lurking in the hearts of these psycho men until the right amount of fury brought it out. Margot gravitated to the stories with the biggest elements of surprise, to the victims who were minding their own business and then got a bullet in the brain.

Her cauterized heart chambers were not the same as these hearts of stalkers who lurked around gas stations, but she wondered a lot about the parts of herself she could shut off; this dark distraction was the right kind of vice to make her own fear seem more ordinary.

Evy

At the last two visits, when Dr. Zimorodi declared *good news*, Margot's face had formed a flat, forced grin. After the last appointment, Evy's friends had filled their group text with happy faces, rainbows, and hearts when she texted them the *good news*, the same stream of teeny pictures they sent each other when someone had a birthday. Cameron texted **ur dad is soooo funny.**

But the *good news* gave Evy a mushy, gray feeling. After the last visit's *good news*, she had gone home and written a GBM Wives post as Pamplemousse7:

Everyone says good news, but it's not la di da around here, I feel like a mean liar, I feel like something's wrong with me, I feel like I want to turn my car around and go back to that hospital and tell them take him, I'll come by and say hi, I'll send him new pajamas and nice pillows, but you said he was gonna die six months ago so that is the exact amount of crazy time my heart budgeted for and it is NOT the kind of thing you make more of like red blood cells or something.

Liz

Brian counted their steps out loud through the cold corridors of the hospital, ten at a time. "Okay, so that's a hundred and ten steps, great," Margot said. "Here's our elevator."

"A lift is what they call them in London, or possibly a great glass elevator might be more appropriate," Brian said.

"I didn't think the woman from the supermarket would go with him to the mountain," Evy said, ignoring Brian and picking up where the murder podcast had left off.

"It's crazy how he had that whole cabin rigged," Liz said, joining Evy on their own little island of info about the murderer. It would have been kinder to talk to Brian and not over him. Someone would tell Liz one day that it was okay that she didn't go along with every free-association idea Brian's rogue brain brought forth, and she would wave them away until they said it a second time, and then she would break open, remembering the airless feeling in this elevator.

"So, Liz, how did the end of your track season turn out?" Dr. Zimorodi asked, after they'd all talked about traffic. Maybe there was a test in med school about making small talk, along with the class on where all the arteries and tendons were located.

Three months ago, Liz had felt fierce when she worked out so hard her muscles broke down and released that ammonia stink. Three months was such a long, long time.

"Oh, I stopped running," she said. It felt good to say this out loud to see how it landed. Dr. Zimorodi nodded and looked to Margot, then back to his computer screen, clearing his throat.

"It's all right to take a break when you need it," Margot said. Her mom's friends were always tagging Margot in online articles about self-care stuff like massages and baths, adding messages like *Take a break to take care of you,* though they never followed up to say, *I'll be over at ten tomorrow to stay with Brian—your Zen retreat at the strip mall spa is booked, on me!*

It's all right to take a break when you need it was meant to be encouraging, but really it was a way of forcing Liz into a space that her mom had jury-rigged out of the broken junk she had around and declared *fine. It's all right to take a break when you need it* sounded supportive and understanding, but Liz felt its subtext in her gut: *It must be nice, quitting when you get sick of something.*

"I give it three more weeks before you're running ten miles for fun again," Evy said.

There were things, like Liz's running, like Evy's friends' gossip, that they only talked about in this way: quick, sarcastic callouts. Liz rolled her eyes whenever Evy complained about hangovers or anything to do with Hailey, and Evy called Liz's track teammates nerds. But they also escaped to each other's rooms and admitted in whispers when their days dedicated to being good daughters to their dying dad had defeated them. Evy helped Liz sound like she cared less when she texted Gabe, and Liz listened to Evy figure out how to be as brave in person around Olivia as she was on social media. Still, neither of them could resist the jabs and the shrugs and sarcasm sometimes. Neither of them could survive this time without the other.

Margot

Margot followed the end of Dr. Zimorodi's pen across the screen, staring as it traced the gray-on-gray between healthy tissue and the creeping decay. The tenor of his voice was a soft legato, his eyes steady and watery brown, but he was direct in his language: the treatments had stopped working, the tumor would take over now. He said it again, his phrasing free of metaphor to avoid any chance of misunderstanding. *There's nothing else we can do.*

Margot's eyes lifted from the contours of the doctor's face, flicking around in panic: to her daughters, who reached for each other; to the door; to the blurred edges of her husband in her peripheral vision. A hot-acid chokehold closed on her neck and only let her get a sharp half-breath of air.

The doctor's delicate explanations of where, when, and how the tumor would take over now—soon—were fine, were necessary, were nonsense. Brian's muscles tensed, and his eyes landed on each person in the room, alert and searching.

Margot had been nudged off the cliff now, and she was suspended in air before the inexorable rush of gravity sucked her down down down, without any nylon rainbow parachute strapped to her back to slow her descent. She was not a winged bird or a weightless soul, she was heavy and human, with her healthy multiplying cells evolving or maybe mutating, with her offspring here, with her big brain and falling blood sugar and melanin-flecked skin, with her fighting or flighting instinct kicking in without her permission, telling her with all its chemical cues: *survive.*

Did that deadened tissue Dr. Zimorodi pointed out protect Brian from what would otherwise have been shock and pain? Margot reached for Brian's hand, but he swatted it away. She folded her hands in her lap, hunching forward, and her head dropped. She waited a few moments, still feeling the warm sting where he'd hit her.

Brian emitted a guttural sound and paced toward the back of the room until he ran out of space, breathing in and out and swinging his arms like a boxer getting ready for his next round.

Did Liz and Evy feel this same dulled-approximation, this artificial-almost-pain, the blessed temporary numbness that she did not trust at all? They seemed stunned and still, their eyes focused on the floor. Had they tried to catch her eye and she'd missed it?

Did they share the same shame at their own failure to really fall apart with wails and howls at this moment, and should Margot fake falling apart like *that*, for them? She couldn't reach their hands from here. She couldn't offer any assurance that the torrent would come one day, and they were not all broken or wrong just because today was not that day. The girls came to her and hugged her even though she couldn't stand up.

Dr. Zimorodi left the screen open to the images. He filled the beats of silence with more professional, relevant follow-up details she didn't hear. Evy interrupted him to ask, "How long, exactly?" He said some *never knows* and *every case is differents*, a few *anything could happens*, but then he said: by the end of summer.

Liz

She was uncomfortable in this instant, but in the same way that repeat 200s readied her for the final kick of the 1600, her body was ready for this: everything fell out of rhythm, but then she found it again, fast.

Her blood pressure spiked and then stabilized. Her throat closed up and then relaxed. Her tears smudged her makeup, swelled her sinuses and throat. Her tears were warm and then went cold when they hit the air. Then they simply stopped.

Margot dabbed her eyes. Brian ran out of rage and eased into his chair, for now performing the straight-backed imitation of himself they had tried and failed to summon too many times to count.

Evy

They were shuffled to the social worker's eucalyptus-scented office. Whenever Evy smelled eucalyptus after this day, she would feel a cold shadow encircle her. The scent would surprise her for so long, even as she deliberately sought out eucalyptus-scented things to desensitize herself, dabbing oils or lotions on her pulse points at times she knew she would already be strong and relaxed.

Margot read over a booklet about palliative care, then handed it to Evy. She read the bullet points inside, nestled between butterfly and flower graphics. There was a stock photo of an old gray-haired woman, whose face looked like it had been given a triple shot of Botox. She was hugging a hundred-year-old man.

"Oh, hello, man who could be my father, or much older husband, if he left his third wife for me sometime in the eighties," she imagined the Botox photo lady saying to the hundred-year-old man. She had already Googled what happened when hospice came to your house, and she imagined the Botox lady saying, "Here in this bag I have enough morphine, Ativan, and Haldol to literally kill you, these drugs really do not fuck around, anyway I don't believe in heaven, the afterlife is a myth, oh, there goes another butterfly!" Evy let the pamphlet fall to the floor.

The social worker handed them steaming paper cups of tea before she rephrased everything in the booklets. It was her whole job to make this one hour softer: the light, the air, the words on glossy paper. She herself was a soft-looking person, wearing a loose-knotted scarf, a flowy beige dress. Her hay-colored hair in loose curls. It was her job to ease them into understanding how fast it would all happen before they left and another family sat across from her. Couldn't they all stay here, together in the muted light coming in through the sheer-curtained window, where someone asked the exact right questions?

Evy watched her mother's pigment-edged lips move, confirming with *ahs* and *uh-huhs* that she understood. And then this part was over, and they were back in the van, which smelled like Margot's Febreze. *The Rocky Mountain Murders* picked up right where they had left off, with a survivor's disguised voice explaining how little she remembered.

Margot

On the drive home to Seaside, Margot anticipated the ordinary landmarks: the Wawas, the diners, the upscale strip malls of the Philly suburbs, and the stand-alone bars with sand parking lots in the Pine Barrens. Mile markers, chapters, months. Files, storage containers, grocery aisles. All ways to make order, to measure and divide so everything wasn't a jumble of disconnected junk.

She looked straight ahead, holding the wheel steady, even when Brian woke up from a nap and said the air smelled like sulfur, even when his request to play some old live version of "Rosalita" no one could find escalated into pounding on the windows and deep-throated grumbling: *bitches bitches, cunts cunts, ridiculous twats*, before he slumped down in exhaustion again.

Margot gave in to the inertia of thinking only *get home, eat, sleep,* as hypnotized by the double yellow lines as she was by the tired voices of the lawyers who'd tried the Rocky Mountain murderer in the 1980s and almost lost.

She bit down on the M&M's Evy handed her, swallowing the softened chocolate as the brake lights flicked on and off in front of her and the textured afternoon daylight faded. A police officer on the podcast remembered how frayed his nerves were when the killer kept eluding him.

The road opened up from the dark two-lanes into the bright lights of the strip malls and car dealerships of Route 37, and Margot pulled into a sub shop parking lot. The girls brought back a bag full of vinegar and onion and yeasty bread smells into the van, and they ate while they drove. Brian lay silent across the backseat.

She thought he would be starving as they neared home, so she'd had the girls order him a number five with extra capicola, extra provolone. But he wasn't hungry at all, even when she said she got his favorite.

Margot turned on the defroster to erase the layer of condensation forming inside the windshield, fighting against the warmth all their bodies were now giving off.

CHAPTER SIX

Evy

"Hey, Dad, you want the usual at Dunkin'?" Evy asked, but Brian was asleep in the passenger seat, still worn out from their trip to Philadelphia the day before. "Iced coffee with cream, got it, yeah, looks like you could use some caffeine!" she said out loud anyway. When it was Liz's turn to be alone with him, she took him for those walks on the boardwalk where he veered into everyone and made her stop at the Buccaneer for beers. Margot would take him to look at towels or paint swatches and then spend twenty minutes trying to find him in the store. Evy took him for drives.

Evy wouldn't be old enough to get a driver's license for another year; she had her permit, and Brian technically still counted as a licensed driver, even though he probably would have careened into the bay if he tried to drive a car himself.

At first, she took a lot of precautions to hide it from Margot, refilling the gas tank, arriving home an hour before anyone else. Then she got lazy, leaving the tank a quarter full, waiting until the last second to pull into the driveway before her mom got home, but Margot never noticed.

The first time Evy had taken Brian for a secret drive was last fall. "I want to call Congress, about HB 798.2," Brian had told Evy that afternoon, the second Margot left them alone. Then he was on the phone for twenty minutes, haranguing some congressional staffer, saying *outrageous* and *unconstitutional* and *anarchy*. Evy Googled HB 798.2 and found nothing except call numbers for library books on horses.

When he finally hung up, he crawled behind the TV, fiddling with wires and yanking them out of the wall before the screen went blank. "*What* are you doing?" Evy asked. "Also, Brian, there's no HB 798.2."

At the soccer practice she had skipped to stay with him, they would be doing passing drills right now. Evy liked drills: the repetitive rhythm of weaving around cones or trapping a ball over and over. She played left midfield, on the JV team, where she was fully responsible for neither scoring nor defense, where she never stopped moving.

She could break out and find an opening, take a shot, but that was a special, every-so-often thing. There wasn't the constant pressure to fire at the goal that the forwards had, or the chaos of bodies inside the eighteen that the defense had to deal with.

When Evy watched Liz win a race, she thought the tunnel of cheering faces at the finish line was cool. But she also saw Liz the night before those meets, picking at her skin and doing plyometrics at 11 p.m. because she was too nervous to sleep. She couldn't imagine competing at anything without a team in front of and behind her to back her up.

"You are a child," Brian had said that day, crawling out from behind the TV. His face reddened with the effort. "You should drink chocolate milk, not make accusations. HB 798.2, in case you were not aware, is a legislation type that provides business owners like myself with a fair way of savings."

Her soccer coach was always talking about *building character*. Evy was almost sure it was all made up—all the character-building bullshit coaches and teachers claimed turned you into a responsible, hardworking adult. She played soccer because it was nice to get some air and kick a ball around for an hour before she went home, not because it was turning her into a team-oriented adult.

She liked Coach B, despite her *building character* speeches. She had some kind of other not-teacher job she called consulting that she wore dress clothes for once or twice a week. She bought the whole team pizza and made them screen-printed hoodies without even collecting money for them; her wife was a fancy lawyer of some kind who brought their labradoodle to games. Was that being a great adult? Marrying a fancy lawyer, living your JV soccer coaching/consulting dream? Coach B, an adult, seemed very happy.

Evy was pretty sure she was going to be a fucking great adult whether she spent her afternoons kicking a ball, running into a forest with thirty other people like Liz at her cross-country meets, or watching Bravo and eating Zebra Cakes. Or whatever *this* was with her dad.

A substitute teacher had once shown their health class an ancient after-school special called *Forgiving Karen*, a cheesy, melodramatic movie about a girl who sneaks vodka mixed with Gatorade to her history class and crashes her car into a guardrail. Evy wasn't worried that too many shots at high school parties would turn her into a teen alcoholic. If she lived in another country, she would already be going to a pub like normal adults did all the time. The drinking age was one more arbitrary rule invented by adults, most of whom—including her mom—drank a lot more than her, they just spread it out over the whole week.

Coaches and parents and teachers weren't deliberately lying—winning at sports and getting straight A's had been the first steps to being a great adult when they were young one hundred years ago. But all the rules had changed. You could get A's and go to an expensive college and still work at Old Navy paying off your debt forever, or you could get F's and smoke weed every day and invent an app, or get a billion YouTube subscribers to your makeup tutorial channel, and none of those scenarios had anything to do with being an interesting person.

That day in the fall, Brian had turned the TV back on, and static shushed at them at full volume. He said, "They've been cheapening the service for years. I'll have Robbie come install a particular spare satellite dish I know he's storing."

She was sure as hell never going to write about this shit with her dad on a college application. Dear admissions committee: nope.

Her dad had droned on, asking and answering his own questions in a breathy, conspiring way about where he and Robbie would position the dish on the roof. That voice made Evy uneasy, like when her friends were drunk but she wasn't, when they slurred their words and whispered too loud. She talked back to her dad the same way she did to them, with lots of noncommittal *uh-huhs* and stupid-bright *sures*.

"Evelyn, damn it, this is necessary equipment," he said, and then some metal bolts clunked down onto the floor. The drill made a grinding sound. When had he grabbed the drill? Had there been a pocket of quiet while she checked her phone, when he'd found it without her noticing?

The girls she used to babysit had made themselves up into little psycho beauty pageant contestants with their mom's makeup once, right before their parents got home—that had also happened in a pocket of quiet. Of course, that mom had never asked Evy to babysit again, but other families still called her all the time, not because she brought crafts or cleaned their kitchen, but because she was good at distracting kids from tantrums. She understood that a quick *grab your shoes and get in the wagon* almost always worked to keep kids from losing their damn minds over a lost Lego but only if you got everyone moving the second you said it.

When Evy spotted the keys on the counter, her babysitter-tantrum-distraction sense had kicked in, and then she was clutching them in her fist. She'd realized Brian still had his license, technically. She grabbed his wallet too.

"We're going for a drive," Evy said. Brian followed her, still gripping his drill. She almost said, *Get in the wagon.* He set the drill in the backseat and buckled it in like a baby, then climbed up front. Evy started the car and pulled out of the driveway, setting them in motion, the only trick she knew.

That first secret-drive day, Evy had taken one lap around the block and then declared, "Mom wants us to check on the K Street house." They'd idled there a few minutes, looking out the window at a vacant bungalow.

"We better check out the C Street property too," Brian said, some part of him both in on it now and still oblivious. Driving somewhere felt like a mission, and the idea of a mission unmired him enough from whatever the f he was doing with the cable and the congressional bill. "This house looks good," he said, "but we'll swing by again tomorrow."

They drove up and down Bayview for another twenty minutes; the whitecapped bay blurred by. "The swans are out already," he said, before he sighed and sank into a light sleep. There wasn't a swan in sight.

One day last December Brian had asked if they could drive to the inlet, where they looked across to the lighthouse. By mid-January, they were driving north on the Parkway, getting off to drive past the empty orchards and horse farms in Colts Neck; they were driving to the Turnpike exit before the Lincoln Tunnel before heading south again, stopping to watch the planes at Newark Airport take off.

Would Margot even believe Brian, if he told her some out-there story about how Evy had driven them all the way to Atlantic City and back? Would it sound any different from his other warped stories?

Most of the motions of driving were easy for Evy: flick the blinker, adjust the mirrors, ease down on the brake when a light turned from yellow to red. The feel of her hands gripping the wheel and the accumulation of miles to their made-up destinations all made more and more sense to her whenever they were alone together, even as her dad made less and less.

But she still made so many rookie-driver mistakes, missing exits or cutting other cars off when she forgot to check her blind spot. "Heard a honk there," or "Sharp turn," Brian said sometimes, only aware of what he could feel or hear, missing everything outside his narrow, blurry tunnel of vision.

One dim winter day Evy had accidentally run a red light in Point Pleasant, ten miles north of Seaside, and then a siren whined behind her. She'd pulled over and the flashing lights flooded the dashboard.

"Yellow doesn't mean try to beat the light, young lady," the cop said. She'd handed over her permit, and her dad's license. A jolt of adrenaline jacked her heart rate up and she felt herself talking a little too loud, upspeaking when she meant to sound assured and chill and convincing. Would they take Brian's license away if he started acting weird? Would Margot have to come pick them up in Point Pleasant? Could they delay her real license because of this?

"I—uh—yeah, my dad said I still needed some practice? Yeah, with passing and everything, so I could go see my grandma next week? So . . . he was helping me!"

Didn't they usually go walkie-talkie all the info to their buddies at the station? Was he going to say, "Step out of the car now" next, or call a direct line to the Seaside cops to confirm her identity?

"Dad, we've got a new driver here, then?" He winked.

"Well, Officer, I did wonder whether the loading zones will be permanent, as I'm sure you're aware there's no standing statute—" Brian said.

"I'm really, like, so sorry," Evy interrupted him, flipping her hair. "It's my fault and he actually told me not to go." The cop's face softened to a fatherly knowing, as if thinking about how silly young ladies could be, and he crossed his arms and leaned down into the car. She knew you had to walk the line, not go full tears-and-snot, but still act a little worried they'd caught you. She'd gotten her friends out of more than one cop visit when things got loud in someone's backyard.

"Evelyn, very old-fashioned name," he said, cocking his head, shifting his weight. "Was my grandmother's name. She was a good woman, raised five kids and never complained about it."

Evy thought that seemed unlikely. "It was my grandma's name too, Officer," she said. It wasn't. She could see Brian pressing against his seat belt like he wanted out—they needed motion again before he followed some urge to reach across her and hold the officer's hand and pray for his soul or something. She said, "I get sooo nervous at those left turns!"

"Well, you keep in mind, that light changes and you stay put, hon." He walked away with a little wave-salute. *Hon* was so condescending and old-mannish, but being able to pass as a *hon* was also a superpower, it could keep her safer and out of trouble. Not all her friends could pass as a *hon*. She got *hon* and a nice grandma story and a wink, and then she got to keep driving. She knew exactly what she could get away with.

To celebrate their escape, Evy had driven through Dunkin' Donuts for coffees, establishing a routine Brian then expected every time they drove together, until this day after Penn when he didn't ask for any iced coffee, when he slept and slept instead.

"Want to go to the inlet?" Evy asked. He was still asleep. "Yeah? Sure, let's go," she answered for him.

She'd already drained her own coffee and felt the caffeine and sugar from her extra-caramel and whipped cream surging through her. She tried some of her dad's, but it had a heavy bitterness, because it was the drink of an adult who didn't need to cover up the taste of coffee anymore. She didn't like it, but she took another sip anyway, and they drove to the edge of the barrier island together one last time.

CHAPTER SEVEN

Liz

Gabe drove Liz home from Sun and Shade after work. That evening, she, Evy, and Margot were going to meet the hospice nurse, Lorraine. Dr. Zimorodi had warned them things would change fast, and they had; in the days since their Penn visit, Brian had slept eight or ten more hours a day. He woke up at 3 a.m. one night, ate cereal out of a mixing bowl, drank a beer, then fell asleep again at the table, where they found him in the morning. Then he descended into some other kind of sleep that softened his muscles and unclenched his jaw, a kind that didn't always separate one day from another, but rushed in to fill nearly the whole day and night.

In the sudden calm, Margot, Liz, and Evy orbited each other, ate their meals standing, and munched on stale chips or softened fruit, as if they were all awaiting further instructions from someone else. Maybe Lorraine would be that someone else.

"I remember when the windows on that house were all blown out after Sandy," Gabe said. They were driving past the restored Victorian, the house that had always been Margot's favorite. Gabe's voice jolted Liz out of her zoned-out state. *Whatever the sun's gonna do, you know the tide will follow,* her dad had said to her that morning, before he slid back under his sheets with his baseball cap on.

"Oh—yeah. My family owns that place now," Liz said. Her parents had managed that property for its previous owner, but the day they bought it themselves, Margot had brought home champagne for her and Brian and sparkling cider for the girls to celebrate. "My mom is obsessed with it."

The people renting the Victorian this week were out on the porch drinking gin and tonics; three Audis were parked in the long driveway. The big American flag stirred. It was easy to miss the E&E sign in front of that house, nestled among the landscaping. It wasn't like they needed the extra advertising—that place was always booked. It was as if all the gin-and-tonic-Audi people who wanted to go on vacation had a bat signal with each other to get out their gold credit cards the first day it was available.

"It's a nice house, I can see why," he said. "Also, you know you hardly ever say anything about your family except when you're turning over a rental house for them? I thought maybe you were an orphan who lived in a closet under the stairs."

Her whole family had, technically, lived under her grandparents' stairs, in their basement, while they rebuilt after the hurricane. Liz had gone to a different elementary school for that whole time, with a dirty mural painted on the side and a stinky hamster in the back of the classroom. Her parents were gone all the time and her grandma made her watch PBS Kids shows that were too babyish.

"Why don't you guys live there, then," he asked, "if your mom loves it so much?"

"That place only rents to rich people," she said. "You don't *live* in the fancy rental houses—people are paying for them to feel perfect. My parents talked—I mean, they *talk* about moving there one day, after it makes them more money, I guess, but it's like they haven't earned it yet."

"So, you guys own, like, half the houses in Seaside, but *you're* not the rich people?"

The way her parents had always talked about money was complicated; they went around and around about interest rates and refinancing the bungalows, about renovation budgets and payroll, arguing and negotiating for hours. It all seemed precarious and convoluted to her, not rich.

There were kids at school who wore the same running shoes for three seasons and got cafeteria food every day, even if it was something gross, because they qualified for free lunch. And there were kids who spent their summers sailing at the yacht club and drove loaded black SUVs like they were in a presidential motorcade. She guessed her family was somewhere in the middle, but an uncertain, up-and-down kind of middle.

Did rich people have to spend so much time arguing over whether to buy a new or used power washer, about whether they could afford to hire someone else for the cleaning crew for five hours of work on Saturdays? Did rich people drive old vans and only eat out at BYOB restaurants? Did they hustle to wash strangers' sheets and clean hair out of the drains before the next people showed up for their vacations? She didn't like how Gabe said *rich*, like he was accusing her of something she wasn't even sure was true. Even if they were rich, it wasn't bank-owner rich, it wasn't influencer or world-traveler rich.

Even if they were rich, she was still on her way home to meet the nurse who was there to help her dad die. If they were rich, what good was it doing them now?

Margot

Who was this woman who would be in her house, enmeshed with them in these last moments? Today, she was a stranger. Tomorrow, Lorraine would work behind a closed door with Brian, taking care of his skin and bowels and sleep and pain, easing him—them—into the fast-approaching phase she was an expert in.

Tomorrow, she would tell Margot what to do, with the calm and confidence of an army nurse who had traveled the world caring for wounded soldiers before settling down near the beach.

Tonight, Lorraine would tell Margot and the girls how her expertise had been earned, from long nights caring for soldiers in the desert, and from her last five years repeating the palliative rituals inside other people's homes. Lorraine lived two towns over and only took hospice jobs on the island. She was tiny and strong, and her skin was smooth and unblemished, her neat half-gray bob tucked behind her ears. She wore a large rubber watch like an athlete, as if she was ready to take a pulse or run a marathon.

Lorraine had a respect for and belief in what people were aware of in the end, a reverence for the meaning of the work, and a practical way of communicating that Margot found too frank at first but grew to trust. Lorraine let Margot ask dozens of questions, keeping her answers short and her tone honeyed but tough. Margot scribbled down Lorraine's first few answers, making her repeat medicine dosages and brand names of supplies they still needed, but then Lorraine reached over and put her hand on Margot's as she gripped her pen.

"You don't have to do that," she said. "I'll tell you the rest again tomorrow."

Brian was already asleep on the recently delivered hospital bed in the guest room, a particular model Lorraine approved of. "Go on in and talk to him," Lorraine suggested to the girls. She and Margot still had to discuss morphine. "People can get overwhelmed," Lorraine explained. "It's all right to say something ordinary, tell him about your day. And keep his windows open if it's cool enough, so he can hear what's going on outside."

A few minutes later Margot was surprised to hear Eddie Vedder's deep voice through the door, layered with the girls' voices. If Brian was listening at all, maybe the music would trigger a dream of that concert he drove to see, three hours alone in the snow, the night before he proposed to her, or of the lyrics he'd scribbled in an anniversary card he bought her the year after Hurricane Sandy. He had attached a fly-in-amber necklace to the card—such a strange and perfect gift to commemorate or apologize for the hardest year of their lives. Before the one she was living through now, anyway. After Lorraine went home, she would go and find the necklace.

Who would Lorraine be to Margot by the time she left them, which was to say, by the time Brian left them? In only an hour, Margot felt unburdened enough to exhale without holding a little air in reserve each time, she felt a gratitude for the one small certainty of this woman in her home at this exact fragile moment.

Evy

The hospital bed was bulkier than she would have imagined. It took up so much space they'd had to shove the dresser and armchair together in a corner and put the nightstands out in the hallway.

Evy still expected her dad to get up any minute and start an argument about whether they could go to Acme at midnight for peaches so he could make the neighbors cobbler and call it gobbled-up cake, to absolutely insist on it, to tell them which neighbors he swore he'd promised gobbled-up cake to, they had to make it. She wouldn't trust this descent into sleep even as it stretched on day after day.

She sat in a pile of pillows on the floor while Liz perched on the edge of the dresser. Brian barely stirred.

"I like her," Evy said. "Lorraine."

"She's going to hook tubes up to him," Liz said. "And give him so many drugs. That's what they're talking about."

"I feel weird in here." Evy scrunched up her face and nose, and hugged her knees up to her chest, looking at the dark rearranged room. She would come in once to be with her dad alone, but seeing his sunken cheeks and discolored skin would make her panic, and she would not go in by herself again.

"I know. It smells like dad-sweat and the rubber from that mattress," Liz said. Evy opened the window as Lorraine had told them to do. The background noise of their neighbors in the summer was a whole mood if you paid attention: laughter and children and guitar strings, the *thwap* of their screen door, the hiss of water on concrete of the outdoor shower. The summer went on without them tonight.

Liz

Margot had paused midway through reorganizing this room to accommodate the hospital bed. Bins of baseball caps, piles of papers, and cords littered the space around their dad's bed. Liz pulled out a boombox and a binder full of Brian's old CDs from a box and flipped through them, holding up individual discs to show Evy, asking if she wanted to listen to any of them and getting vetoed every time.

"They're all scratched up anyway," Evy said. "I don't know why he kept them when you can literally stream any album anytime you want. Here, I'll look up a dad-rock playlist."

"Let's try a few more actual CDs, I don't know, I kind of feel like he'll be able to hear the difference?"

Evy shrugged, and Liz held up Billy Joel, Queen, Pink Floyd, Jimmy

Buffett; she held up Ben Folds, Stevie Wonder, Foo Fighters, Fleetwood Mac, the Cranberries; she held up Tom Petty, Nine Inch Nails, Nirvana. The huge binder had no particular allegiance to any time period or genre. Liz held up Elvis Costello and Beastie Boys CDs side by side, and Evy shook her head. "I didn't know Elvis *had* a last name," she said.

"Different Elvis, you idiot," Liz said.

"You can just play whatever old CD you want," Evy said.

"Should we be talking *to him*? Like Lorraine said?" Liz held up Pearl Jam's *Vitalogy*.

"Sure. *Dad*, Pearl Jam is a *very stupid* name," Evy said. "Like maybe they thought that was cool twenty years ago, but now it sounds gross."

"I'm putting this one on," Liz said. "Here's some dad rock for ya."

She picked a random track from the album, "Better Man," which started quiet and which Evy hated right away. She shook her head and tried to make her case against listening any longer, but Liz shushed her so she could hear it.

Halfway through, the quiet guitar gave way to drums and bigger chords, like an answer to the beginning, and Liz remembered this part of the song from when Brian used to play it in the car, nodding his head along up front while they stared out the windows in the back. She'd never paid close attention to the lyrics, but they were sad, about a woman who comes back to a guy who treats her badly because she can't find anyone else, or she's too scared to be alone, or maybe both.

"I mean, this music is depressing," Evy said, "but so is all this, so, you know." She waved her hands around to indicate *all this*.

They all went to bed early, but Liz couldn't sleep. There were no texts yet from Gabe—he usually waited until the middle of the night to text

hey this made me think of you and send her links to songs she would listen to in the dark, scrolling through the lyrics and memorizing the lines as barely coded signals. Evy agreed that sending songs was a sign he definitely wanted to have sex with her; you did not send songs to girls you did not want to have sex with.

She dragged her dad's CD binder into her own room. She flipped on the light and sat up in bed and turned each heavy page, pulling out the ones she wanted to listen to with him and flipping through the little booklets of lyrics wedged behind each disc. In one of the back pages, stuck between Led Zeppelin and John Denver, next to No Doubt, Liz found a gold CD with the letters *M&B* Sharpied on the front. She plugged her headphones into the CD player and tried to play it, but no sound came out, so she sneaked into the hall closet and dug out an external CD drive from a box labeled OLD COMPUTER STUFF to plug into her laptop.

When she opened the file, it was a mess, copied and pasted and reformatted so many times, but readable: *M&B* wasn't an audio CD, but a big file called margotbrian.txt. She locked her bedroom door and started to read.

9/6/94
Subject: hey
To: margotmeyer@stanthonys.edu
From: brian-dunne@rutgers.edu

Hey Margot,
    I couldn't wait (I know you said you'd write first)
    How's the Midwest?
    Rutgers is . . . big. It's easy to let your mind wander, and it wandered to you more than a few times. I miss

you. What if I drove out to see you this weekend?? I'm
getting in the car tomorrow if you don't tell me not to.
    -B

9/11/94
Subject: re: hey
To: brian-dunne@rutgers.edu
From: margotmeyer@stanthonys.edu

I know you're driving back to NJ now and won't get
this until you're back. . . . If you play the tape I made
you eight times, you'll make it all the way home.
Anyway I hope your mind keeps wandering.
    -M

9/18/94
Subject: re: hey
To: margotmeyer@stanthonys.edu
From: brian-dunne@rutgers.edu

I love you.
    I know I'm not supposed to say that, especially in a
dumb email, and because we're definitely NOT "long-
distance dating" and everything, but I do.
    I'm gonna build a house near the ocean one day. I
want you to live in it with me.
    You don't have to say if you will or not. I hope you will.

Liz slammed the laptop closed, her heart racing, and she held her
body still in case she heard her mom's footsteps in the hallway. There

were so many more emails to read, but Liz didn't think she should keep going. Not tonight, not alone, not all at once. You weren't really supposed to know this part of your parents' lives. But: you also weren't supposed to know the parts of them that would be left if their impulses took over everything else they'd ever learned or felt, and she knew all that about her dad now.

Even in these first few emails, she'd found out that her dad had said he loved her mom first, he had thought of her from far away and gone to see her, and promised to build her the house they *lived in now.*

He'd known, when he was only a year older than Liz was this summer, that he should risk telling her mom how he felt from some computer lab a thousand miles away. And her mom hadn't ghosted or been afraid it was all too much.

The idea of her parents staying up late to tell each other how they felt in front of a big old glowing computer screen was so sad, if you knew how the story turned out, but it was also like the old rom-coms she and Sonia loved to watch, like *You've Got Mail* or *Bridget Jones's Diary*. She was rooting for them and wanted to see if they ever broke each other's hearts.

She also wanted to show Evy before she read ahead to exactly how they'd found their way to each other in Seaside again, because all she knew was the supercondensed version their parents always told, devoid of all the best details: they'd met working at the Cranky Crab the summer before college, then they ran into each other at the Buccaneer after not seeing each other for a long time.

While she was reading, she had missed a text from Gabe: **I tried to write a song tonight and everything felt forced and fake—too much on my mind . . . if I'm late tomorrow, just tell Carl, Gabe had to write some terrible songs last night. I'm sure he'll understand, boss.**

Maybe she would save these texts and love Gabe forever, or maybe they would disappear with her next phone upgrade, and he would take off at the end of August for a tour of the West Coast and never text her again. Tonight she didn't care.

She did a quick Google search for "songs that took a long time to write" and texted back: **Did you know Dolly Parton wrote Jolene and I Will Always Love you in ONE NIGHT? But Born to Run took six months. So keep going.**

Everything they said to each other felt more important now; she wanted to tell Gabe everything.

Part II

Chapter Eight

Margot

After their first meeting with Lorraine, Margot found a crumpled Post-it with the word *emerald* scribbled on it in Brian's room. She set down the armful of clutter she was shoving into a box and sat at the edge of his bed. Was *emerald* just one of the dozens of words he had been cataloguing, a random output of *em-* words unattached to any meaning or message?

On her left hand, she wore the emerald Brian had given her when he proposed. It was tighter now, the band scratched and the stone clouded. Brian had bought it in an antique shop years before he gave it to her, and he and Margot had made up so many stories about how the ring ended up there: it was pawned in a crazy game of poker; it was sold off from a grand estate; it was some stubborn Taurus woman's birthstone, lost one day when she set it down in a fancy hotel.

The ring had confused plenty of diamond-wearing women, but Margot had never been the kind of person who wanted too much glitter. Give her the somber deep green and the imperfections of this cheaper stone. Give her a guy who went all-in when he was too young to know better and brought her along with him. Brian buying this ring had been such an old-fashioned gesture, such a brazen symbol of hope, such a statement that he knew her and what she really wanted. Who would ever know her that way again?

Evy

"We should show these to Mom, right?" Liz asked.

"Terrible idea. She's not good with nostalgia right now," Evy said. They were supposed to be doing a house turnover before their shifts at Sal's Sweets and Sun and Shade, but instead they were swinging on a rental house hammock. Liz had emailed the whole margotbrian.txt document to Evy, and they were both reading it on their phones. They held their small screens over their heads and shared the dregs of a coconut iced coffee.

"I feel like such a stalker reading these," Liz said. "They only wrote them for each other."

"If you didn't want to read them, you would have slid that CD right back in there with all the dad rock," Evy said. That morning, Margot had written a new post on the GBM Wives forum, less emotional and more logistics-focused, asking about which small cities were *best for the arts*, as if she were super into Shakespeare and needed to see *Hamlet* every month instead of obsessed with murder documentaries and fantasy novels.

Liz checked the time. "We need to get this house done."

"Whatever, the house will be easy, and why would you show me these if you were gonna make me swoosh the toilets right away? That's mean," Evy said. "You don't have to read the rest if you don't want to. But I'm going to." Evy was not afraid that reading something she wasn't supposed to would make her sadder; that was impossible.

"We do only know the story Mom and Dad tell," Liz said, shrugging and slow-nodding, her usual signals she was really thinking about something.

"*Oh, we met in a bar after being apart for a long, long time,*" Evy said, doing a breathy impression of Margot, fluttering her eyelashes. This made Liz laugh, and then she set her phone down and convinced Evy to at least finish the house first. Evy went inside to clean with her headphones on, experimenting with a playlist of dad rock, giving it another chance. She listened to *Rumours* and decided Stevie Nicks was an ethereal witch; she could get on board with that particular brand of dad rock.

As anticipated, it was an easy turnover and only took half the time they'd allowed. The renters hadn't even used the kitchen or second bedroom at all. "Mom should only rent houses to tidy old people like this from now on," Evy said.

"Yeah, she should change those listings she always obsesses over, from *idyllic haven for your perfect family* to *elderly non-slobs only,*" Liz said. "Okay, I want to read the rest. But doesn't the idea of reading them knowing how it ends mess with you a little? Like these poor people in the emails, they have no idea."

"No. I think it's worse for the people in the emails if all the stuff they said gets ignored. Also, Stevie Nicks is a dark angel, I am partially open to dad rock now."

They sank into the hammock again and shared their screens. They read everything Liz had already read, then an exchange in October where their parents mostly talked about *Pulp Fiction,* their favorite Elliott Smith songs, and their Philosophy 101 classes. Then they kept reading.

11/6/94

Subject: homesick

To: brian-dunne@rutgers.edu

From: margotmeyer@stanthonys.edu

Sometimes I feel so homesick here and worry after
awhile I won't feel at home anywhere. Sometimes I
feel myself starting to love it here.

Are you ok on Sundays? For me, those are the worst.
I think I made a mistake going so far away!

11/7/94

Subject: re: homesick

To: margotmeyer@stanthonys.edu

From: brian-dunne@rutgers.edu

If it helps, I feel homesick too, and I'm much closer to
home. You didn't make a mistake, I've seen you there
on Saturday afternoon. I think Sundays feel kind of
homesick everywhere.

I love you.

11/18/94

Subject: re: homesick

To: brian-dunne@rutgers.edu

From: margotmeyer@stanthonys.edu

I'm counting down to Thanksgiving—I have a
Kierkegaard paper due first—but anyway, I'm glad we
didn't spend our first semester waiting by the phone

and whining when the other person sounds tired. I'm
so excited to tell you the long version of everything. I
got your mixtape for the ride home but I listened to it
already.

12/3/94
Subject: re: homesick
To: margotmeyer@stanthonys.edu
From: brian-dunne@rutgers.edu

I know, we shouldn't be waiting by the phone, but
what if we did, maybe just sometimes? Maybe only
Sundays.

12/4/94
To: brian-dunne@rutgers.edu
From: margotmeyer@stanthonys.edu

I could say a lot more, count how many Sundays until
Christmas, the point is I love you too, but what would
Kierkegaard say about that?? He would say, "Life can
only be understood backwards, but it must be lived
forwards." So I'll talk to you next Sunday. And maybe
the next one.

That was the last message they exchanged for months. Before they
jumped to their parents' 1995 emails, Evy Googled a picture of what
computers looked like then: half the size of a small refrigerator with
tiny screens. She read Liz a section of an old article where the writer

said *one day* people would send pictures and shop for things online, like that was the craziest thing anyone could imagine, like it was some kind of magic.

They kept reading.

8/30/95
Subject: sorry?
To: margotmeyer@stanthonys.edu
From: brian-dunne@rutgers.edu

Hey, this is a few weeks too late but I promise not to start any more bullshit fights with you like I did our last day at work together in Seaside, what a dumb way to spend a night in August, drink enough sangria to forget it happened, ok?

I know you're in Madrid by now, no idea when you'll get this. I already got your postcard, I am supposed to tell people it is from my international-exchange-student pen-pal and not my girlfriend, right? I don't want the embassy to get all confused, if you get called someone's girlfriend in the USA, does it affect your visa??

Have all the Spanish adventures, abrazos.

9/2/95
Subject: re: sorry?
To: brian-dunne@rutgers.edu
From: margotmeyer@stanthonys.edu

Abrazos! I WAS being weird the day before I left!
(See: already homesick and very nervous.) Internet

is a little unpredictable here, but I'll try to call you soon.

Did you know in Seville the air smells like oranges? I will keep sending you postcards, but you HAVE to make up cooler stories about your pen-pal if anyone asks. Make me very interesting.

Let's drive to Seaside over Christmas for locals' winter.

Another gap. Another chance for Evy to imagine them missing each other across an ocean, to imagine her dad checking his dorm mailbox every day, looking for a note from her, to imagine them typing away at those big machines.

2/20/96
Subject: (no subject)
To: brian-dunne@rutgers.edu
From: margotmeyer@stanthonys.edu

It's been awhile—again—I have to tell you I met some-one . . . and I know, we said only say something if it's serious, so that's what I'm saying, it is.

What are the rules, for international pen-pals and secret admirers, if they meet someone?

3/2/96
Subject: re: (no subject)
To: brian-dunne@rutgers.edu
From: margotmeyer@stanthonys.edu

Hello?

3/6/96

Subject: re: (no subject)

To: margotmeyer@stanthonys.edu

From: brian-dunne@rutgers.edu

I know we tried to be so careful, so if this happened no one would get hurt, right? We tried.

I swear this isn't a payback thing or some girl I just pulled in off the street so I could be like, me too. But I did meet someone. Her name is Claire, and she knows more about solar energy than you, but she also doesn't sing to herself when she thinks she's alone like you do. She did like Pulp Fiction, all that blood didn't bother her as much as it bothered you.

I hope being back there doesn't make you too homesick. I hope it feels like home by now.

Evy and Liz ran out of time and had to get to work. Evy imagined what had happened in between the emails, wondered about messages on worn-out answering machine tapes, postcards with stamps from Spain, quiet winter days their parents met in Seaside. Margot and Brian had been so brave, saying they loved each other from so far away, letting each other go for a while, all when they were so young.

"If they'd had texting it would have ruined everything," Liz said.

"We're reading the rest, right? To see how he gets the girl?" They were outside Sal's by now, sidestepping some seagulls. Irene was tapping her watch to tell Evy to sign in, and Liz had to hurry to get to her shift.

"Yeah, we'll read them later."

Talking through the emails, and having someone else to weigh their meaning with, had made Evy feel like the GBM Wives posts she had typed, reread, and obsessed over—especially all the new posts about moving—were way too much to keep to herself.

She was already late for work, but she knew she would be distracted all day if she didn't send her sister the GBM Wives posts right now. She forwarded the link as she signed in to work at Sal's, following up with one text before Irene took her phone: **I'm Pamplemousse7. don't tell me I shouldn't have done this. mom sounds serious about moving, right? help.**

CHAPTER NINE

Margot

She spent hours weeding outside their own house while Lorraine spent her first day caring for Brian inside. She piled up those deep-rooted monsters while the late-summer sun reddened her shoulders. She listened to podcasts of other people's stories: an interview with a comedian, an actress promoting a movie and admitting to an eating disorder, an investigation of a bitcoin scam. No murder podcasts today.

Her back ached and the sandy soil coated the crevices of her palms and stuck under her fingernails. She stared down at the ground, she sweated and stank, she still had hours left but no idea how many she'd spent with her hands in the dirt.

She grabbed her clothes and went to an empty rental house to rinse off in the outdoor shower. Margot would get used to working, showering, puttering with Lorraine around, but not today. After her shower, she updated the GBM Wives Forum:

> *I read all the bad reviews people are writing, about all the*
> *things I'm neglecting in the houses. The worse they are, the more*

times I read them, but I never fix the water pressure or the miss-
ing tiles that ruined their vacation.

Does anyone have experience with these federal loan pro-
grams? I'll drop the link below . . . good options in towns we
might move to with lots of fixer-uppers??

I figured out what I think all our houses will sell for. Brian
and I were playing a three-dimensional chess game of debt and
income and risk; we have dozens of spreadsheets, an accoun-
tant, lines of credit; we had a five-, ten-, and twenty-year plan
for E&E, but when it comes down to it all I needed were two
columns on the back of an envelope, in pencil. It will be enough.

Liz

Liz stopped by Sal's to see Evy on her break. *In fact, I have thought only*
of my daughters had echoed in her head all morning. She had been so
distracted after reading the stuff Evy sent her from the GBM Wives
that she forgot to take two deposits. How could Evy work in this as-
sault of primary colors and sugar all day? It was giving her a headache
already. "We can talk to her about all this—people say stuff—" Liz
stuttered, "—they say stuff on the internet all the time—*you* say stuff
on the internet all the time, right? Pamplemousse7?"

Where would Margot make them go, and was there any way to
stay? What if they absolutely refused, but she took off alone and left
them? You had to say it out loud to make the rabbit-hole feeling let up
a little. The idea of her sister's suburban-mom alter ego and of their
mom selling off their *entire* business was starting to register as *a lot.*

Liz considered all the times she should have known Margot hated
it here now, but all she could remember was her mom on the deck

looking at the sunset, her mom arranging flowers in a vase at the Victorian, her mom taking them the long way home on Ocean Avenue to check out the waves after a storm.

"Talk to her. Sure," Evy said, shoveling gumdrops into the display case. "Like you talked to her about quitting running? That went great." It was all still fresh and overwhelming for Liz, as she imagined the possible outcomes. Evy already sounded resigned and a little hopeless. She'd had weeks, not just a few stolen speed-scrolls between customers, to get used to this.

"You read the posts—especially the ones this week," Evy said. "You know when Margot asks boring questions, she's serious." She made Liz follow her over to a tree made of ten-inch-wide lollipops, cartoon-sized swirls that would take a kid all afternoon to eat.

"It is possible she would not be thrilled about . . . the nine months of being catfished. That might not be great," Liz said. "And yeah, she's getting wonky with her questions, also not good. I logged in an hour ago, she already asked the Wives today about Kansas City's zoning laws."

"Kansas?" Evy dropped a lollipop back into a box and it cracked in half.

"Well, it might be Missouri."

"Right, Missouri, much different."

"Well, maybe we—you—double down, and you get this Pamplemousse mom to tell her to fuck off with this idea."

Evy looked at her as if offended at this suggestion. "I have written ten drafts, actually. And they all suck."

Liz blinked back at her like, *And? Why don't you write eleven, or twelve, until it doesn't?* Had Evy's internet-persona-muse decided she didn't want to help with this now, all of a sudden, after nine months of inspiration?

"Pamplemousse is really good at, like, telling people about her bananas husband," Evy said. Irene glared at Evy, and she grabbed a broom, sweeping an already-clean floor. "But I kind of screwed myself because how can she say she's definitely staying wherever she lives if she has never talked about the actual place she lives before?"

When Irene went in the back, Evy gave Liz a handful of the salted caramel almond chocolates she liked. She turned up the doo-wop music she'd turned down when Liz arrived. When the bell at the front of the store dinged and a customer walked in, Liz knew she had to get back to work.

"Let's go this way instead," Liz said. She and Gabe had closed up Sumner Ave for the day and she steered him north, toward the lights of the pier and the fireworks-night crowds instead of south toward the quiet stretch of dunes closer to her house. Tonight Margot would be calling the last of the extended family to tell them Brian was in hospice. And probably posting stuff online to strangers about what a good mom she was for lying to her kids. Liz was staying away for a few hours.

Not home for dinner tonight, Liz texted Margot. **LMK when you're off the phone and I can come home whenever!** she added, feeling fake and wanting to text **Oh, also, are we moving? Did you decide where? Fun! Also LMK!**

Liz's head throbbed, thinking about how much she missed the mom she thought she'd taken such good care of, the mom she'd thought had her back. It was nauseating going back and forth between the versions of herself before and after this anger and distrust, and asking herself if Margot had been like this all along.

They walked past Miss Della the psychic and the raw bar, past the whirring wheel games, ignoring the guys yelling at them to try to win oversized SpongeBobs. They didn't stop at Sal's, where Evy was still working. They moved into the flow of the crowd and its backlit shadows.

What version of Margot would she find when she finally went home? The one repeating the halting, hoarse script one last time into the phone with an I'm-fine lilt; the one giving terse orders to Liz to *take your junk back to your room, for Christ's sake*; the one drinking wine on the patio and staring at the fence? Or would she find the one asking strangers online if some new, anonymous place was what her daughters needed instead of asking her daughters themselves about that?

She still thought: *Those phone calls will be hard.* If a message from her mom buzzed saying to come home, she didn't know what she would do. For so long, she would have done exactly what she thought her mom needed. But Margot texted **No hurry, I'm fine**, and Liz shoved her phone in her back pocket.

Liz asked Gabe where his band had traveled, and she listened to his stories about staying up all night, about driving around in vans jammed with equipment. She had guessed he was smart from the way he name-checked books from her AP reading list, but when he told her about his earned and rejected college scholarship, that gave his band-wanderlusting an extra layer of glamour.

This stolen time with Gabe before going home was like the one-minute break between 400-meter repeats on the track, where she gulped in air, felt her heart rate ease but never enough, where she anticipated the pain ahead and counted down to it and willed her body and mind to recover and find their rhythm before she demanded they do more.

Gabe teased her about how tough she was with the Sun and Shade customers, and about the playlist she put on her little portable speaker while they were packing up at the end of the day. Liz turned away from the gray-on-gray pattern of clouds hanging low over the ocean and toward the rainbow strobe lights of the bars, toward him.

Evy

Evy sat on the counter at Sal's ignoring the trash she was supposed to take out and the sticky floors she was supposed to mop before closing for the night. A new girl named Miranda was on shift with her, unloading boxes and ignoring her. Evy stole her own phone from Irene's basket in the back and scrolled through the GBM Wives forum. Margot had posted something new:

> Dreading these calls to update everyone, hearing that beat of silence and scrambling to fill it for them. Then I'll write some emails pretending to care about other people's vacations.
>
> I'm not hanging on, I'm not making it work, I'm neglecting what we've built. I'm making these calls and going to sleep alone, then I'm doing it all again tomorrow, alone.
>
> I know my posts have been emotional—especially when it comes to the girls. I've been reading a few self-help books you all recommended that give great scripts for conversations like the one I'll have to have if—when—I tell them we're going to move. I have all the pages I'll need marked. I was skeptical of those books, but the FLHC method (feel, listen, honor, calm) in Radical Change for the Better is really interesting, and I'd love to hear if anyone's used it with teenagers??
>
> I promise I'll tell you all as soon as I'm sure where our new place will be (!!!!). I've been clicking through to see the cafés and libraries, the theaters and the parks, scanning house listings,

*and I've got it narrowed now, and it feels so much like in the
early days of our business, this balance of imagination and logic,
doing all the research you can and then going for it.*

PHXmamma9 responded:

*Good for you! You can't stay in that town. I left Boston for the
desert, I sold our business too. I gave away my furniture and flew
my family here, and now we swim in the pool all winter, we
made brand-new friends who never knew him. The grief follows
you, of course, but you're more in control of it, if every damn
landmark you drive by every day isn't reminding you of him.*

Evy left Sal's five minutes early and made Miranda finish closing
up, walking past three E&E signs on her way to a party.

Staying out after work tonight, Evy texted Margot. Liz was staying
out too, and Evy texted her: **don't tell mom about GBM Wives stuff until
we talk again, ok?**

Margot saying she was alone in her post confused Evy—she and
Liz were there all the time; she wasn't alone. Even if Evy spent the rest
of the evening with her, it somehow wouldn't count?

Margot texted: **Sure—don't walk home alone after midnight.** That
was the protective, instructing-mother Margot, not a broken-open woman,
not a self-help-scripts woman. Evy needed a break from all of them.

Evy hit send on a Pamplemousse7 post she'd saved to drafts. She
still hated it, but it was better than nothing:

*It might seem like a good idea, to change everything, but what if
it's worse? What if the girls don't want their town to be different
after everything else already is?*

Margot

She poured a glass of cabernet and sat on the edge of the bed as she proceeded through her scribbled-down notes, through her *we don't really knows* and her *we'll just have to sees* and her *I need you to know that it will be soons* to the extended family.

She had tried to listen to what people said back to her, but fragments of old, naughty little non sequiturs that had wormed their way into her long-term memory interrupted other people's *I'm sorrys* and *if there's anything we can dos.* Time to make the donuts! Roto-Rooter, that's the name, and away go troubles down the drain. Every Good Boy Does Fine. He measured out his life with coffee spoons. Call me maybe.

It was her weakened defenses doing the best they could, scattershot searching, reordering and rewriting reality, shortcutting to anything familiar while what she said out loud to all these people was the opposite: decentering and dizzying. So many patterns and facts stuck in her memory without any effort, but she couldn't learn to survive this quiet the way she learned the order of the notes on the treble clef.

Margot saw her daughters' texts about staying out, and she wanted them home with her immediately. She wanted to sit on the couch together and then she wanted to know they were in their rooms, she wanted to have another presence in the house besides Brian and her own untethered mind. She knew they needed time away, a luxury she hadn't had since last September, but, really, she hadn't had in seventeen years.

She tidied up their rooms for them and left them each a stack of magazines. She changed their sheets, emptied their clothes hampers, and opened their windows to let in the cross-breeze. She opened a few packages, new contact lenses for Liz, allergy medicine for Evy, and sports bras she'd ordered for both of them when she noticed how old their other ones were getting. She sat on the edge of Evy's bed; along the baseboard she could see the tiniest shadow of yellow paint, the color this room had been when she was a baby, peeking through the dark blue.

Then she brought her cabernet into Brian's room. Lorraine had tucked the sheets in so even and smooth, set a small night-light on his table so there would always be a little glow over him while he slept. Margot took a big sip of her wine. How did she begin these one-sided conversations with him? She imagined all the ways she'd invited inertia and momentum to take over before, the times she'd been awkward and stubborn but undaunted, a true beginner.

"Do you remember how bad I was at tennis, when I first started to play?" she said. She'd bought a racket and a case of tennis balls when they finally moved back to Seaside after Hurricane Sandy, when long walks weren't enough to calm her down and she wanted to whack the hell out of something. She didn't even set foot on a court until she'd hit the ball against the concrete wall ten thousand times. Then she served wild, crooked shots to no one, collected the balls in a bucket, and tried again until she got her serve to arc into that sweet spot somewhere near where it was supposed to land.

"You came to the court with me a couple times, but you were lobbing that ball high and slow, not keeping score or anything, and I was still so bad but hitting it hard, throwing that racket around and yelling cusswords—I think I scared you a little."

She'd finally figured out how to get her shoulder, elbow, and grip into a rhythm consistent enough to play against some other people. "And then"—she paused—"you called and got the town to keep the lights on for me at the courts an hour later? I don't know how you convinced them, I never asked."

She beat some other beginners right away, but it had taken another year before she beat her first intermediate player.

"God, I was obsessed," she said. Tennis made her feel agile and alert even off the court. She hadn't played now in over a year. She'd neglected every part of her own body since Brian got sick; the trap muscles between her shoulder blades and the base of her neck were always sore, but every other muscle had gone soft. "Anyway. Yeah."

She would survive this quiet by forcing herself to do it again, and again, even when it felt unnatural. She texted her daughters and told them she was fine.

Liz

Liz caught the eye of a guy she knew working at the soft-serve stand, a shot-putter who rated the entire girls' track team on a fuckability scale. She inched a little closer to Gabe, putting on a show that said, *See, this is how it turns out for girls like me, the sevens and seven-point-fives on your scale, you neckless piece of shit. We get interesting, tattooed band guys.* The shot-put guy finished ringing someone up and then saw Liz; he grinned the same dumbface grin he did when he was around all his friends, and yelled across the boardwalk at her, using his hands as a megaphone, "The gun means go!"

He and the other shot-put guys had started yelling that to her at the end of the season, after she'd frozen on the starting line of the state championship meet in May.

An hour before her race, Brian had gotten lost in a crowd of sprinters in the paddock area, then insisted on napping on another family's belongings. When Margot said he had to move, he'd called her a shrivel-titted bitch loud enough for half the crowd to hear. She'd dragged him away, and Liz had followed them to the car.

When she came back, Liz's teammates had stared at her, waiting for her to make a joke like she usually did, but instead she jogged past them and stretched by herself in the shadow of the concession stand. She'd tried to focus on the race she still had to run by staring at the dirt and listening to her headphones, but it didn't work. The gun went off, and she froze.

After that she stopped running, stopped showing up at practice and meets. She ignored her track coach's calls and texts. This summer was the longest she'd gone without running since she was twelve.

"Thanks, got it, Randy!" Liz yelled back. The shot-put guy's name wasn't Randy, it was Zach, but Liz had started calling him and his friends middle-aged guy names whenever they yelled, "The gun means go!" at her. She couldn't tell if it bothered or confused them, but it always got them to leave her alone.

Randy/Zach was also a football player. Only a few people could escape the strict categories in high school, like the few students who started midyear, the Olympic-hopeful figure skater, and the daughter of parents who died in a tragic car wreck.

A parent dying of an organic disease wouldn't do the trick, though. That would only make teachers give you extra time for assignments if you missed class, or allow you three or four passes to the guidance office during times of acute emotion.

She wanted to tell Gabe everything about her dad, but she was still afraid it would feel like spending too much money on something you really wanted, only to find out it was cheap and flimsy, and you wished you could take it back and have the money again instead of the thing, to feel the heft of a wad of warm cash again instead.

"What was that about?" Gabe asked. "'Cause that guy is huge and I probably can't fight him."

"Oh, inside track-team joke," she said.

"You're on the track team?"

"Not anymore, I quit."

"Because of Randy?"

"No, definitely not because of Randy. I would never decide anything because of, uh, Randy."

"Well, why, then?"

"Oh, I pulled a quad muscle," she said. She waited for him to hear the fakeness in her voice.

"Should you be spending all day running around the beach dragging giant umbrellas around with a pulled quad, boss?"

"I'm doing some hamstring strengthening, which actually helps the quadriceps, so it's a lot better now," she said, marking the first thing track-team Jesse had ever said to her that had been officially helpful. Jesse's favorite topic was his hamstring-strengthening regimen.

They got ice cream from a different non–Randy/Zach place, and then a couple, hands wrapped around each other's hips, stumbled out of Jimbo's, drunk-weaving in and out of the crowd. The guy was dressed in a tight shirt, with bulging biceps, and was doused in body spray. The girl had black flat-ironed hair and wore tiny shorts with *SEXY* written across the butt. They were both spray-tanned to a smooth shade of orange-brown. It had been years since Snooki and The Situation spent their summers here, and Liz had been too little to watch their show when they had, but these two were their doppelgängers.

"Well, if it doesn't interrupt your hamstring-strengthening regimen or anything, you want to come over tonight?" Gabe asked.

She didn't know if she would ever win a race again. She didn't know how many more times she would play her dad's scratched Radiohead and R.E.M. albums for him before he was gone, but she knew *you want to come over tonight?* meant Gabe didn't think she was too young, too awkward, too quiet, too serious, too sad, too nervous, too shy, too all-of-those-things she believed about herself whenever she'd been ignored.

"Tonight?" she asked. She wanted her first time to be private, important, a necessary transformation from awkward adolescence to whatever came next. A way of staking her claim on some fraction of this summer as hers, and on this place, especially if she had to leave it soon. A way of wielding a new kind of power and proving that all the Randys had always been wrong about everything, especially her, and always would be.

"I—yeah—I mean, yes." She was ready, but she didn't want her first time to be at the end of this confusing, complicated day; she didn't want her burgeoning anger at her mom's lies to distract her. "But I can't tonight? Another night?" she asked, or maybe she said it like a fact that was already true: "Another night." She wasn't sure how it came out. He told her that after tonight, he was staying at his mom's house across the bridge for a few days, while some people rented his aunt's place. But then he'd have his aunt's house to himself again.

"I'll cancel the band's show at Giants Stadium next week, you know, if you're free then," he said, fake-texting someone on his phone. "There, I did it, it's done."

"I *am* excited to check out the rental house competition your aunt has going on over there," she said. "Maybe she'll put us out of business one day." She didn't say, *At least until my mom does that herself.*

"It's probably not up to your standards," he joked.

She didn't know whether he'd ever call her on a Sunday and make her laugh from a thousand miles away, or whether her first time would give her everything she wanted. When she went home tonight, she didn't know if she would blurt out everything she knew about Margot's plans to make them move in a righteous stream-of-consciousness speech, or choose to sit with her mom on the couch and wait her out.

She did know that the feeling of Pop Rocks crackling in the back of her throat distracted her from the day's secrets and sadnesses, making them feel so far away. She kissed him, faster than she wanted to, before she pulled away.

Margot

Liz came home without her usual whispered "Hey" a minute into the opening credits of *Ted Bundy Uncovered*. Margot heard the shower, then Liz's footsteps slipping into Brian's room; then she heard her in the kitchen, slamming cabinet doors before emerging with a bowl of chips. She slumped down in the chair on the other side of the room.

"Evy's still out?" Liz asked. "You finished all the calls?" She stared down into her bowl.

"Yeah, Ev's out, and I think I called everyone. Your aunt Eileen is such a mess."

Liz shoved a handful of chips into her mouth and nodded once, which Margot took to mean she did not want to hear about the other ten awful calls. "You didn't have to come home early," Margot said.

Margot paused the show during an interview with a woman half-hidden in a shadow: an invitation in case Liz wanted to say more. Liz said, "Mom. It's fine," so Margot hit play again.

The girls hurled accusatory, acidic *fines* at her sometimes, but this tone was different, more detached. Liz looked at the TV screen, leaning forward at the pivotal reveals, then staring off past the TV or down to scroll on her phone. Margot knew enough not to ask anything more of her in this moment—the fact that she was sitting here, and not behind her bedroom door, said she didn't quite want to be alone, but whatever was on her mind was protected and private, inaccessible to her mother.

Evy

Cameron worked at the rides on the pier with all the foreign students who came to Seaside for the summer on work visas. Hailey and a few others were going to a party at their house, but Olivia had texted, **I have class again** and sent a sad-face emoji hours ago.

By the time Evy arrived at the party after work, Cameron and Hailey were deep into a game of flip cup with Declan and his friends. She wandered inside to the too-bright kitchen, where she recognized a Russian girl named Inessa who had a second job at Sal's Sweets.

"You guys have anything to drink?" Evy asked her, surveying the sea of half-empty bottles on the kitchen counter, and Inessa handed Evy a paper cup of warm vodka. The only time they'd ever worked together, Inessa had asked Evy a million questions about New York City, which Evy had no idea how to answer. The rep from the company who organized all the student visas and jobs sold Seaside as more convenient to New York than it was when they got people to sign up to work here all summer.

"Wait, I got some gummies from Sal's, I made these little guys," Inessa said, handing Evy a cup full of slimy vodka-bloated gummy bears. Even the sugar couldn't cover the poison acid taste, but Evy chewed them up and then finished a second paper cup of vodka. She chased it with a warm Dr Pepper from her purse.

Someone scored a goal in a soccer game on the TV and the house erupted in cheers and boos, and a guy wearing sunglasses and a red and white soccer jersey handed her another shot.

It always seemed to happen this way: someone handing Evy drinks she never turned down, then this sudden blur. She wandered out to the dark backyard, where Hailey hugged her and squealed, "You're heeeeeeere!" and dragged her down into a lawn chair, giving a garbled play-by-play of their last three games of flip cup.

Some people were dancing in the yard to reggaeton, and the sunglasses-soccer-jersey guy tried to grab Evy's hand to drag her up and dance, but he gave up and let go. The slower release of the vodka-soaked gummy bears hit Evy then, with the weight of Hailey still on her, still talking. The dark yard spun, the bass and the Spanish rap and the rising tide of voices all collided and confused her. Then Hailey jumped up and ran back toward the plywood table covered in cups, hopping up and down and hyping everyone up for another game.

Did Evy close her eyes, or did a floodlight kick on and off? Had Hailey played a whole game of flip cup, or hadn't it started yet? The drum machine and synthesizer beat repeated on the speaker, the same song or a new one, and then Olivia was standing in front of her, a streetlight halo softening the edges of her floral flowy dress while Evy slumped lower in the lawn chair.

"Evy? You okay?" Olivia asked, and Evy tried to stand, but some invisible weight held her down. "Inessa hadsome gummy bearss," Evy said, still looking up at Olivia from the lawn chair. "You weren't sss-poseda be here, because your class." Evy pulled out her phone and saw seven missed texts, direct to her, not on the group text: **Hey, I'm still skipping the party then but let's hang out instead??**, then **evy, u ok?** from Olivia in the last half hour.

"Yeah," Olivia said, looking around. Even through her cheap vodka haze, Evy sensed how much Olivia hated it here. Hailey waved and yelled, "Liv, come join my teeeeeam," and Olivia ignored her.

"S'Inessa's fault," Evy said. "I wanted . . ." She had wanted space between Sal's and home; she had wanted to forget the GBM Wives and their dumb idea to make them leave Seaside. Now she wanted to re-wind and read Olivia's texts half an hour ago and meet her somewhere else—alone, not half-sick, not in this shithole backyard.

"Me too," Olivia said. "Let's get you home, okay?" She was already calling a Lyft from her older sister's account, then waving good-bye to Hailey and Cameron in the middle of their next game of flip cup and guiding Evy through the broken gate, then easing her into one side of the passenger seat and going around to the other. "My mom says, she says you know, don't walk home alone," Evy said, tapping on the seat between them. "I'm glad thiss is a car. Can we get some pizza with a shit fuck ton of pepperonis?"

Olivia handed Evy a plastic bag from the seat-back pocket, which Evy promptly puked into, bits of gummy bears and bile lurching out of her. "Pizza's probably not a great idea tonight," Olivia said.

"Ssorry I'm sorry," Evy said. "My mom says, she says she wantssusto move." Her eyes teared, from the vomit and the sadness that rushed in to take its place once it was expelled from her body.

In the few-second window of relief, Olivia said, "It's okay, I know how . . . this is," and handed Evy her own full stainless-steel bottle of water. "Drink *all* of this," she said.

The bay air rushed in through the open windows, and Olivia's hair blew around, loosening from her ponytail. "You're so pretty," Evy said.

"You're so drunk," Olivia said, tying off the top of the bag to contain the stench. When they pulled up to the house, all the lights were off. Olivia asked the driver to wait and brought Evy to her room, shushing her when she said thank you too loud, so they wouldn't wake anyone up.

"Ssmydad in there," Evy whispered, pointing to the guest room, where you could see the outline of a hospital bed in the dark. "We're ssposta leave the window open ssohecan hear summer, and we're sssposta talkto him, sept he can't hear it."

Olivia left her water bottle on the nightstand and slid Evy's sneakers and socks off, and Evy was asleep before Olivia eased the screen door closed on her way out.

Evy dreamed of a night when she was a little girl, crying into her cotton candy and begging her parents to let her ride the roller coaster, even though she was an inch too small. In three months, she somehow knew in her dream, the hurricane would sink the whole thing into the ocean.

In her dream, Liz wouldn't shut up about how great the ride was, how it had turned the world upside down. Nothing, not another spin on the Tilt-A-Whirl, not a round of Skee-Ball, not a vanilla orange twist cone, could lift the fog of absolute unfairness Evy felt at the way time worked and what she wished for on that particular night.

Her dad pulled her into the Scrambler cars and said, "See, you can hold your hands up high and scream here too." He pulled her through the haunted house and she barely flinched at the zombies; he gave her coins to spin the wheel for another stuffie, and she won a sequined snake, which she dragged behind her like a fancy tail between her legs. All night that roller coaster distracted and obsessed her, ruined everything. The boardwalk vibrated every time the cars went clattering and looping around.

Her family dragged her up to play rooftop mini-golf, and at the third hole her friend tapped on her shoulder and said hi, then ducked behind the windmill. They both exploded into giggles, and Evy showed off her dirty, glittering snake.

In the dream, the friend was Olivia, even though Evy hadn't known her as a kid, and she wasn't tall enough to ride on the roller coaster either. "I like the pirate ship better anyway, have you tried the pirate ship? It gives you the stomach flips," dream-Olivia said, and then it was so much easier to shrug off this thing she couldn't do anything about. Evy said, "Yeah, I'm totally gonna try that pirate ship," and all that roller-coaster sadness and disappointment vanished because a friend had found her and said the right thing.

When she woke up, little flashes of her worst moments the night before bled into her dream. But despite her regret at the ugly, sad side of her Olivia had seen, and despite her sour mouth and aching head, Evy's stomach flipped in the exact way it did on the upswing of the pirate ship ride when she saw a text from Olivia.

You ok today?? Evy knew from Olivia's last social media post, a montage of five photos of brackets and symbols and words all nested inside each other, with sparkle effects and a caption about caffeine, that she was taking a break from some long coding assignment to text her. All the words on Olivia's screen meant something different than they did in real life: *bold*, and *if*, and *then*.

I was a mess! thank you for getting me home. vodka gummy bears=bad idea. Feelin it today ugh.

it happens

not to you tho!

I . . . no, I have not been wasted on vodka gummy bears. true.

I don't recommend

I have been drunk enough I needed help, though.

???

. . . it was at a frat party when I went to visit my sister at college . . . not gummy bears. Jell-O. And something they called lucky juice???

ew. (but tbh I would probably drink it). I swear I never mean to get like that!!!

yeah I know . . .

I really, really wish I wasn't so
drunk last night.

I'm sure!! u need Advil!

Yeah . . .

Evy paused a second, typed and deleted, then texted: **but also I thought . . . it was just gonna be Hailey & Cameron there . . . 100% wouldn't have gotten so drunk if I knew you were gonna show up . . .**

Olivia's three typing dots appeared and disappeared, and then the screen went blank for ten minutes. Evy was sure she'd just screwed it up—she might as well have sent her beating heart across town in a FedEx box to be refused and sent right back where it came from.

Then Olivia texted back: **well I did promise drunk Evy last night that we could get pizza some other time . . . when she was less drunk . . . ? you requested a shit fuck ton of pepperoni, I think those were your exact words?**

They were probably-slurry, almost-puking words, but still—Olivia remembered them. Did she also remember the door to the guest room, wide open, where her dad was in the hospital bed? What about when Evy said *you're so pretty*? If Olivia remembered her exact words about pizza, *then* was this code for saying she remembered that too? Evy knew she was supposed to say something cool and either-way to Olivia next, but she wanted to show she remembered too.

Evy texted: **Oh yeah, I remember that.**

Another endless thirty seconds of three dots, appearing and disappearing, from Olivia, and then: **You do? I was wondering. what you remembered.**

CHAPTER TEN

Liz

Now, as the languid August days bled into each other, Brian was asleep when Liz left for work and asleep when she got home. She was glad to be rid of the rotating cast of jerks (and toddlers, zombies, and Rain Men, according to her new friend Pamplemousse7) who used to inhabit his body, but still wary of the temporary calm of this in-between.

Playing Brian's binder of CDs gave Liz something to talk about when she visited him in his room, some script to stick to when she wasn't sure what to say. Today she told him she was sure "Sloop John B" was the saddest song on *Pet Sounds,* and that *Bleed American* was the only album from his emo-pop-punk music that held up.

She grabbed his soft hand. She still expected calluses.

"Springsteen again? Maybe some R.E.M. or Tom Petty?" An album was a whole unedited conversation, a complete, flawed story. There were always songs on albums that didn't seem to belong. There was always that half-second whir in between tracks on these old CDs after you pressed the button to skip ahead.

She played "Free Fallin'" from *Full Moon Fever.* Sometimes during the first chords of a song, Brian's eyes fluttered behind his eyelids, and sometimes he swatted at the air, reaching for something. Liz liked to think he was having a dream about seeing a friend at a concert and was waving across the room to say, *Hey, I'm here! Over here!*

Liz had listened to *Full Moon Fever* enough times that she expected the first electric guitar notes of "I Won't Back Down" to come a beat or two after the end of "Free Fallin'," anticipated them now as she paged through the rest of the CDs in the binder.

Each tiny-printed lyric booklet and CD slid together into the proper sleeve; she loved looking at the old album art: the rainbow shooting through the prism on *Dark Side of the Moon,* the red baseball cap in Springsteen's pocket on *Born in the USA.* While "I Won't Back Down" played, Liz pulled a live album out of its sleeve and read the huge track list, anticipating the recorded roar of a crowd's cheering from before she was born.

If Evy joined her, she whisper-critiqued Liz's music choices but then settled in and listened, and sometimes said, *Yeah, this one is all right.* If Liz missed a day, the next time she was in her dad's room she would notice his skin more drained of color, his mouth drier and wider-open. If she left any CDs lying around, Lorraine would play them for Brian and leave little notes on them if a song had evoked a small reaction with a note: *2:10 pm/ track 5/ calm.*

Maybe the sound of Liz's voice and the guitar chords activated some long-atrophied neurons in Brian's subconscious. Maybe some distant half-here version of him heard every word she said. Maybe nothing made it through anymore at all.

But all these lyrics about loneliness and love, in "Heart of Gold" and "Tupelo Honey" and "Wonderwall," would become Liz's secret weapons for making it through long drives and winter afternoons after her dad was gone. She would play all these songs even when her own daughters wanted to listen to Disney music instead in the car, dropping them off at a classmate's birthday party with the words still in her head. Then she would take her girls' coats off and hand their friend a wrapped gift, she would scan her children's faces for worry to make sure they'd be okay there alone at the party without her.

Evy

An hour into her shift at Sal's, Olivia showed up—while Evy was out doing an errand for Irene at the Acme. Irene told her when she came back, and Evy badgered her for details: How long had she stayed? And did you see which way she went? "You can give her a free bag of the old licorice if she comes back," Irene said, and actually winked.

Liz confirmed that the next move was to reciprocate Olivia's visit.

When Evy showed up at Olivia's vintage store that evening, she acted interested in the misshapen boots while some woman made Olivia bring out every belt they had in the back. Olivia caught Evy's eye and did a little *I'm sorry* shrug when the belt woman wasn't paying attention.

When the lady finally left, they were alone in the store. It was so jammed with clothes, Evy had to weave through a maze of three racks to get to the counter.

"I, um, needed a belt as well? So yeah, do you . . . have any?" Evy asked.

"No, we have no belts, no more belts," Olivia said, laughing, shoving armfuls of belts back into a box. Olivia's phone buzzed on the counter three times in a row, and she let a pile of belts fall across the counter and picked it up.

She texted with her back half-turned to Evy, hunching over her screen and holding her breath, then letting it all out. "It's my mom, sorry," she said. "She's—um, I guess she's having a bad night."

Olivia's phone rang. "Mom, I'm at *work*," she said, and Evy said, "I got this," waving her hands to show she would watch the empty store. Olivia slipped into the back, and Evy rearranged some of the shirts by color. Through the door to the back room, Evy heard her say, "Just breathe, Mom, stop saying that." Her voice was so, so calm. There were long silences when Olivia only got out a syllable. Evy got through all the red shirts and was halfway through the orange ones when Olivia came back.

"I'm so sorry," Olivia said. Her usually smooth makeup was smudged.

"For what?" Evy said. She thought, *You too.* "So, where's all the good stuff?" she asked, and Olivia's eyes lit up. She showed Evy the formal-wear section, an explosion of tulle and sequins, and Evy tried on every dress Olivia handed her through the fitting room curtain.

Evy peeked out and then paraded around, moving to the Whitney Houston music playing in the store, letting Olivia zip her up and fasten and unfasten the hooks on the dresses, feeling her fingers graze Evy's spine and press against her shoulder blade when she helped her with a poufy purple taffeta minidress that made them laugh. Olivia found her a silver lamé Jessica McClintock and said, "You have to spin," and Evy did, five times, until she was dizzy enough to grab Olivia's arm for balance and hold it a second longer than she needed to. The last one was a Calvin Klein halter dress, cool against her skin, a rare find with the tags still on. She reached around her own neck to tie it herself, but Olivia said, "Wait, I'll do it," and tied it twice to make sure it was even, and they made up stories about all the galleries and banquets and glittery cocktail parties she would wear this dress to one day.

Liz

"How do I sabotage the rest of these people's vacation?" Gabe asked one evening after work. This time of August was always more booked with renters at his aunt's house; the current ones would be there a few more days, and he was counting down how much time was left until he got her empty, rent-free house back. He kissed Liz as the last of the beach crowd made their way to their cars, sun-drunk, and then Gabe drove away too.

Liz spent an hour that night taking and then editing sexy selfies for Gabe, but then sent him a link to a live version of a song by The Machine Is Red instead. She didn't delete them, though. Gabe had never directly asked her for any pictures, but he joked about it, in a way that Liz heard as not quite a joke. Sonia texted: **SEND THEM**; but to Liz, sending him sexy pictures now felt like doing things out of order, exposing herself that way when she hadn't done it in real life yet.

So many nights this week, Liz had had to hurry home after kissing Gabe good-bye, to meet whatever relative was at their house. They all asked her how she was doing and looked her up and down like *Why are you in a yellow uniform shirt and not something sadder, where's the black velvet?*

Then she'd sit down, alone or with Evy, who was still in her own hot-pink, fudge-covered work uniform, and eat whatever IDC Margot heated up. She would ask Aunt Eileen about her cats or her grandparents about their tomato garden or whatever each visitor's thing was they liked to talk about besides when they thought her dad was gonna die, though nobody said that exactly.

During her hurried hangouts with Gabe, she kept her secret about her dad being sick. She still refused to risk disrupting the balanced chemical reaction that happened every time he came close to her.

Evy

"Oh god, look at this one," Evy said. She and Liz were scrolling through the GBM Wives forum together on the screen porch, while Margot was out. Hockeymom87 had sent a picture of herself in front of the RV she lived in now, encouraging Margot to move once Brian died. *Do it, do it for you, spread your wings and fly*, she wrote.

"I do want to drive cross-country one day," Liz said. "But I don't want to *live* in a van next year."

It wasn't that they never wanted to leave Seaside. Evy dreamed of traveling, and of living in a big city one day, or in a lot of different places before she picked one to stay in. She did want to know what it felt like to have a warm winter or a view of the mountains. But first she wanted a few more years here, where her friends knew her already, where the beach was empty and all hers in September, where Olivia might love her back.

"I asked Mom if she was thinking of doing anything differently in the next few months," Evy said. "And she handed me a grocery list and explained the difference between garlic powder and garlic salt."

Liz

"I didn't know why you wanted to join this thing, but yeah, she's so *different* here," Liz said. Since Evy had given her the login info, she'd read all the old posts again. Margot had a way of remembering a story a Wife had told months ago and using it as evidence the woman could face her current crisis. She was still so generous in asking for more of their stories, and in talking the other women out of their shame and fear spirals and into the next right thing. *Been there, you're not alone, here for you*, she wrote.

Like Evy, Liz had tried talking to Margot offline, sometimes stealing word for word from the forum in hopes of steering her into sounding the way she did there. She asked open-ended what-happens-after-Dad-dies questions to see if real-life Margot was really as into the idea of moving as her online persona was. The most Liz ever got her to say was, "We'll see," like she used to say when they asked for candy at the grocery store.

Conversations with Margot about what happened after Brian died were DOA, and so was any opportunity to compromise or to explain to her that moving was a cruel, undeserved punishment for her daughters.

Evy

Evy wrote more drafts of posts by Pamplemousse7, bringing her total up to more than a dozen. She tried to say something convincing to Margot about staying in Seaside, but she could not find the magic feeling of her hands flying across the keys that she'd had all year.

"I think Pamplemousse7 got you through a lot," Liz said. Evy's most recent Pamplemousse7 post had been three useless words: *Thinking of you.* "But that's the problem. You made her up to help you deal with toddler, zombie, jerk, and Rain Man, right? And now that part is over, those guys are gone, and she's sad about it. That's why she's not saying what you need her to say anymore."

The Wives all felt like her friends, and she had loved reading their posts about Mardi Gras parades, homeschooling, and Canadian maternity leave when they weren't talking about brain tumors. Evy had learned about winters in Minnesota and life on military bases. She didn't always agree with them, and they could be cliché (*Spread your wings!*) but the Wives were always there for each other. No one's post went unanswered.

"Maybe this forum needs more trolls, to scare these very opinionated women away with links to penis enlarging creams," Evy said.

"I think it is time to say thank you for your service, Pample-mousse7," Liz said. "We don't need trolls. But we do need someone new."

Evy had invested so much time in Pamplemousse7 that abandoning the role had not occurred to her. But Liz was right: they needed someone specific and stronger and self-assured, someone who could call bullshit on Margot's idea to move. She didn't have to leave the GBM Wives altogether just because Pamplemousse7 had lost her voice. Evy opened a new browser tab and her fingers flew across the keys again, making a new GBM Wives account, with a new username: Scrabblemary45.

She and Liz considered killing off Pamplemousse7's poor husband, but then they decided to make her family move—but only across her unnamed town, so as not to encourage moving too far. She would be away from reliable Wi-Fi for a while. That would get her out of the way.

"Okay," Liz said. "Now, who is Scrabblemary45?"

They decided she would be from Seattle, a place they'd never been but that they knew was both beautiful and interesting, a place that you wouldn't want to leave, even if something sad happened there. In fact, it felt to them like a place where people might get used to and even love the sadness of rain and clouds.

"She should be like Ms. Thrall," Evy said. Ms. Thrall was a teacher they'd both had for tenth grade English. She wore black-framed glasses and red lipstick, and she could keep the asshole kids in check with one look. She paced back and forth in front of the room gripping whatever novel the class was reading, asking questions that made you sit up straighter. She had a compass tattoo on her forearm. Her bookshelf was bursting with brand-new best sellers, graphic novels, and thrillers. She assigned choices for projects instead of boring papers and helped you choose books instead of always assigning the ones the curriculum dictated; Evy had made a poetry podcast she got an A+ on, and devoured a queer YA sci-fi series she found on Ms. Thrall's bookshelf during free reading time.

In the GBM Wives forum there were already Jesus-y women and sporty women, ambitious corporate women and older conservative women. A Seattle/Ms. Thrall type was just what the girls and Margot needed now, someone interesting and stylish, funny and kind, who could tell Margot why moving was a terrible idea and how she wasn't actually alone, who could reassure everyone with her cool confidence.

Evy introduced Scrabblemary45 to the group and ended her first post saying:

> *I took the kids to the Space Needle after grading all my AP students' essays at Starbucks with a latte. I can't sleep, but not from the coffee.*

"Ev, she's *from* Seattle," Liz said. "So she wouldn't go to the Space Needle. And she definitely does not drink Starbucks. And don't forget, she has to never want to leave." Evy deleted the last lines. Liz Googled some things Seattle people might actually do, and Evy wrote:

> *I put on the Mariners game for my husband as background noise, even though he can't hear it. He's always liked baseball. I'd rather go to a poetry reading at Elliott Bay than listen to baseball, but now I think the sound of baseball is comforting too. The idea of being in any crowd seems strange.*
>
> *It's raining, but I went on a hike at the Discovery Park loop trail, and it helped so much. It's wonderful to still have all these familiar places, especially now. My kids asked questions I*

couldn't answer today. Our hospice nurse is so nice, but I wonder how many people she watches die in a year. I don't really pray, but thank God for her.

"Okay, good," Liz said. "Let's have her go jump into another thread while she's here."

Evy clicked on a thread WineNChocolate12 had started, where the women shared the worst things their husbands had done to them before their tumors had transformed them. There were posts about shady financial deals that screwed with the retirement savings, about business-trip affairs. Several stories about chronically neglected child-care and chore duties. If Evy got married one day, she did not want it to be to anyone who thought wiping their kids' butts or making dinner at six every night should be exclusively her job.

This thread really seemed to help the women, reminding them that the stranger they were taking care of had been far from perfect even when he was 100 percent himself. But these unresolved, accumulated hurts also seemed to mess with the Wives. They'd always assumed they'd have more time to figure them out.

"Have Scrabblemary45 write her own post here, before she responds to Margot's, since she's new," Liz said. "So we can talk about her wife secrets *before* we make her talk about moving? Make it bad, but not, like, divorce-him bad."

Evy made Liz Google gambling debt, DUIs, and video game addiction; then she wrote:

A few years ago my husband got a DUI, and I had to drive him to work for six months. We had to get up at five every morning, to get us all to work and school on time driving on 405, where traffic can be terrible! The worst was we kept it a secret, because

*it was embarrassing. I wish I could say it was a big wake-up call
and he never drank again. . . .*

They closed the laptop, but then their phones dinged, with the
little alert from the app that Margot had also posted in the thread.

Her post was only one line:

This is not the first time he's left me.

Margot

There. She'd said it. Well, not all of it, but enough to feel that she was
being as generous as she could be about this particular secret. There
were so many ways to break someone's heart and leave them when they
needed you. She felt compelled to share, to add her voice to the chorus,
but she left this confession incomplete.

"We never needed all this," Brian had said. It was a week after Hurricane Sandy. The day the storm hit, they'd evacuated to her parents'
house in Cherry Heights, only ten miles away, but far enough from
Seaside that it had been safe from significant storm damage.

The last of the inland November light framed the blackout curtains, which Margot's mother kept drawn to avoid triggering her
migraines. Brian was half-obscured in shadow on the couch. "We're
done," he said, "E&E is done."

As *we're done* hung in the air between them, ten-year-old Liz ran by in a set of cat ears Margot had found at Walgreens and Evy followed in an old sequined dance costume Nanna had dragged down from the attic. The girls made cat dance monster sounds up the stairs and stomped around, high on the Halloween candy Nanna let them eat.

"We haven't even seen the houses up close yet, so maybe—" So much of what she said out loud since the storm came out as unfinished fragments. "If FEMA comes through for our primary residence, then—" "We can stay at my parents' until—" "Maybe some of the properties will be—"

Hearing Brian say *we're done* before they'd even assessed the damage was like a coded message saying *send help* from the Brian she knew, who would never utter such a defeated, depressing cliché. He believed in figuring things out and finding a way; he believed in DIY and ROI the way Evangelicals believed in Jesus. He was the one who always convinced her to be brave and to ignore the voice that said smaller, slower, sensible was always better.

By saying *we're done* before they'd submitted one form, insurance claim, or tax write-off, before they'd stepped over the waterlogged mattresses and ripped away the unwieldy, mold-eaten rugs, before they'd shoveled the sour-rotten bay grass or imagined the low-slung bungalows all raised up another story, Brian was demanding that Margot convince *him* now, and at any time his faith or patience ran out, that they were not *done* but only beginning, not *done* but only in need of a cash infusion, another few phone calls, another subcontractor. He was handing off something so heavy to her, and if she set it down for even a second it would be swallowed up by the ground and take them both along with it.

Of course, she didn't know then whether they could or should rebuild, or whether they should buy up even more properties if they went on the market for cheap. But the Brian she knew would never declare *we're done* without fighting, without showing up to day one, without seeing it all through the bitter end on their island.

Call it by any name: checked out, shut down, depressed. Call Margot a hostage negotiator, a therapist, or a hopeless, currently homeless romantic. She had no language for what to say next, but she knew it would be impossible to say the right thing, so she said nothing and let her weak half-formed thoughts stand in for her rage and disappointment and fear.

On the TV, a reporter in an NBC-4 windbreaker stood on a mountain of debris between overturned cars and smashed sailboats. Then they cut to the aerial footage. A monster wave had washed away half the pier; the Tilt-A-Whirl teetered on what was left of it. Lone jagged walls stood where whole homes had been. In the familiar footage, Margot searched again for any red E&E sign, for any half-salvaged structure amidst the wreckage.

When she finally stood up from the couch, she was seized by hunger, by a clawing in her gut. She had not eaten a full meal in two days. Her mom set out the odd snacks: saltines and a blob of jelly, stale pretzels and a container of crusty old pub cheese. Margot's mother rarely remembered to plan whole meals. It was a sign she was getting old and was overwhelmed by the number of steps required to shop for, put away, cook, serve, and clean up food for six people, so Margot did it: she ordered pizza the first day, cooked spaghetti and diced tomatoes she found in the pantry the second. She ran out for rotisserie chicken and dumped a bag of lettuce in bowls with some Wishbone Italian dressing the third day, before she got the message and went ahead and grocery-shopped for everyone from then on.

PB&Js and bruised apples appeared for the girls from whoever was around when they said they were hungry, but if Margot didn't decide what all the adults in the house were eating, they grazed and fended for themselves.

How was she supposed to summon some *Friday Night Lights* big game speech to give Brian about how they'd make it through together as a team when she had spent the last two days running errands for kid-sized toothbrushes, deodorant, and allergy medicine, when she was spending all her emotional capital competing in some subpar *Top Chef* quickfire challenge with whatever she found in her mom's freezer?

Days into an indefinite displacement, she already ached for the ordinary comforts of home: her own stocked bathroom cabinet, her own bed and the familiar weight of her quilt. She'd only seen video so far of the obliterated houses, but imagined the pieces of their own life destroyed: the forgotten photo albums, their old Scrabble set, Brian's T-shirt collection, a bin of the girls' old art projects, a box of scribbled old recipes from Brian's mom. She even longed for her own replaceable things: her drawer of warm sweaters, her favorite electric teapot, the girls' *Harry Potter* books, and their bin of a thousand glass beads.

The insides of the rentals were less sentimental than their own home in some ways, but she'd curated and renovated and reimagined every property to make each one into any renter's hoped-for ideal of a beach vacation, and she was always finding ways to brighten and soften each room, to make them feel fresh and welcoming; these rentals were their life's work, and now they were their liability, their mess, their nightmare.

How had she ever felt at home here, in her parents' threadbare chairs and yellow kitchen, in the dim brown-flower-wallpapered hallways where crooked-toothed kid versions of herself stared back at her every time she walked by?

She was not ready to give in to Brian or to convince him, or to interrogate the uncertain space between them. Exhausted as she already was, she knew better. They needed more time and real rest, they needed to eat, and they needed a drive through the deserted suburban streets of her hometown.

"We're going to the Starlight," Margot said, surprising herself with the sudden authority in her own voice, with the unfragmented expression, with a solution to one small problem they could fix with twenty bucks including tip.

She needed to slide into a booth at the Starlight Diner, where Brian would have no choice but to look her in the eye; she needed a cheeseburger steeped in its own grease and a plate of disco fries dipped in off-brand ketchup. She needed the nostalgia of the other nights she'd spent there, after the Cherry Heights High dances, when she let down her fancy hairdo and felt the warm adoration of the first boy who had ever kissed her. She needed the efficiency and indifference of the night-shift waitress, the hypnotic rotation of the pies in the dessert case, "Daydream Believer" playing in the background.

After they'd ordered at the Starlight, the space between them felt as charged and unsettled as the air at the center of the massive storm. She watched Brian hunched over his cheeseburger. She promised to buy him new underwear and razors when she went to Target tomorrow. *We're done* still hovered between them.

Brian's face was thick with stubble, his skin gray. How could this dim detachment have set in so quickly, when Margot was still flooded with adrenaline, still riding waves of panic and holding her breath waiting for even one definitive piece of news about when they could go back to their island for even an hour?

He was asking too much of her, but what choice did she have?

CHAPTER ELEVEN

Evy

What did you mean, when you said it's not the first time he's left you? Evy wrote in the GBM Wives thread to Margot. She was surprised no one else had yet. Margot responded:

> *The last time he left me alone, our versions of reality were not the same. I felt more alone than I ever have in my life. I don't mean to be evasive. Does it matter that what he did to cause that wasn't sneaking off to a motel?*

"What do you think he did?" Evy asked. She was helping Liz unload her umbrellas before she headed to Sal's. She tried to plant a display umbrella, and then Liz did it over again. The green-headed flies inflicted fierce little zaps on their legs, distracting them.

"You can cheat in other places besides motels," Liz said.

"No, I don't think that's what it was—I found another forum all about this," Evy said, "for women who have been, like, kicked out of the husbands-who-cheated-at-motels forums because the women *there* were all like, 'That's not cheating, get out of here.'"

"Of course you did. Is Mom there too?"

"No—I mean, I don't think so, I did look—anyway, some women there freak out when their husband gets dinner with a lady coworker once. Some are like, 'Um, I'm not sure this counts,' and it turns out their husband sent like a hundred sexts to the babysitter."

"*Ew.* So . . . you think Dad was sexting someone. Cool, cool, totally normal thing for us to know."

"No . . . I don't think it was that either, and not just because the idea of that is *ew* . . . it's the way Mom said she was *alone*—stuff like sexting, or like not-cheating cheating, the women usually are more disgusted and pissed off. They don't say stuff like, 'He left me alone.'"

Liz pushed an umbrella back and forth deep into the sand, then pulled another one out of the box. It was already hot, with a heavy land breeze that offered no relief.

"Maybe Mom deserved it," Liz said. "And maybe Scrabblemary shouldn't waste her time on this." Evy was stunned, hearing Liz say that. But she had thought the same thing.

Evy imagined all the posts she'd have to compose, delete, revise, and finally post, to engage Margot in this how-did-he-leave-you-alone-before thread, when she could be getting her to admit what a dumb idea it was to move.

"We're pretty sure Dad wasn't a creep," Liz said. "Even if she tells Scrabblemary everything, we'll only know Mom's side of the story, and we still won't know if maybe she was lying to him, like she's lying to us now, and maybe he'd had enough."

Liz

Liz loved the way the hand-painted boardwalk signs endured year after year, and how the sudden shift from a land breeze to a startling salt-cool chill gave her goose bumps. A half-mile stretch of boardwalk had burned down a few years ago, another disaster after the hurricane, when a frayed wire sparked an explosion. The fire had left heaps of melted rides and blackened pilings. The tarred smell lingered until it was all bulldozed away, leaving a temporary swath of naked, splinter-littered beach. The imitation-wood boards on the rebuilt stretch were smooth and even now. This section of sturdier, fireproofed kiosks had a too-new uprightness, a temporary aura that felt disconnected from the rest of the boardwalk.

An old Sublime album played at the Buccaneer and those foamy beers flowed. The bar had survived the fire, then stood alone, an odd island atop the wreckage, for the year it took to rebuild the burnt-out boards around it. Robbie had left the one blackened section of siding where the flames had threatened it like *come at me, bro.* The Buccaneer went about its business in the tourist season and the off-season, indifferent to the changes in crowds. Robbie was behind the bar, and gave Liz a little wave. When he came by to visit Brian now, she heard him in there telling stories about their bartending-together days and going through his Sysco order.

After the Buccaneer, she crossed from Seaside Heights into Seaside Park. A double yellow line separated the towns. On the Park side: cruiser bikes, tidy green and white gazebos, a quiet boardwalk with only dunes on either side. Her mom would say *weathered charm, uninterrupted sunsets* in her ads. On the Heights side: tricked-out cars straight out of *Grand Theft Auto*, dance clubs shooting spotlights skyward, airbrushed tank tops. Her mom called it *where all the action is.* Between the double yellow lines on Porter Avenue: a few inches of in-between that wasn't one place or the other.

Liz always texted Sonia when she was halfway home. This time of day Sonia was always bored out of her mind, waiting to go to Florida early-bird dinner with her grandma, so she responded even faster than usual:

is Florida retirement community living still luxurious? what's for dinner?

tuna casserole and wet lettuce and weak decaf coffee? kill me. sext him tonight. don't wimp out this time.

I literally can't.

do it. how's ur dad?

kinda checked out?

well I'm around . . . everyone here will be asleep by like 7pm, so kinda whenever, esp if you're sad . . . don't act all tough if you're not, really, ok?? promise.

I promise. I'll call you later

also don't forget to send tit pics to band guy asap. or a vag shot

right, will get on that. I'll keep you updated . . . on everything

When she got home, Lorraine was opening the window wider, swapping out Brian's pillow for a fresh one, and smoothing his hair back. "It's Liz here, Mr. Dunne." She had arranged all the containers on Brian's nightstand in perfect rows. In the background: the neighbors' crescendo of voices, tires on gravel, the cadence of laughter. After Lorraine left, Liz played *Hot Fuss* for her dad. It was one of her favorites to play on her own walk home too. She would turn up "All These Things

That I've Done" at its biggest chorus, when she was so tired from work but feeling that end-of-the-day energy.

Maybe wherever her dad was now felt like her walk home from work after a long day. Maybe it was not one place or another, but full of familiar landmarks, like an extended version of the moment when she stepped on the thin strip of asphalt between the double yellow lines while big bass lines and electric guitar played on her headphones, knowing to the minute how long it would be before her own screen door slammed behind her and she was home.

Margot

After so many months of dark-eyed impatience, rage, and blank disconnect, Brian's face was now smooth, his mouth upturned at the edges. She shared the space beside his bed now with the parade of people passing through. They told Brian the latest baseball scores or about the times he mattered most to them. It was Margot's job to let them each stay for an awkward five minutes or an endless afternoon, to insist it was fine if they overlapped with someone they'd never met or if they settled in for an extended vigil. Some people didn't behave the way you might guess or play the part you pegged them for. Some people didn't know the cues and rules that seemed obvious to Margot.

Brian's brother, Pete, canceled three times, then showed up with a car full of gifts for the girls from a business trip to Chicago he'd been on and asked if Margot had a certain craft beer he liked; when she said she didn't, he drank a Coors Light but seemed confused by it.

But then Jimmy would stop in after working overtime to keep their houses from totally falling apart, and he would play old movies in there for a few hours. Margot actually found it comforting to hear him in there laughing at the old *Point Break* catchphrases in the background.

Robbie was drunk the first time he came to visit, still wearing his sweaty Buccaneer T-shirt. Then Margot gave him Lorraine's advice about saying something ordinary, and she'd hear him in there telling Brian how much money they were making on these spiked seltzers; people loved the low-carb stuff, Brian wouldn't believe it.

Margot's mom resurrected her cooking skills and brought down triple portions of stews to eat while they all watched *Jeopardy!* Her mother commented on the girls' cutoff jean shorts. But she also washed every dish and left an Entenmann's and strawberries for the morning, and both her parents gave Margot long hugs when they left. Margot's sister, Melissa, didn't come down from New York, because of her job, but she sent Margot expensive candles and a set of gleaming new wineglasses she would never have bought herself.

Brian's mom was in her own assisted-living facility, too off-kilter and old herself to really get what was going on with her son. Margot would be the one to try to explain to her, probably more than once, when her son finally died.

Chapter Twelve

Liz

Liz filled out the green swimsuit more now than she had last summer. She was conscious of the fine prickle of hair under her arms, the faint blue veins on the backs of her legs, all the exposed skin. Gabe's sunburn had become an even tan, and the reddish hair on his chest was lighter. His swim trunks sat low on his hips. She could see from his tan line how his other shorts sat a little higher, see his tattoos that had only peeked out from under his shirt. He handed her a rash guard and showed her how to practice popping up on the board while they were still on the sand. Without water underneath, it was like pretending to drive with the engine off.

"You got this," Gabe said, paddling ahead on his own board, looking back after each wave to see that she'd pushed through it. She wasn't afraid and she didn't pretend to be. She'd learned to surf with her dad when she was twelve, but she hadn't told Gabe that.

He had shown her how to sit with her back straight and watch for the next set in the distance, how to paddle as fast as she could when she felt the wave building behind her. Twelve was old enough to learn to surf an easy set—but it was also old enough to notice the teenage boys racing down the beach in their black wetsuits, holding their boards with bright brand-name stickers on the bottom. She knew their names: Brock, Emmett, and Hunter, from the bus, but they all called each other by their last names, laughing at some joke that had nothing to do with her. In the middle of a perfect set with her dad, she said she was cold and wanted to go home.

"It's all right, kid, it'll get easier," he'd said, and at the time she thought he only meant surfing. The next time he asked if she wanted to go up and check the waves, she said no, even though it had felt like flying when she stood up for a second. She'd never surfed with her dad again.

"Now, when the wave comes, you just paddle like hell," Gabe said. "Then one quick motion to pop up."

She gauged where the wave she wanted would break. You never knew which kinds of muscle memory would come back to you even if you'd stopped short of learning something by heart. Sometimes it was harder to reconnect with a rhythm you'd once had than to start fresh.

"Got it," she said. It was getting easier to curate herself for him the way she did her social media feeds, which were full of boardwalk scenes: sky-ride benches and bumper cars with a filter that made the photos look like old postcards.

"That one's yours," Gabe said, but she had already turned around and started paddling, feeling the gathering strength of the wave pinning her to the board. "Yeah, I guess you do got it, boss." When she fell, she freed herself from the tangle of the leash, breathed through the sting of saltwater, and tried again.

They stayed out until the waves were dark, pulsing shadows, until the last streak of red-gold sun rushed out of the sky, until they could see half-moons of purple under their fingernails.

Gabe reached up to put the boards back on top of his car, and her feet made wet marks on the asphalt. She pressed him against the hot back bumper, kissing him with her hands around his hips. Her kiss was more insistent than it had been before, and he insisted back; she was exhausted after getting knocked down so many times.

The dashboard lights flicked on. She didn't feel like leaving his front seat that smelled like coconut and sand. "Do you mind if we drive around a little longer?" she asked. "If you don't have anywhere to be?" He accelerated faster than he needed to. She cracked the window.

It drizzled, but people lingered on the motel balconies. The neon signs made ripples of glare in the puddles. The car next to them had the bass turned so high that the windows rattled. Through the rain-streaked windshield, their wobbly reflections looked back at them. The flags at the miniature golf course sagged. Gabe turned south again, past the empty playgrounds and floodlit docks.

They hadn't eaten, and Liz felt a light-headed spell descend on her. When they pulled into an empty parking lot looking out at the black bay, the cattails fluttering and bending away from them toward the water, he killed the engine.

Her mind went blank when he leaned in and kissed her again across the console, an unbuzzing space that felt so special and so apart from this constant waiting for whatever was next.

Margot

Margot read *The Girl with the Long Shadow* on the screen porch from five in the morning until Lorraine got there at seven. She listened to the news in the car, alone, and spent an hour in Acme, browsing and lingering in front of the fancy cheeses and the wall of yogurt flavors. She took the long way home and listened to an interview about the president.

People who came to see Brian asked her whether she thought this president was guilty, dangerous, or a genius. But the feeling she got trying to respond was like what she used to feel as a sleepless new mom meeting a still-single friend who told her about a wild night out. She had only the vaguest sense she used to be like them.

When she unloaded the groceries and got back in the car, the interviewer on the radio was asking whether democracy still existed and what exactly the limits were for decency. She went over to the Victorian house, watered the geraniums, and dropped off a bicycle pump and a basket of fresh beach towels.

Margot went to the Victorian to take care of every detail the same as always, even though she had stopped responding to her other renters' emails and texts with any regularity. If the crew took too long with a turnover, she said they could promise the renters a discount. She paid all her workers, but missed schedule changes and didn't bother to scramble or do it herself if someone didn't show up.

Jimmy did his best to fix what he could without bothering Margot, but he missed a lot. If renters complained about mildew, ripped screens, or weeds, she imagined revising her online descriptions from *Beautiful family-friendly property, blocks from the beach, bring the kids for sun, sand, and fun! Grill, parking, hot tub—the perfect getaway* to sound more realistic: *Adequately maintained house, but people take vacations here and it's a real bummer what they do to the place. The sheets are probably clean, bring your own if you want to be sure. I'm going through some stuff, so how about you leave me alone and you can stay in my house proportionally cheaper to how many fewer fucks I give?*

What suckers had they been to waste energy making sure every crack was filled and weed killed, obsessing over that sacred bond between renters and owners and over their five-star reviews? Maybe she'd been the sucker after Sandy too—maybe Brian had been prescient, maybe his slow fade then should have been a warning, and she'd missed it.

After that night at the Starlight in Cherry Heights, Margot had taken the lead in the early plans for rebuilding the E&E houses, fielding all the paperwork and playing unanswered voicemails, then plotting their course through the chaos.

Brian did what she asked: stayed on hold with utility companies for an hour, called around until he found a dumpster, bought the girls pajamas or whole milk at the Walmart near her parents' house. But he waited for Margot's instructions and dragged himself through every task. He lacked the capacity to decide anything important himself or to force away the stubborn fog that seemed to have descended on him and dampened his sense of reality.

It had felt like a betrayal then, Brian being suddenly so unlike himself, but Margot understood now that you didn't get to choose which imperfect coping mechanism kicked in and when. With incremental, near-invisible work, you could come back to yourself, but never on the schedule everyone around you expected.

When she suggested anything—a doctor, a drug, or anyone better at this than her, to help nudge him nearer to who he had been before the storm—his refusals were unsubtle and absolute, which was the cruelest irony, the impossible equation she couldn't solve for him even though the answer seemed so obvious.

They slept in her parents' basement, between the cat's litter box and the crafting supplies, in the shadow of the gurgling hot water heater. Their clothes were piled on their suitcases, and their phones and laptops charged in a tangle of wires atop the plastic bins of Christmas ornaments. The girls were supposed to sleep upstairs in Margot's old room, but often ended up down there with them, scared of the upstairs creaks and darkness. The mean cat peed on their comforter. They showered in the basement bathroom where they'd displaced Margot's dad from his favorite place to take a shit (though they still found him in there sometimes, acting like he was looking for a screwdriver but really lurking around his spot). Above the smudged bathroom mirror hung a single bare lightbulb, so whenever you caught your own reflection you imagined what you would say if you were being interrogated for murder.

It was never the right time or place to reach for each other. When they most needed the reset that sex gave them, they had the least opportunity for it. They tried sneaking off to a parking lot behind a strip mall, but it wasn't romantic and secret, only awkward and cramped and sad.

Margot felt an edge and irritability increasing in Brian, a disinterest and impatience whenever she asked a question, no matter how small. Margot was quicker to pick a fight, less willing to wait a beat before saying whatever snarky variation on *if you would only* popped into her head. She drank more than she should, and blamed him more when she did.

They needed sex to remember again the ten thousand hours of expertise in each other's moods and weaknesses, to access the reserves of grace and forgiveness and occasional optimism that sex somehow shortcutted to; they needed the tension-release it allowed so they could go back to joking about the cat pee and the zeros accumulating after their debt, so they could be sarcastic and silly about their tiny basement bathroom instead of getting in each other's way and saying *it's fine* in an edgy, passive, default tone of voice.

Nothing special, a little overpriced. Before heading home to relieve Lorraine, Margot read a two-star review of one of their properties, a house they'd raised after Sandy so it could never flood again. By the time Margot got home, it was late afternoon and Lorraine had to leave.

"E&E sure is not what it used to be," she yelled to Brian after Lorraine was gone, sitting on the screen porch finally answering an urgent text from Jimmy about a clogged toilet. "It's a real shame! Someone should do something about that! I'm gonna write them a bad review!"

Brian's brother arrived while she was still in the shower, and she stayed in there an extra ten minutes and let Pete wander around their house alone. He'd brought over three six-packs of beer, as if they were about to throw a party, but it was sweet: he included Brian's Coors Light, and Corona, which Margot used to drink when she was in her twenties and Pete was in college. The first thing he asked Margot when she finally came out of the bathroom was the same question about the president the reporter had asked the senator on the news that morning. She said word for word back to Pete what the senator had said, as if she had thought of it herself.

Chapter Thirteen

Evy

Evy had never considered finding an online group called something like "GBM Teens." She spent enough time with people her own age in real life. Most of them probably had no idea when she suddenly felt the urge to hide in a bathroom stall and stare at her feet. They had no idea about the sadmonster.

Evy always knew, the whole time her dad was not-himself-sick and now that he was fast-fade-sick, that the dark little sadmonster wasn't gone when she forgot about him for a bit. That motherfucker, he was just shoved into his monster hole, where he was eating protein powder and getting all jacked up on monster steroids so he could come bite her in the freaking neck as soon as she got home.

Evy thought Olivia might be the only one who got how the sad-monster felt. Something had shifted between them since their Lyft ride home, since Evy's visit to the vintage store.

They mostly texted things like **heyyyyyy! ugh, still at work? Omg, Irene is awful today, did u see this video??? coding=v hard, do u like this hat?** But they also let little details about what was happening in their families slip in.

Evy texted: **tough night here, can't sleep. Shld I steal my mom's ambien?**

Olivia texted: **My mom was just sitting on the kitchen floor holding an empty coffee cup when I got home. My dad posted another picture with him and his new barely-legal girlfriend, at Disneyland, UGHHHH.**

As hard as it was imagining her dad gone, it would be so much worse if he was not himself forever. Evy spent two hours making a playlist of songs for Olivia, about silver linings and bastards, about not being alone, about worry and shaking it out, about landslides and dancing.

They texted in all their stolen moments, and Olivia's new-message pings pierced through Evy's busiest hours at work on the August weekends, through her saddest evenings at home when she wondered if her dad could hear anything they were saying to him.

Olivia made a simple game for her coding class and sent it to Evy: a magic 8-ball where you typed in questions and it answered *yes*, *no*, or *maybe*. Evy typed her questions in and clicked on the 8-ball picture for answers: *Yes*, Olivia loved the playlist. *No*, she didn't care that it was late and they both had to get up early. *Maybe* one day with more practice she would build a multiverse with her code instead of a magic 8-ball.

They kept showing up to see each other at work too, as if they needed more candy or clothes. They memorized the best times to visit, when it was slow, when their bosses were gone. Except for a few minutes at a time between customers, they still hadn't been alone together since the Lyft ride home from the party at the end of July. Evy was wondering whether they'd ever have the chance, with Olivia's mom and her own mom and Lorraine and all the family visitors always around, when Cameron texted the group: **my house, tonight.** She texted Olivia:

Are you coming to Cameron's
pool (plz say yes!)

CLASS until 9. But coming right
after . . . don't eat too many
vodka gummy bears before I
get there this time, ok??

wut, wld never.

Evy felt the stomach-flip again. She promised herself she would not get too drunk at Cameron's before Olivia arrived. She set a reminder on her phone for 9 p.m.: *1 drink!!! No more!!!!*

Olivia had to go finish her homework, and Evy had to finish her GBM Wives post, which was taking a lot of work to get right. Evy had tried a few more times to see if real-life Margot was as into the idea of moving as her online persona. But still, Evy never managed to say exactly what she wanted to say.

In English class, Ms. Thrall had written poems on the board every day. Evy loved how the ideas of plums in an icebox, or hope as a feathered thing in your soul, stayed with her. Images from poems popped into her head when she least expected them, while she was waiting around for the bus to a soccer game and a robin landed on the field, or when the lunch lady handed her a cold piece of fruit with her soft, wrinkled hand.

Scrabblemary45 was supposed to be a teacher, so Evy thought a poem would be a good way for her to connect with Margot and say something about sadness that someone had already said better. She hoped a poem might make Margot see the world differently, like a beautiful little ambush.

She wanted to do for her mom what Ms. Thrall had done for her by making her see ordinary slamming locker doors and muddy soccer fields as less ordinary, as things to capture in memory.

Evy knew one reason Margot wanted to move was that she thought staying in Seaside would be too hard, because everything here reminded her of Brian. Maybe with the right kind of words, she could make her mom see that moving would not help her escape anything, but would only add another self-inflicted loss to the one they were already staring down.

Evy Googled "poems about death" and scrolled through what she found: death as a ship that sailed away without you, death as a storm, as a visitor, as an obliterated place. She wrote a new response to Margot's last post, pasting in "One Art" by Elizabeth Bishop:

Hi. I'm sure you've read this poem before. My students all ask about how loss can be art whenever I make them read this poem. She (the writer) went through a lot in her life and lost a lot, too. It's harder when you lose the person a little at a time, right?

She says, "I lost two cities, lovely ones," and some people might read that as her saying look how strong I am, losing people and places over and over, forever, even choosing to! I don't read it that way. When she was a kid, her dad died, and her mom couldn't take care of her, so she had to live with her grandparents. When she was older, the woman she loved committed suicide. I don't know why she moved so much once she could choose. I don't think saying it wasn't a disaster means losing cities was always the thing she needed.

I would never lose my city, if I could choose.

You will feel like yourself again, someday soon, I hope. If you ask, your daughters might be able to help you (you could help each other) more than you might think?

It's okay you're thinking about it, but it doesn't mean you have to do it.

Anyway, I'm still not sure moving is the right thing.

Margot

Hi, Scrabblemary45. Thanks for the poem. I was a teacher too, but of younger students. We did a lot of Shel Silverstein, who is very dark, in his own way. "One Art" is perfect for our group. I have read it, but I understood it a bit differently from you. By leaving these places, she can miss them, but also find something new in herself.

So many of the stories I read with my students were about finding your way after losing your parents, or about being an outcast. I'm sure it's their biggest fear, at that age, though I guess it doesn't go away, does it? It's scary at any age. I'm afraid of it.

Your city is bigger than mine. That matters.

I know I'll be different after he's gone, and I don't want to be that different person in the same place. Does that make sense?

Maybe I can show the girls how a new place can change you—they don't know that yet. I chose to come back here once to be with him, and now he's leaving me forever, and I'm choosing another place. It will be what we need.

I used to make my students memorize poems. Speaking of art, that's a lost one. Once you've memorized something, you can call on it anytime you want. It's good to have something to remember when you need it. It's good for it to be a part of you.

It was so thoughtful of you to post this poem. I am on my way to memorizing it.

Evy

All right, Evy thought, Scrabblemary45 would keep trying. Evy imagined all the times, in the heat of real-life arguments with her mother, when she'd threatened a thing she would never do. She'd once sworn that she would drop out of high school if she had to take higher-level Spanish instead of art. She knew the effect these threats had, making the actual thing you wanted more attainable, and so she didn't panic at Margot still insisting on this idea that they needed to leave. She would do what Margot usually did when Evy made her own threats: give her some space and change the subject, leave it alone for a while because it was so ridiculous.

Scrabblemary45 wrote:

I'm glad you liked the poem, though I guess all good poems can be read in different ways. . . .

I have some friends I like to meet on Orcas Island for the weekend sometimes. I would not want to lose them, even though they're not perfect. I'm sure you have friends like this too, who are there for you as best they can be, and will be after.

Not everyone is going to understand—how could they??? Spoiler alert: they won't in a new place, either!! There is no GBM Wivestown you can move to. This is it. Sometimes I don't even tell my friends how hard my week was because they are too busy, or they drink too much when we go to the pinot noir wineries around Washington. Sometimes I think they're not really listening to me. That's a reason I'm glad for everyone here, but I'm not going to trade my local friends in for some strangers.

I know you don't want to talk about whatever time it was your husband left you alone, before he got sick. I won't make you say what happened to make you feel that way. But won't you be forcing your girls to be alone, away from their friends, and their town, if you move? Won't you be making them feel exactly the way he made you feel, when he left you alone, in a way? Is that what you want?

CHAPTER FOURTEEN

Margot

Of course that feeling of being alone is not what I would ever want for my girls . . . but we wouldn't be losing Seaside. In fact, if we leave, we would get to keep all the good we've built here. Leaving a place is not the same as losing a place, whatever Elizabeth Bishop meant by that.

When I started to lose Brian this time, it felt like some circuit breaker inside me flipped—to protect me. I felt that the last time I lost him, too, and I wonder what it would have been like (harder? at least less familiar) if that feeling had been brand-new this time around.

Brian had first messaged Claire on Facebook one night in December, two months after the hurricane hit. He and Margot had spent the day wading through frigid mud and pieces of broken bungalows. Margot didn't go looking for the messages; they were right there on the still-open browser on his laptop. While Brian showered, Margot only had a few minutes to scan them, but she sent screenshots of them to herself and did a deep dive later.

Brian had dated Claire in college, when he and Margot were broken up. After graduation, Claire had moved to Seattle, a city on Margot's mind more lately since Scrabblemary45 from the Wives' group seemed to love it there. Claire was married to a tech-startup type who liked to hike, according to his own social media posts.

In college, Margot had imagined Brian and Claire up late, telling each other their life stories, wasting long afternoons with music and cheap beer, while Margot played at being some kind of Kennedy-wife wannabe with a wealthy, immature new boyfriend from Chicago. Sometimes she was sure she had purposely chosen someone so wrong for her during that time apart from Brian, so she wouldn't risk falling in love.

That December after Sandy, Claire and Brian sent a hundred middle-of-the-night Facebook messages over one week. No wonder Brian could barely remember how a sledgehammer worked or whether he'd heard back from the plumbers. He was up all night.

In the chat, Brian might as well have been transcribing everything Margot had said to *him* since the storm. He took full credit for running the numbers and eking out a way to fund the construction projects; he described *his* plans to expand, not sell off, E&E's real estate assets, even though it had been Margot who mapped that out and convinced him that selling it all would be a mistake, she who figured out that expanding was a huge opportunity.

With Claire, Brian played the confident provider, the shrewd businessman, the devoted dad, which was only true if you considered watching TV with the girls devoted. Margot was also not exactly a model parent with the girls then, but she managed to drag them to the park or the library before it got dark some days, at least.

For weeks Margot watched Brian glance at his phone and then leave suddenly for unnecessary errands, feeling the energy between him and Claire build when she read their messages later (his password was the same one he used for everything, and the disregard for taking even basic steps to hide the connection was as confusing as it was cruel). Claire had a more athletic body and a sporty Seattle style; she had child-free weekends on the Oregon coast (hiding from her own husband while walking the beach) and long afternoons *alone* in her perfect Green Lake house with wildflowers outside. Margot's gray roots had grown out, and her skin was raw from working in the cold houses. She had not bought any new makeup in her many recent Walgreens runs.

Margot held on to the secret like Emma Thompson in *Love Actually*, when she realizes the ridiculous necklace her husband bought is for his girlfriend and then goes to their children's Christmas show anyway. Margot even fake-enthusiastically fucked Brian in her parents' basement once when they had the rare chance, as if that would be enough, competing with his idea of someone else, acquiescing to something, negotiating something, sacrificing something, hoping somehow that day he heard her say: *stay closer to me.*

When he didn't stop messaging Claire on his own, Margot asked Brian one night in the basement what exactly he thought he was doing, and did he think she was stupid? She said *what is wrong with you*, and she shoved all the screenshots she'd sent herself in his face and said *I've seen* all *these* and left it there. Then she read as many messages back to him as she could manage and wouldn't let him interrupt her, she said he better knock it off because this was the last thing they needed. It was all whispered, it was already late, and then it was hours later, and it was awful.

The fault line that opened up when he said *it's nothing* separated them from the reality required to proceed any further.

After that, Claire and Brian switched to texts and phone calls Brian didn't bother to hide. Margot found the messages intimate and wanting, each challenging the other to take the next step into explicit (**I like being up late with you; I've been thinking about what you said all day; What would it be like if we weren't so far away? Can I tell you a secret?**). They didn't exchange pictures of their body parts, but photos of book passages (he even sent a paragraph from *The Girl with the Long Shadow;* she sent him Pablo Neruda, ugh, ugh).

When Margot and Brian had finally finished demolition and started renovations on most of their ravaged bungalows, Brian sent Claire pictures of the progress with descriptions of the stone or tile they'd used as if Margot hadn't done most of the work, as if she hadn't called seventeen concrete companies and bribed a drywall guy to get his ass there from three states away.

He sent Claire pictures of the ocean, and she sent pictures of the Seattle snowcapped mountains and her black coffee with little captions about how she knew he took his with cream, how she remembered little things about him after all this time.

Margot told one person about Claire and Brian: her college friend Tracy, who lived in San Francisco. Tracy had just divorced her husband after she found out he'd sent ten thousand dollars to a nineteen-year-old woman in Florida whom he liked to talk to late at night and have her call him daddy. It was a relief to tell someone, but Tracy had a particular point of view. Tracy had refused to wait around to see if the husband she recognized would return. Tracy had kids little enough they wouldn't remember anything else, a job unrelated to her husband, and an intact house going for her too.

Tracy was the one who'd explained that Brian was not himself, without offering judgment or drawing any lines between Florida scammers and Facebook messages between exes. Tracy used the word *compulsion*, and that scared Margot. Compulsions told any convenient story; compulsions rewrote the whole narrative in order to hijack your obedience to them, to distract you so wholly that you no longer acted like yourself.

Tracy said seeing it this way was the only way to survive, whether you stayed with him a hundred years or signed a paper dissolving it all, because if this was really the Brian that Margot had known all along, then that made her the sucker. And she was no sucker.

The next several times Margot told Brian his messages to Claire were hurting her and she was not okay with them, he said she *sure was the detective, huh*. It was so measured and mean, not a promise to stop but an accusation of unfounded jealousy when right in front of her any idiot could see these two people fondling each other's egos and activating each other's tummy butterflies, which was no better or worse than a different kind of affair where your skin and mouth touch another person, but a kind of hurt all its own, an awful kind of turning away, a particular version of withholding and redirecting the fragile and finite resources of love and attention at the time when Margot was so desperate for them.

Margot had no choice but to navigate through the wreckage both Sandy and Claire had caused. It was always going to be her conversation to start again and again, would always be her own voice insisting that this person hurting her could not be her husband. Margot stood wobbly and weak at the helm of the ship, guiding them through the narrow strait not because she was a seasoned and optimistic captain who knew calm seas were ahead, but because the only other choice was steering into jagged rocks and drowning.

While so many E&E houses were still half-razed, still broken plumbing and unfinished foundations, Brian kept right on communicating with Claire. He still said that Claire was *going through a hard time and I'm her friend*, still said Margot was overreacting, it wasn't like he was sneaking off to a sleazy motel, and emotional affairs were fiction. Tracy asked, "Has he made the at-least-it's-not-a-sleazy-motel argument to absolve himself yet?"

Margot and Brian exchanged necessary information as the renovations moved forward. The circular saws and spackle, the elderly electrician, the shady flooring guys who stole a thousand dollars from them, the shopping carts full of caulk and grout and gallons of paint were nothing when she assigned them to Brian to handle one at a time, in short texts and legal pads full of handwritten notes. He did his part, and they didn't ask questions about what would happen when everything was done.

She took her own pictures of the early spring Atlantic and the still-broken pier and posted them online for whoever might want to see how destroyed Seaside was. One April night, restless and awake because she'd had a cup of her mother's Folgers in the late afternoon, Margot dragged Brian downstairs at midnight to their basement bed. She had quick, silent sex with him again, not out of some want of him, specifically, but because of a desperate untethered need that seized her the same way that hunger had when she took him to the Starlight that first time after he'd said *we're done*. She wasn't fucking him to get him back, but because she wanted something he had taken from her and she knew it was the only way to get it, because it was her battered heart and not her conscious self that took over and told her to.

Afterward, quiet with each other in the shadows of all the basement junk, she did not ask, she demanded. She did not threaten but said in a deadened monotone: *enough*. And he said *okay*.

Did it matter how many more messages Claire and Brian exchanged after that night in the basement? Brian had been an economics teacher before he gave it up for E&E, and maybe he understood that bankrupt is bankrupt and you might as well have one more fancy dinner on the corporate account before the people you owe divvy the rest up tomorrow, right? But he did stop. However unromantic or un-subtle their encounter on the basement bed had been, it neutralized some toxic vitriol long enough for them to hear the loneliness in each other's voices.

The day after *enough*, Brian brought home a bag of fancy ground dark roast for Margot, plugged in an old coffee maker he'd found in one of the rental houses, and made them their own secret basement pot while Margot's mom drank all the Folgers upstairs. He poured Margot a cup with cream and sugar and handed it to her before her alarm went off, and he made a joke about the mean cat.

It would take a thousand gestures like this before they excavated the lies and cruelties that had taken hold the winter after the hurricane, before Brian said out loud how sorry he was, how grateful he was, how he knew he didn't deserve the grace she'd found for him, until she found a way to admit her own imperfect ways of coping: shut down, drink, blame, repeat. He brought her coffee every single morning after that, even a few weeks into his tumor taking over, though the actual coffee then went downhill fast; he once flavored it with cayenne pepper.

Tracy texted Margot updates when she went on dates with men she met online. *Some days I'd take three Florida mistresses over this,* she said one day.

Margot and Brian lived out the rest of the next year in the same twenty square feet of the half-finished basement, rebuilding their bungalows to withstand another few decades on a slowly sinking barrier island. After Margot's *enough*, they were able to ask each other about the gas lines, the mold, and the HVAC systems, just as they had before, but now they faked patience with each other until it became real again.

Weeks after Margot's *enough*, Carol, the owner of the Victorian, called. Before the storm, they'd still been managing the property, the only E&E rental they didn't hold the mortgage for. Carol was sick, and she wanted to sell it to them—at a price so low it was nearly a gift. She wrote up a generous contract that even gave them time to make the first mortgage payment.

Carol's daughter didn't fight the idea—the house was a small fraction of their wealth, and in its battered state, more of a liability. The work Margot and Brian had already done on it as property managers had made her mother happy, from far away.

There was so much work yet to be done on the other E&E houses, and on bridging the distance between the two of them. But when they began to work on the Victorian together, Margot and Brian found a separate space where the lingering tensions stayed at bay. They cheated on the other E&E houses to spend more time on it, together. They used the new asset to support other projects. They made it beautiful again.

When Brian's tumor left its first imprints on his brain tissue, Margot sensed some unbalance in his sleep and his mixed-up, distracted way of getting an idea out. Weeks before the MRI last fall, she wondered if he'd reached out to Claire again.

Did this second round of Brian being not-himself feel any easier for Margot because of the year they'd fled one natural disaster and then succumbed to another? It was as she'd explained to Scrabblemary45: not easier, but familiar. It had felt familiar to use her own will to disengage from moments that would otherwise break her, and to imagine, when she closed her eyes, the miracle of her own cells dying off and regenerating themselves, making her into an entirely new person.

Chapter Fifteen

Liz

They sat together in Brian's room for the first half of *August and Everything After*, Liz's new Dad-CD-binder favorite, before moving next door to the screen porch, leaving the door ajar so they could hear him, and the music. They were still in their work uniforms, comparing battle scars.

"Cotton candy machine broke," Evy said, holding out her hands and pointing to little red spots. "It kept getting too hot and spitting out these sugar bullets at me!"

"Green-headed flies were disgusting today," Liz said, stretching out on the sofa. "They bit the shit out of my legs."

They reread Margot's last GBM Wives post. "She hasn't asked any boring questions about other towns' recycling programs recently, at least," Evy said. "That's a good sign."

"Scrabblemary's just getting started," Liz said.

They scrolled through their phones, tapping hearts and tending to the text threads and stories. Gabe's message to Liz said **see you tonight**. She wrote and deleted seven texts before she sent a smiley face with heart eyes back. She'd Googled "what does sex feel like" three times that week, and people on the internet said it was as if God whispered in your ear or people said it hurt and was *meh* until you got very good at it (and sometimes even then, there were people who had all kinds of other tricks they liked better).

There was no Google answer to her other question, because it applied only to her: What would happen to the all-consuming feeling of wanting this, once it was done?

Evy

"I mean, just trust me," Evy said. "Use this nice lotion, I don't even care that it cost like a whole day of work, I'll share it."

Liz dabbed some on her legs. "Okay, this is way better," she said. "And it does smell nice, what is that?"

Liz didn't come right out and ask when she needed help. She disguised it, hanging around longer in Evy's room, trailing off midthought, or sighing. Evy had learned the ways she could take care of her sister, the ways Liz wouldn't help herself. Liz always bought cheap beauty products, but sometimes you needed the nice ones.

"Eucalyptus," Evy said.

Liz sat on the edge of Evy's bed. "Gabe invited me over. Tonight. I'm ready, I think—if he wants to, you know—"

Evy looked up from her phone, giving Liz her full attention. Liz twisted the ends of her hair around her fingers. Was she *telling* Evy she was going over to his house to have sex with him, really, or was she *asking her* if it was okay, trying to decide herself?

"Isn't he leaving, soon, with his band?"

"Yeah—and I actually haven't told him anything about Dad. At all."

Evy nodded. If Olivia had only been here for the summer, Evy was sure she would have kept it secret too. She had asked herself the same questions about her and Olivia that she was sure Liz had on her mind: *Is it okay if I do this even though we're in this shitty holding pattern? Is it okay that this is all happening at the same time, am I a horrible person for wanting these things right now?*

"And Olivia's meeting you at Cameron's tonight, right?" Liz asked. **will try to leave class early . . .** Olivia had texted, and Evy imagined the dark corners of Cameron's yard, imagined drinking only a few sips of something, so she would stay clearheaded with a little buzz. She had told Liz she hoped Olivia liked her, but when she imagined finally sitting next to her at the edge of the warm lit-up pool, she asked Liz if she had maybe actually misunderstood all Olivia's texts, and her hand on her back zipping that Calvin Klein dress, and the answers to her magic 8-ball questions.

"Ev, she's not showing up at that party to play flip cup with Cameron and Hailey," Liz said. "And didn't she come see you at Sal's, like, three times this week? That's not because she loves saltwater taffy."

Evy remembered the ding of the bell on the door of Sal's, the same one she heard a hundred times a day when customers walked in, and how its sound punctured the air differently when she looked up and it was Olivia there. She wanted to make Liz read twenty saved texts she'd already seen, assure her again that Olivia wanted her, but Liz was nervous enough about her own night.

Evy felt protective of her sister, an unfamiliar role reversal she was growing used to. She sensed she had the power to dissuade or reassure, to encourage Liz's excitement and experimentation, or to unravel and undermine it. She would never do that, especially now that she understood Liz didn't expect this band guy to love her forever, now that she felt like her sister had already considered the likely end-of-summer heartbreak and decided it was worth the risk.

"Hang on a minute," Evy said, and she came back with her makeup kit and some jewelry, and then she made another trip to Liz's closet to pick some tops out, and to her own closet to get ones she might want to borrow. "Let's get you ready."

Liz

"Welcome," Gabe said, spreading his arms as if his borrowed bungalow were one of the mansions on the beach in Mantoloking. He handed Liz a bottle of Yuengling. There were glass lamps full of broken seashells on a tarnished brass side table, watercolors of umbrellas, and a crab with a painted-on smile: a messier version of all the E&E houses.

She and Evy had picked out Liz's dark denim shorts, a soft cotton tank top, and Evy's gold star earrings. Evy had done Liz's hair in loose curls and brushed pale pink onto her cheeks and eyelids. It had taken them an hour but looked effortless.

Gabe put on some dissonant indie song she didn't know. They sat close on the couch, his arm light around her shoulders, and she reached for a yellowing paperback from the shelf, a copy of *The Girl with the Long Shadow*. Liz had finally read it this summer.

"I love this book," Liz said. "This main character is a badass, but it's only after lifetimes and lifetimes of going through the interseams that hold the space continuum together."

"Should we invite the other members of book club over tonight?" he said. "Maybe Linda and Janice want to join us?"

"Oh, no, I was just—" Oh god, had she really rambled about a *fantasy book*? But also, if you loved something, it was mean for someone to say it was silly. She gulped her beer, hoping a few more sips would let her slip back into the ease she'd felt with him before.

He unbuttoned her shorts while he kissed her, pressing his fingers against her underwear. He asked her *hey, you cool with this*, twice, which reassured her. Under the outfit she'd picked out so carefully, she was wearing the light-pink bra and panty set from the photos she'd never sent him. The *tink-clunk* of the neighbors' game of quarters spilled in through the window. Liz stared at her half-finished beer sitting on the table, and at every particular kitschy-beach-house detail of this room.

They kissed again, and Gabe pulled off her shirt and unhooked her bra, letting it fall before he picked it up and flung it away, a gesture that was overly dramatic and funny and made her feel less awkward. He disappeared into the bedroom, then set the condom on the glass-topped table and spread a sheet across the floor.

"It's nicer out here," he said, taking her hand and pulling her onto the floor in front of the couch. "Right? That room's a mess."

"Yeah," she said, nodding, shrugging, nodding. "Totally."

Under the couch she saw popcorn kernels, a sock, stuff they would never leave for renters to find if this were an E&E house. The ceiling fan whirred. He pulled off her underwear, and then she thought, *THIS IS HAPPENING*, and then he said the word *sexy*—in the middle of something else, but that's the word she heard—and that broke the spell for a few seconds and made her wish he hadn't said it.

Her real life was glitching, but here she was, leveling up and capturing the castle. Gabe took a drink of his beer and asked her again if she was ready and if she was sure.

And then she felt the dull ache, the suffused pain. His eyes were closed, and his mouth was open but no sound came out, then he was saying her name. The rest of the world, the voices and the quarters clunking in shot glasses and the music from passing cars and the sounds of tires on gravel, went on. He fell onto the sheet, the thin bars of light through the blinds shifting across his skin.

His arm was heavy on her. She felt like someone had told her a secret that she had always suspected was true.

On the way home, they stopped at one of the photo booths on the boardwalk and fed it two dollars, then waited for the bright white flash. No one but them would see these, comment on them, or like them. They smiled for the first photo, and then he kissed her for the next two. They made monster faces for the fourth photo, and when the machine dropped the four black-and-white frames, he said she could keep them all.

Evy

Evy was shedding her bikini in Cameron's backyard, joining a group of girls she didn't know in their echoing shrieks, saying *ssssso funny* and *are we doing thisssok letsgoletsgo*.

Evy had only drunk half a cup of that sweet red juice, but it was so, so strong and gave her a little buzz she would have wanted more and more of on any other night, but not tonight, when Olivia said she would come, when they might be alone.

Then the other girls were saying *heyyissmystraps, cansomeonedo mine*, and she felt like maybe those few sips had been too much. The edges of the lit-up pool blurred. She felt the rise of a wild giggle, the grip of another girl's hand, her own elbow jerking forward, and then she was submerged in the pool, she was nightswimming, cold and exposed, only skin and water where usually she felt the stretch of a tight swimsuit.

Evy opened her eyes underwater: trails of cloudy bubbles and the backyard spotlight, the tangle of limbs. Then she surfaced and saw every guy (all wide eyes and *fuck yeahs*, who were these guys? where were Cameron and Hailey?) at the edge of the pool, looking at the girls' distorted bodies through the water before they all plunged in, flinging their own trunks away like flags of surrender, and her ears cleared out and the girlshrieks and chatter and the deep boyvoices crested and fell, and she felt another body next to her then space when it kicked away, and she pushed off and dove under the churned-up choppy water again.

Then a heavy arm was pushing her against the side of the pool, a boy but she couldn't see his face, then he was hardening against her leg saying *come on* and pulling her toward him. Some voice inside her said *get away* and she dove deep, until her chest was about to burst, then she resurfaced and climbed out of the pool. She stood hunched, cold, and naked for a full five seconds at the edge, grateful she was more alert now, eyes darting to see who it had been up against her saying *come on*, but it could have been anyone. If Olivia arrived now, this was how she would find Evy: exposed, with only humid air blanketing her skin.

She grabbed an Elsa towel, someone's little sister's favorite she was stealing, and wrapped it around her midsection before she slipped inside, making wet footprints on the carpet, and no one said to come back in the pool because they were all churning up water and stuck inside their own chlorine cocoons, and she was a little clumsy and slow scooping up her clothes, finding buttons, moving her wet fingers over the buckles of her sandals. She willed herself up from the soft bathroom rug and out to the front porch.

Olivia texted Evy: **leaving class now! how's the party?**

**CAMERON HAS LUCKY JUICE
BUT I ONLY HAD A TINY BIT.**

> Ssshh don't tell anyone but I
> brought some of my mom's
> Campari w me, having some
> now, watch out, fun Olivia is on
> her way

Evy had not tried Campari, but it sounded fancy. She sent back a screen full of party-face emojis.

> Good bc I am also fun EVY, woo woo (but not wasty face Evy this time!!!!) party is ok, just me and my friend Elsa here on the front porch (she's the best princess, fight me).

> Elsa=queen w ice powers, not a princess?? um . . . driver is taking a weird way and just said, hey, party girl and stared at me creepy in rearview mirror. Stand by???

A stab of fear cut through Evy's buzz. She pictured Olivia alone in the backseat, on some dark back road. She texted: **send car details and where u r, then I'm calling you!!**

blue Civic, license plate had a TY. On 37 near Wawa. 10 min away, Olivia texted, and then Evy called her and asked, "Hi, are you kidnapped yet?"

"Oh, hey, yeah, ha-ha, I mean, no, going over the bridge in a sec." She sounded so fake, and scared, Evy hoped the driver didn't realize it. "So yeah, class was so boring but we turned in a huge project, oh, totally, yeah I know. . . ."

"Is he acting more normal?" Evy asked. She heard a man's voice over Olivia's fake-casual small talk. She heard him say, "This town, it's a crazy town."

"Ha-ha, no way, you're kidding, I know right," Olivia said, to him or Evy or both. Olivia said, "Yeah? Wow, okay," a couple times like she was listening to Evy tell an interesting story.

"Are you close?" Evy asked, keeping her voice low.

"No. Yeah, nope, I guess, kinda? Anyway, so what were you saying about the thing the other day?"

"Just hang on, at least you're over the bridge now," Evy said. She imagined Olivia opening her door and rolling out onto the road like a stuntwoman.

"Right, right, you're sooo right," Olivia said. "Uh-huh."

The Civic finally pulled up in front of Cameron's house, and the driver leaned out the window, casual.

"Five stars, thanks," Olivia said, opening the back door before the car had stopped all the way and looking at Evy with wide-eyed relief. The driver leaned out the window and looked Evy up and down, and Evy glared back at him and curled her lip, saying *fuck off creep* with her eyes. He said, "Party girls, yeah, okay," before he drove off.

Olivia exhaled and took a pull on her bottle, then passed it to Evy. She liked the citrus aftertaste, the watered-down icy bitterness of the Campari. The bass and voices drifting from backyard blended together.

"Thanks," Olivia said, "he was *probably* not a murderer?"

"I have watched thirty murder documentaries with my mom this summer—he checked a few boxes," Evy said.

Olivia's eyes fell on Evy's damp Elsa towel, the dry swimsuit in her hand, and her wet hair, trying to piece it all together. "Did I miss skinny-dipping?" she asked. Someone shrieked in the backyard.

"That screaming person sounds naked still, we can go back there, if you want to?" Evy said, but Olivia shrugged.

"I don't," she said. Then they left the half-light of the front yard and turned the corner into a dark pocket before the next streetlight, headed toward the beach, when Olivia's hand found Evy's, and held on. Evy felt a surge of nerve-numbing-magic.

They debriefed on the not-murder Lyft drive, funny now that it was over. They laughed at how Olivia had been a good actress and Evy had been good mission control, at how it was silly and scary at the same time. They wondered, what if Olivia hadn't done everything right? What if Evy had been drunk on more than a few sips of lucky juice and hadn't been on the phone the whole time?

Evy pulled Olivia down the path through the dunes, and said *come on,* and then they were all the way to the end where the path opened up onto the beach. The broken light scattered across the black ocean, and when they kissed, when Evy tasted the bitter citrus they'd shared, and felt Olivia's hand on her hip, she didn't hold her breath, but breathed in the salt air and Olivia's rosemary shampoo and the lingering chlorine, and no, it couldn't have been anyone, it had to be her.

CHAPTER SIXTEEN

Margot

Margot poured her second glass of cabernet. She sat on the screen porch next to Brian's room, as attuned to his breathing as she had been to her newborn babies, when she had convinced herself she couldn't be trusted to keep them alive. She'd listened to each of her infant daughters breathe in those weeks, waiting in a half-second of panic for each exhale. She'd sniffed their warm talc-and-milk heads, rocked them after their 3 a.m. wake-ups, and quieted their long, low cries of loneliness or hunger. In the morning she'd breathed in the smell of brewing coffee, the only thing that separated night from day.

Sixteen and seventeen years after those babies, Margot listened to the labored letting-go of their father, to the slight wheeze and little hum, the occasional sigh that signaled either temporary relief or awe at the constant dreams that were blurring into the end for him.

Where had the girls said they were going tonight? Margot considered the inevitable, awful truth that the girls would eventually have sex with someone, someday, the not-all-that-reassuring fact that they'd at least had sex ed in school.

When the cabernet really kicked in each night, during the forty minutes while she worked on her second glass, a soft-focus feeling finally descended on her, the edges of everything softened, and her pulse slowed. Her worry receded like a low, warm tide.

She looked forward to this moment all day, counting the hours until it arrived, longing for her thick-cushioned chair on the screen porch, the soft glow of the outside floodlights, the almost-quiet except for the strangers' voices next door.

No one ever told you how much hosting dying involved, how people expected you to usher them through it even when they acted like it was the other way around. Her parents meant well and loved her, though she was sure she would vomit if she had to eat another mushy stew or watch them guess the *Wheel of Fortune* words with their mouths full one more time.

Brian's sister always stayed too long, talked about her cat's medication, and finished off an entire block of cheese. Eileen was too much in the best of circumstances, the kind of narcissist who turns every conversation into a story they think you'd probably like to hear about them, the kind of person who asked her if Evy was going through a phase with all the rainbow stuff and if Liz was going to go on a diet to lose the five pounds she'd gained since she stopped running.

Through the neighbors' fence, Margot heard the crack of a beer, the whir of a blender. Let the neighbors have their vacation drinks; cabernet was the drink of women with too much to think about, the drink for women who couldn't stand anything too sweet, or bubbly, or bitter, for women who wanted smooth and room-temperature. Red wine at night felt like an ancient ritual, a way of easing away from another day and into the knitted sleeve of sleep. She poured a third glass, but only half-full; she knew the exact amount she could consume and avoid the head-pressed-between-two-walls feeling in the morning. She adhered to these self-imposed limits about half the time.

She scrolled through all the emails in her inbox from summer renters. She knew weeds were creeping through the concrete at their properties, paint chipping; she knew some renters were getting wilder than their rental agreement allowed. She put it all off and felt nothing: no worry, no mind-racing fears of the consequences. Those were the choices, when you were triaging debts, leaving hospital envelopes unopened: feel every red number's pull and power, or feel nothing. What masochist would choose the former?

She had more of the details worked out for selling off the E&E properties at the end of the summer. She'd narrowed down her search for where to live when they left Seaside to two small cities, one bigger city, and a small town, and the idea of pouring herself a glass of wine in the evening in a place where she remembered nothing, where she'd invested nothing and lost nothing, where she would see only strangers when she ventured out to get coffee, where she would never pass a house she'd poured her heart into, felt close to being real.

Margot read the Wives' responses to more of her requests for realtors, tax info, and cold-weather gear recommendations in the places she wanted to move.

Scrabblemary45 had responded:

You do seem to be getting more into the details! I am a detail person too—are you sure it's not planning something exciting, something new, and not this PARTICULAR new thing that's making you feel this way?

My first date with my husband was at Dick's Drive-in for burgers, and I know when he's gone, I'll take my kids there and tell the story, and it might be sad, but the alternative is forgetting and I don't want that either. I always want to send you a poem, because there's nothing new to say, someone has said it better (don't tell my students that, they won't want to write essays).

This is called "The Raincoat," by Ada Limón, and it's about a mother, protecting her daughter, and about the day the daughter realizes how her mother has been doing this for her for so long. Don't you think that's a mother's job? Don't you think your girls' home is a place they deserve to stay in after their dad is gone?

Margot read this line in the poem, in the daughter's voice. She reabsorbed the images of a little girl's spine and a storm, this gesture of a mother sliding a raincoat onto her daughter and the speaker imagining her own mother's protection, her childhood, "thinking it was somehow a marvel / that I never got wet."

That woman speaking to her in the poem carried some message Margot wanted to quiet, so she closed her laptop but heard some silent whisper say *enough*, interrupting her wine ritual. She flipped the screen open again and clicked on the other threads, and did not respond to Scrabblemary45.

FLMom99 was schlepping to a clinical trial in Maryland all the way from Tampa, bringing her in-laws who insisted on fancy restaurants even though her husband hated the noise and couldn't read the menu. FLMom99 discussed meds: costs and side effects, insurance coverage, out of pocket, and off-label, and then a little rant on socialized healthcare, though it was unclear if she was for or against it. She had three kids under ten and a spray tan and manicure Margot could tell from Facebook that she *always* maintained. When her husband totally lost his speech and punched through all the screens in their house, the tan and nails got fresher.

FLMom99 sent Margot invitations to buy some face lotion she

sold on the side, which Margot didn't mind, and long passages of scripture, which Margot did mind; she didn't care if people read the Bible to help them through hard times, but throwing it around felt too much like a performance to her.

Margot's faith was private, fragile, and buried, full of contradictions and questions that she did not have the time or bandwidth to unpack. She'd come to expect so little in return from the rituals except a quiet hour in a pew, until they couldn't do that anymore. It didn't feel right to cherry-pick a beatitude or a psalm and ditch everything else, at least not now, especially not right now.

Michelleruns5 was a real type-A lady, from what Margot could tell. She'd run three marathons since her husband's diagnosis, started a charity for brain tumors, and earned a promotion. She name-dropped surgeons and sent the other women in the group care packages in the mail with samples of holistic remedies, which Margot threw in the trash. But she was so generous and so full of energy that it was impossible to hate her.

Margot clicked on a thread where the women were making jokes about their future online dating profiles, and listing the ways they were coping this week: by bingeing *The Real Housewives*, by eating entire boxes of Little Debbie cakes, or by filling their Target carts in a fugue state and then returning it all when they realized the total was four hundred dollars. All the acceptable escapes available to moms with other shit they had to take care of while their lives fell apart.

The screen door creaked open as Liz came home. Margot heard her filling a water glass before she came out to the porch and sat down.

"How was the movie with Kaylee?" Margot asked. "Isn't that where you said you were going?" She closed her laptop again. It was good that Liz was here, sitting with Margot again, good that she hadn't said a hurried, "I'm home," and headed straight to her room. There was no need for Margot to know everything, but she wanted to give her daughter the unspoken okay to tell her if something happened that she couldn't handle.

"Oh, it was fine. We just watched Netflix at her house, so." Liz looked at a place four feet above Margot's head.

"Netflix, huh?" Margot asked.

When she was still teaching, Margot had mastered the art of wait time. If you gave a class three or four seconds after asking a question instead of calling on the first hand that shot up, you would get more students to volunteer answers. It was an especially good trick to get the shy kids who had thought the most about the question, not the gold-star-addicted ones up front. But standing alone in front of a room of thirty eyes staring at you for four seconds took discipline. Four seconds of wait time was awkward. It never felt natural. But she always did it.

Margot took a long sip of her wine, then left Liz alone on the screen porch. She adjusted Brian's sheets, then went into the kitchen, opened a nicer bottle of cabernet, grabbed a second wineglass, and set it down in front of Liz. She poured a half glass of the wine and raised her own in the air as if she were going to make a toast. Maybe tonight had been momentous for Liz. Maybe you made a night momentous when you opened a better bottle of wine.

She remembered her own first time, months before she met Brian, with a boy a year older. They'd dated when he was still in high school, and she went to visit him at his college. They'd squeezed onto his bottom bunk, bass thumping at the party next door. It wasn't traumatic, or ceremonious, or at all romantic. It was ordinary, but it was memorable: the smell of Right Guard tinged with sweat, the low static on his radio in the background, the way he offered her a warm beer after and then cracked the window. She remembered the mess of flyers tacked to his bulletin board. When she left the room to buy a soda from the vending machine, she could feel the eyes of the guys from the party next door on her while she walked down the hall. It was lonely, the feeling she had done something important and was supposed to be casual about it.

"Is this for me?" Liz asked, raising her glass when Margot raised hers. "When did you decide to let me drink wine with you?"

No, she had never offered Liz a drink before and had in fact swiped a half glass of champagne out of her hand at a wedding and told her to go get a Shirley Temple if she wanted to be fancy. Well, tonight she was offering. It got her daughter's attention, at least. It broke the spell of Liz's recent experiments with aggressively ignoring her.

Margot had always resisted rushing in to make things safer and easier for her girls. She waited, willed herself not to break up a preschool fight they could figure out themselves, not to buy them a brand-new version of a ruined toy, not to email a teacher about a low grade. Brian had always reminded her about times she had screwed up or fought for herself, figured it out or failed; he'd always reminded her how much the girls needed to do the same, even if it was a mess or unfair.

She could make tonight a special ceremony with the wine, but the loneliness and discomfort of the next fifteen years, of moving into adulthood one awkward, lonely night at a time? Liz would be on her own for those.

"Tonight," Margot said. "I decided tonight."

Liz

Evy got home after Liz was asleep, but sneaked into her room to whisper, "I kissed her," which made Liz's heavy eyes open wide. "And did you guys—did you?" Evy asked, and Liz nodded. Evy flopped down next to her, and they stared at Liz's ceiling and traded whispered details of their nights, re-creating the time lines that led to the big moments, play-by-playing every little thing Olivia and Gabe had said and guessing at its subtext. They wondered what Margot knew, since she had let Liz have that half glass of wine with her. When Evy slipped back to her own room, Liz was wide awake for another hour.

Chapter Seventeen

Margot

Lorraine still called Brian Mr. Dunne, a final insistence on formality during even her most intimate tasks. She was so gentle and competent, so delicate in her simple instructions to herself and to Margot, so practiced in her routines.

"You might want to stay a little closer the next couple days," she said, which was a kind, coded way of saying: *get ready*.

Margot went in, wanting to be near him. She was not a poet or a time traveler. She had no metaphor or space-time escape hatch to another place to gather strength or faith. She did not confess, pray for, or promise anything. There was no highlight reel, no rage, no inside joke or last song. There was one last, ordinary gesture: her head on his chest.

Evy

Olivia texted Evy on her way to work the early morning shift at Sal's: **Hey! 1. I am up because . . . um I couldn't sleep?! 2. I like Campari now 3. I'm glad I didn't get Lyft-kidnapped so we could hang out . . .**

Evy texted: **also glad you did not get kidnapped, gonna quit Sal's and work for FBI as a hostage negotiator now I'm so good at that**

Olivia texted: **class out at 8 tonight—since you went out last night figured you were home w the fam tho?**

Evy wanted to spend the rest of August with Olivia, Olivia, Olivia, but in a magical-thinking version of summer where there were no casseroles because there were no women-who-meant-well-and-wanted-to-feed-you, because there was no tragic, imminent end of all the versions of a person who loved you and had left you already, over and over; in a summer with no collateral damage destroying her mom's sense and her heart, too.

Evy had peeked in to see her dad before she left for work. Her mom was in there with him, curled up asleep on the chair in his room, wearing her pajama pants and one of his old Buccaneer T-shirts.

Yeah, gotta stay in tonight, Evy texted.

> prob good for me to stay in to-
> night . . . long story, about a
> very confusing call from my dad
> and my mom's Lladró statues . . .
> will call you later? xx

Evy stared at the **xx**, wanting to send a longer message, but she was already late. So she texted, **I want to hear the long story** and all the cat emojis. Then: **xx**.

When you worked the early shift at Sal's, there was a whole hour before the doors were opened, when Irene made coffee, when the work was uninterrupted routine: stocking and fudge-dipping and counting out the cash and cranking open all the yellow-and-white awnings while the joggers ran by. Irene played Emmylou Harris for that hour and blasted the AC.

Evy always liked the busy ease that occupied her mind these mornings, stacking boxes of taffy into a tidy pyramid, Windexing the huge front windows, no matter what worries lingered.

When there were little pockets of time during that shift, there was nothing to look at except the broken-up brightness of candy around her, no one to talk to except Irene, who was such a gossip, but all the gossip was about people Evy had never met. Irene's cousin Kenny still owed her money and sounded like a liar.

Hailey arrived for her own shift during the last hour of Evy's. Irene was in the middle of a story about a bartender at Jimbo's who wouldn't make her another margarita, and Hailey rolled her eyes and huffed away like she couldn't stand another second of Irene's story.

When Irene went on an errand, Hailey took her phone out of the bin and scrolled through, instead of wrapping up the taffy. "Um, Olivia needs to not wear dresses like these, she looks like a grandma," she said, showing Evy one of Olivia's social media posts.

In the picture, Olivia was wearing a blue dress with the empty boardwalk behind her. Evy thought Olivia seemed happy and the dress had cute ruffle sleeves. She thought that the spill of little freckles on Olivia's forearm matched the ones on her cheeks you could see when she wasn't wearing any makeup.

Hailey had never liked that Olivia also hung out with her friends from the vintage store, or with her older sister at Rutgers. Maybe that was why she was being mean about Olivia behind her back. Or maybe Hailey had noticed that Evy and Olivia had ditched Cameron's party, and had expected them to livestream their kiss to her so she could know everything immediately instead of them telling her about it when they felt like it.

Hailey wasn't always *such* a ten out of ten version of herself like this. She could be different when she wanted to be. When she talked about her little brother, who was a chess prodigy, she geeked out about his next tournament. When she showed up to decorate for school dances, she talked to the DJs and balloon-bouquet guys like a pro, sounding more like a CEO than a teenage girl, because she really wanted it to be nice for everyone.

Usually, Hailey turning up the Hailey was Evy's cue to ask what was wrong, which would make her sigh and explain who had wronged her. But Evy didn't feel like playing that part today.

Hailey set her phone on the counter, put some fudge in a box for a customer, and rang her up without making eye contact. "I'm going to a barre class tonight after work," Hailey said to Evy, "and you're coming, I have a guest pass, but it's only for one person, so don't tell Olivia."

On the oldies sound track they played at Sal's, the long *whyyyyyyy* part of "Build Me Up Buttercup" echoed.

"I can't tonight," Evy said. She grabbed Hailey's phone, entered the passcode—Hailey's birthday—and opened the app to the picture of Olivia's dress. She tapped the screen a few more times. "Here, you unfollowed her."

Irene appeared again and confiscated Hailey's phone, then Evy gathered her stuff before it was time for her to sign out from her shift. Hailey said *rude* under her breath.

Evy stepped from one black-and-white tile in Sal's to the next until she was all the way to the other side of the store; the bell dinged when she pushed the heavy door open to the humid afternoon.

Liz

Gabe's **good morning** and **hey** texts made Liz's heart kick-drum when they buzzed on her phone, waking her up. She started a text to Sonia to catch her up on her night with Gabe but didn't send it; she was sick of talking to her one line at a time and sending her tiny pictures and GIFs and wished her friend were here again in person.

When she emerged from her room, the house was quiet. No one had brewed coffee. Evy was gone, and Lorraine hadn't arrived yet. Sometime last night, Margot had baked cinnamon rolls, which they only usually made on Christmas morning; they sat cold on the counter, but the house still smelled doughy and sweet. Her mom had cleared away all the clutter: the mail and phone chargers, the spare keys and bowl of change. The counter gleamed, smooth and empty. Margot's bedroom door was wide open, and the bed was still made.

All these unsubtle signals could be saying *get ready*, or could be saying *wait, it will be a little longer*. Liz had never called out of work once, or even left early, but standing alone in the quiet, clean kitchen, the end of her shift in eight hours felt so far away; she pulled up Carl's number on her phone, but talked herself out of calling out, convincing herself that *today's* lonely internal echo was not some new frequency.

Liz wanted to work, as she'd done every day this summer. And she wanted to see Gabe, even though she knew all the questions she still had were her own to answer, not his: Did last night give her a new story to tell about this summer, besides the sad one? Did it distract her and give her something that was just hers, did it give her the little thrill she was so gung-ho to get? Did it convince her she was an adult, did it work as a trade-in for the times she was ignored? Was she happy to have crossed that threshold and checked that box and joined that club?

She calculated how much time she had—not enough to make coffee or stop to buy one. After one bite of cinnamon bun, she lost her appetite and tossed the rest in the trash. Out loud to no one, she said, "Okay, you can go. But then you can come home! It's okay. You can just . . . come home." She texted Gabe: **Hey again, this is so last-minute but can you take over at Sumner for me at noon today? I have a thing.**

Gabe texted: **Cool sounds fun? (sure mysterious boss, I got you)**

At Sumner Ave, it was sunny, clear, and seventy-nine degrees, according to the Pepsi-sponsored time and temperature sign, and the ocean sparkled. A light layer of fog shrouded the pier. The boardwalk smelled like it always did before 9 a.m., a mix of humid salt air and the rotting uncollected trash. Liz texted Margot to tell her what time she'd be back, but got no response.

She wore her invisible new had-sex status like an expensive garment. No one would tell her today about the other kinds of sex that would not be the first-time kind: the transcendent, maintenance, or reconnection kinds. No one would tell her about the late-Saturday-morning kind, the angry kind, the last-time-together kind. No one would tell her about the reinventions and the relief, the absences, the experiments. No one would tell her today that one day she would become an expert at reading cues and responding to a touch, at steeling herself and playing a part, at asking for what made her light up, at refusing what made her recoil.

Carl dropped off her bank, thinking out loud about umbrella repairs as the first customers showed up. He explained to them why wooden stakes were better than metal and why he always bought the same yellow umbrellas with zinc-coated joints, rivets, and steel ribs. Sometimes they held up for five seasons!

Carl gave subtle cues when you'd done something right: an approving grunt, or the very rare, end-of-the-day, "Thanks, kid. Nice job today." Liz wanted to do well because when Carl noticed, a flood of confidence surged through her.

"Hey, you feeling okay today, kid?" he asked, and she realized she had been staring at the Ferris wheel's hazy outline for a few seconds too long. She was thinking about Gabe and her too-quiet house, and she still needed coffee.

"I'm good!" she said, lunging forward for an umbrella, emerging from her daze. She forgot to even mention that Gabe was taking over for her at noon.

After Carl was gone, a man in a leather jacket and work boots wandered down the ramp, sat himself down in one of the display chairs, and pulled off his boots. He buried his yellow-toenailed feet in the sand. He was far from the first strange visitor who had made himself at home here.

"Uh, sir?" Liz said. "Chairs are five dollars. To *rent*." She stood ten feet away, hoping he would get up. He had greasy hair and a bare chest under his jacket. He reclined like he was going to go to sleep. "Sir?"

He closed his eyes and sank down lower. He smelled like dirt and death, and he blinked open his bloodshot eyes, smiling at her without showing his teeth. She waited and hoped he would get up and leave, though he only seemed to settle in more.

"Sir?" Liz said again.

"You new?" he asked, squinting. She told him he was not supposed to sit there and that the chairs were for *display only*. "The other girl who worked here let me stay. She was prettier than you." He laced his fingers together.

She could call a bike cop or radio for Carl, but calling someone made this a *thing*. "Well, you've got to leave," she said, trying to sound more forceful.

"I ain't leavin'."

Then he was up and lurching toward her, and she froze even though she wanted to back away, and then he was squeezing her forearm and slurring, "I ain't leavin'," again, and she tried not to retch at the smell of him. And then she knew in a half-second that he could hurt her, that he was slow and drunk but his rough hands pressed into her skin, and there were people around but he didn't care.

"Hey!" Gabe yelled down at them from the ramp. Did she yank

her arm away, finally unfreeze herself from the sand? Or was the man the one to loosen his grip, distracted by Gabe jogging toward them? Liz clenched and unclenched her fists. This was a part of the job it was impossible for her to be good at because she was a seventeen-year-old girl.

"Larry, buddy," Gabe said, and Larry backed away and dropped back into the chair. Gabe furrowed his brow, acting like the good cop. "You have a rough night last night or what?"

"Eh." Larry sat up and squinted. "Went over to EJ's."

"You got somewhere to go get some sleep, man?" Gabe was friendly and stern at the same time, and Liz wondered why her voice couldn't sound like that. She wasn't interested in being sweet to Larry or hearing his dumb bender-at-EJ's story, she just wanted him to leave.

Gabe was wearing his Hawaiian-print swimsuit with his yellow shirt—not the regulation khakis—and he acted like he was taking Larry seriously while he stole knowing glances in Liz's direction.

"Stayin' over on Blaine," Larry said, nodding in the direction of the street. "Where's Amber?"

"Amber doesn't work here anymore." Gabe was so chill, and this dude had drunk-lunged at her. Liz rolled her eyes and thought about the pathetic girls at school who pretended their cars wouldn't start or that they were scared of loud noises and the guys who came to their rescue.

"Listen, you gotta go, all right? You can't be hanging around here right now. You remember our deal, right?"

"Huh?" Larry squirmed a little.

"You gotta get out of here for a while, man," Gabe said. He stood in front of Larry with his arms folded. *For a while?* She wanted to chime in and say she would stab him with an umbrella stake if he ever touched her again.

"I was just resting," Larry said. Then he grunted, levering himself to his feet, holding his boots and socks in his hand, muttering under his breath. He staggered up the ramp back to the boardwalk and disappeared into the men's restrooms.

Liz hated how easy it had been for Gabe to get rid of Larry. She hated even more that Gabe had had to save her, and that Larry had stolen the fun and distraction of thinking about last night.

"Was this your first meeting with Larry?" Gabe asked.

"Yeah," she said. *Larry virgin,* she thought. "I don't know who he thinks he is, or what Amber was doing if she actually let him sit here, there's no way Carl would have been cool with that and he definitely would have fired her if it was a regular thing like he said it was." She folded her arms across her chest, then unfolded them.

"Liz, you're overthinking Larry a little bit," Gabe said, laughing. "I mean, the guy uses a car air freshener for cologne and drinks a forty for breakfast." There was something about Larry that made her furious and also sad and afraid; laughing about him felt wrong.

Larry was probably this way because of an unfair, hard life, and Larry probably picked on girls like Liz because he thought they didn't know anything about that. Larry would probably live forever, poisoning himself with EJ's beer and whatever else he could find, a loser who had won only one thing, a body and brain that no chemical or internal cells sabotaging each other would destroy.

The fog all burned away, the rotten smell lifting when the trash cans were emptied, and Liz's nervousness receded when Gabe stole a quick kiss. Her gulp of water tasted plastic and cold like it always did, and the Pepsi clock counted down the hours until noon.

Chapter Eighteen

Evy and Liz

It's the father-daughter dance, and when the last song ends, the patterns of light on the gym floor evaporate when the sudden, bright overhead ones flick on. Evy and Liz are little girls, and the bows on their party dresses are undone. Their hair is matted against their sweaty necks, hearts still beating catching up to the last song, where they spun holding on to their dad's fingers.

All the dads help stack up the tables and chairs, push the cafeteria tables back up against the cinder-block walls—the heavy lifting of cleaning up. The moms on the dance committee will be in tomorrow to sweep the crumbs and fold the decorations into the plastic bins for next year, to ball the streamers into a hard wad and throw them away.

Lily and Julia are jumping up to grab the helium balloons, gathering them into big weightless bouquets, begging to take them home. Julia is unbuckling her fancy shoes with the low heels and dangling them, stuffing the last cookies in her mouth. The voices echo louder now that the lights are on. The girls all grin, red-faced and big-toothed, frizzy French-braided and feeling still-glamorous in their dresses, and their dads shrug; there's no rule against taking the balloons.

Evy and Liz hadn't been paying attention to the time at all, and they keep singing along with Lily and Julia and Sonia and Hailey like they could keep the party going even though the DJ's already got his speakers stacked up on a little cart. Evy sticks her face into the water fountain and takes long, deep gulps of the freezing metallic water, so much thirstier than she had known. Liz peeks down the hallway to spy on the unreal, empty school at night! She wants to open the door into her classroom and see the uncluttered desks and blank blackboards, to show Dad the water cycle poster and the animal facts reports her teachers tacked up on the wall of fame. But he's calling his girls, he's standing in front of the trophy case near the door with the other dads. He grabbed one balloon for each of them (yellow and pink, the colors of the bedroom walls he painted for them), and the wind from outside blows them all around.

It's time to go home.

Brian dies quietly, alone in his bed, on a summer night when the girls are sixteen and seventeen, while they are with their mom in the kitchen eating takeout fried shrimp.

When Evy crawls into Liz's bed later that night, they flip open the laptop to read the rest of their parents' old emails, merging their fresh shock into a temporary, shared distraction.

4/16/98

Subject: sorry?

To: margotmeyer@stanthonys.edu

From: brian-dunne@rutgers.edu

I was at a secondhand store with Claire and found ten of those ugly green uniform shirts from the Cranky Crab (pristine—no grease!) and took it as a sign to at least ask if you were still homesick. And can I say I'm sorry in an email? (Obviously, if not, ok.) How's Serious Guy?

Did you start student teaching this semester? I did and it's not what I thought it would be. Teaching is only part of the job. Do they call you Miss Meyer?

Do you remember the time we cleaned out the walk-in freezer at the restaurant, playing Never Have I Ever? That job was disgusting, and that was one of the best days. I was expecting to do that all alone and when I showed up to work you were there.

4/18/98

Subject: re: sorry?

To: brian-dunne@rutgers.edu

From: margotmeyer@stanthonys.edu

Hey, again. . . .

Yes, you can ask. But it's different after so long.

I AM student teaching! Serious Guy (he DOES have a name . . .) only has one class this semester, and I'm getting my butt kicked by nine-year-olds!

I love the confidence kids have at that age, right before they care about being cool. Glad to have someone tell me they're in the weeds with all this too. I can imagine you forgetting to answer when someone calls you Mr. Dunne.

4/21/98
Subject: re: sorry?
To: margotmeyer@stanthonys.edu
From: brian-dunne@rutgers.edu

Is that when you start caring about being cool? Fourth grade? God. Claire tried to make me give away half of my CDs and only keep the ones she thought were cool, whatever that means. I thought I could convince her to be less cool, but she'll be cool forever, in a never-listening-to-Billy-Joel way.

Last Sunday, I graded a stack of tests, then had a beer and thought about next year. But I never want to tell you too much, or even say something so obvious (like I do still miss you). How do I tell you about all that, without saying too much?

I better stop there.

4/22/98
Subject: re: sorry?
To: brian-dunne@rutgers.edu
From: margotmeyer@stanthonys.edu

It's a good question: how to really tell someone what's keeping you up at night without asking too much of them.

I think you keep it short, you tell the truth, and you don't try to change anyone's mind. I guess that's how you start. So . . . after graduation I'm moving to Chicago. With Serious Guy. It's a hard decision, whether to make your plans fit someone else's.

I do think about the beach all the time, but what if I go back there too soon?

Have you ever thought about living in a city, or across an ocean, or looking out at some mountains or rivers before you build your house on the beach?

I want to know your plans for next year, of course I want to hear everything.

4/23/98
Subject: re: sorry?
To: margotmeyer@stanthonys.edu
From: brian-dunne@rutgers.edu

Ok: you sound, not excited, but READY for Chicago.

I do want to go see the sunrise from a mountaintop in Colorado and drink coffee at some café on the Seine. But I know where I want to come home to. That's not better or worse than being far away for another year or forever, like you're doing. (That was hard to say). You need to know how Chicago turns out.

I can't say I feel as sure about making my plans and Claire's fit each other's as well as you and your boyfriend are. I'm not sure what she's going to decide for next year. I'm sorry if that's saying too much. But who else would I tell?

I've never even told Claire about the house on the beach. Well, I'm telling you: I'm gonna do it next year. Not a thing I talk about forever, but a real thing. I'm gonna live in my parents' basement and tell my dad to go fuck himself if he comes down there drunk and tells me I'm a loser, but I'm gonna save enough money and do it.

If I work every weekend shift they'll give me at the Buccaneer, then I can do it sooner than you think.

You might love Chicago. Would you make your plans fit someone else's if he wasn't the kind of guy who would do that for you too? Would you admit if you were only moving far away for him, and not for yourself?

5/10/98
Subject: re: sorry?
To: brian-dunne@rutgers.edu
From: margotmeyer@stanthonys.edu

I know we promised we'd say if it was too much, right, if these emails started saying too much?

I'm the one who has to ask for a break now.

I'll be honest: I can't answer your questions yet. I'm glad you asked them, and I can promise I'll be honest in answering them for myself because you did.

I can't handle knowing so much about you, at least for now.

You will build that house, and it will be beautiful. Claire will come, or she'll leave. You have to tell her about it first, tell her the whole plan, see if she's too cool for it. I think it's perfect.

If I ever go back to the Buccaneer, I'll ask around to see who bought the most falling-apart place in town and made it beautiful.

PS–this email address changes in a week when I graduate, so if you write it will bounce back.

Evy and Liz closed the laptop and let their eyes adjust to the dark. The emails had built a little buffer between the earlier evening and the fatigue that finally found them. Their cold fried shrimp had tasted bland and rubbery, the high-pressure shower had hardly felt like a tickle, the sounds of the neighbors' voices were silenced with a closed window and the hum of the air conditioner, their stunned senses were all dulled in the pressure chamber of his fresh absence.

"She broke his heart there for a little while," Liz said. "What if she had never shown up again?" Soon they would hand these over to Margot, but tonight they guessed at the still-missing details, rereading all the sly ways their parents told each other they were still in love all that time.

"He didn't want her back until she was sure, though," Evy said. She guessed the Serious Chicago Guy was a banker with money to burn, but Liz insisted he must be cooler than that—someone who made art and drank at underground bars. Either version would have been a counterpoint to Brian's smaller barrier-island dreams. Was Margot lonely the whole time in Chicago, or were there some afternoons looking at Renoirs at the Art Institute up close and nights out seeing shows and doing tequila shots with her friends, where she forgot all about Brian?

They would fill in the missing parts of their parents' story forever, arguing over who had wanted whom more, over whether the way their parents reached out to each other was ever possible for anyone again now that the computers their parents had had to find and sit down in front of were in everyone's pockets at every moment, now that messages were constant, expected, a new art and language that hadn't existed when Brian and Margot were young.

Margot

Between her cabernets that night, she had one of Brian's Coors Lights. It went down like water and tasted like the end of summer, which it was now, again. How many thousands of these beers had Brian poured for other people, to pay for this house?

When she drove back from Chicago, she had gone straight to Seaside. She spent an hour on the beach alone and then went into the Buccaneer. She wore her yellow dress over her swimsuit, and she fed the jukebox a stack of quarters. The humidity had faded, and the almost-September sky went brighter blue. Her hair was loose and damp.

She picked "Rosalita" so everyone would *hey hey hey* along at the end like they always did here when that song played, and when Brian saw her he abandoned his place behind the bar and walked toward her; the crowd parted or he pushed through them. He swallowed half his beer and handed her one.

Could he see, up close, where the freckles had come out across her shoulders? Those expensive earrings someone else had bought her? She stared at his thin, ripped Buccaneer T-shirt and said, "I was hoping you'd be here."

No one wanted summer to end, but it was almost Labor Day.

"God, it is so good to be home," she said, even though she didn't live here yet. She sat at the bar while he finished his shift.

When they got to the bungalow, it was the stop-everything time of evening when the sun hazed gray and pink over the bay, and the cattails rustled. He said that when he bought the house, it stunk of cigarettes and cat shit inside and had knee-high weeds outside. Brown water-stained wallpaper peeled in the hallways, and small dirty windows barely let in any light, obscuring the whole view of the bay and the bridge. That was the only kind of house a teacher could buy here, a mess no one else wanted to touch. He'd painted the shingles navy and the front door red, mulched under the bayberry and beach plum trees, and added seagrass and stones.

Big-bulbed white lights hung across the pergola. Inside, he showed her where he'd knocked down the interior walls to let light flow through. She ran her fingers along the edge of the lacquered kitchen table.

Some Sundays in Chicago, she had been so lonely, even when she was with other people. He said some Mondays he was so tired after working all weekend, on the house and at the bar, that he missed his exit for school and pulled into a rest stop to crunch peppermint Life Savers to wake up. He showed her where he'd fixed a huge leak and re-wired the lights. It had taken all of two winters and it still wasn't done.

"So, you're heading back to Chicago soon, then?" She knew he wouldn't take her into the other rooms in the house without knowing.

"No," she said. "Not heading back anytime soon." She didn't want to ruin the moment or say too much. All she owned fit in a suitcase, and she had never built more than a three-shelf bookcase with an Allen wrench. Margot admired the small details he had paid such attention to in this house. She would ask him later what he would have done if she had never shown up at the Buccaneer, but he would only shrug and say, "You're here."

The neighbors' voices carried through the window as they always would, laughing like they still had a lot of summer left. "You want to see the rest of the house?" he asked.

He said the bedroom wasn't done yet, but she was already pushing open the door. The dim room was almost bare: a queen bed on a frame with a blue sheet, a coat of white paint, a brass garage-sale lamp on the floor. He kissed her, hesitant, then familiar and warm, and then he reached for that swimsuit under her dress, and she kissed his neck that still tasted of salt from surfing at sunrise. She said the house was beautiful. She thought of the postcards she'd sent him from Spain that said *wish you were here*.

Part III

Chapter Nineteen

Liz

When your throat closes and goes hoarse and dry, when your voice cracks into an older-sounding, lower octave, settle into it. Excuse yourself and fill up one of the little paper cups near the water cooler over and over until the wax wears off the edges and the paper dissolves on your tongue like the bland host the priest shoves toward your mouth and you swallow.

Stand under the stained-glass window of St. Agnes in her rainbow glow, listening to the thunk of the kneelers and the rise and fall of prayers unpunctuated, uninterrupted by his loud *AMENS*.

Uncle Pete gives the eulogy and it's a relief that it's all about baseball, but then he looks at you and Evy when he says "his girls," but he can't quite finish that part, he has to go back to the baseball.

Evy

Inhale incense, your grandmother's mothball-scented dress and her perfume, the dentist-office smell of the funeral home. Exhale the mint-tinged carbon dioxide your body is still making because you're still here.

Stand so close to your mom and Liz that your fingers brush

against their dresses, but face forward, turning toward all the kinds of embraces people give: bony hugs and pillowy fat-tummied hugs, stiff hands placed on shoulders, uncertain quick pats, and delicate, waist-encircling squeezes. Your eyes tire, your underarms dampen, and your breath sours as the hours go on and on, as most of the familiar and strange faces blur into each other, saying the same phrases. Except Jimmy, who says, "Hey, take it easy," instead of "I'm so sorry." Everyone else is in a suit, and he's got on his flowered shirt. When he moves to Hawaii in the fall, he'll post pictures of humongous waves, captioned with quotes from old surfing movies and your dad's initials.

Your friends encircle you in synchronized chatter, steer you away from everyone and into a corner they commandeer. On your phone, find the picture of you as a kid, on your dad's shoulders, on the beach, the one where he's wearing that old Pearl Jam concert tour T-shirt. Post it and caption it with his birthday and the date he died.

When Olivia stands close, hug her.

Liz

Stand until your flats give you blisters along the edge of your little toe. Dead skin hangs off, limp and graying, chafing against itself until you rip it off and press a sweaty Band-Aid against it: the quick exposure to air and then the comfort of the pad pressed against the skin.

You can do this and other people can't.

Evy

Your dress doesn't look like everyone else's. Olivia helped you pick it out: a floral flowy pattern and gold sandals, because the dresses your mom bought for you made you feel like a nun or a judge and this dress makes you feel like you're floating. It has navy *in it*, and some of your aunts always have to make some little comment about what you and Liz are wearing anyway so why not make it about this dress.

Liz

Wear a black sheath dress, cut to flatter your hips and collarbone, a deep almost-black navy. It wasn't on sale, and the girl who helped you left you alone, then brought another size without asking, held it high in the air as she walked it from the fitting room to the register and then folded it lovingly between two pieces of tissue paper. She walked the whole bag around to hand it to you instead of shoving it across the counter like they do in other stores.

Your dress gets a little outline of white in the underarms from your deodorant, but the fabric absorbs it. The people who made this dress knew women would sweat in it. This dress is here to shield you and keep you cool on the inside, this dress is here to hit you above the knee in the right place, this dress has pockets for more mints and a folded-up twenty-dollar bill your grandpa gives you and the soft, fresh Kleenex you keep to give your mom.

Evy

Hailey, Cameron, and Olivia stay. *Hey, I know: sloth videos,* Hailey says, and then you're all huddled around her phone awwwwing at them.

You steer clear of Aunt Eileen, you can't with her today.

Aunt Melissa stands next to your mom for an hour. She's moving people along and shutting it down when some relative gets going too long or confuses generations. She takes your mom outside, where all the Casserole Bitches are sitting in a circle in the Adirondack chairs, and your mom stays out there almost an hour with them. From their faces you can tell they're saying nice things to her before leaning in close to share the good gossip she's missed in the last few months.

Liz

Everyone raises their drinks when Robbie gives an Irish toast: "May your joys be as deep as the oceans, your troubles as light as its foam. And may you find sweet peace of mind, wherever you may roam." Everyone else will think it's all about the ocean, or maybe heaven, but you know it's also a nod to those exhausting hours at the Buccaneer when your dad wouldn't shut up about the foam on the beers.

Eat some small dry sandwiches, the crunchy edges of a baked ziti, tiny nibbles of fruit. Drink LaCroix, Diet Coke, scalded coffee, cold water, two swigs of whiskey from a cousin's flask, then eat again: banana bread, room-temperature fried chicken, a sheet cake with no message written on it.

Your dad's Subaru won't start when you turn the key. You have to move it out of the driveway to make room for Uncle Pete's car. Your dad taught you how to use the jumper cables, so you do, without asking anyone's permission. That engine turns over like a champ, humming over the whoosh of the air conditioner, the too-loud NPR station echoing inside the car. You back it out and reposition it, and then you think about scrubbing the small streak of grease off your hand and leave it there instead.

Evy

Olivia touches up your makeup, using concealer to offset the dark circles under your eyes. It's a good excuse to close the door to everyone for a few minutes and sit on the edge of the bed together.

Later Hailey shows you sympathy texts from everyone at Sal's. Hailey can be like this too, really trying. You can tell she feels awkward because she's biting her nails. "You guys don't have to stay," you say, but she, Cameron, and Olivia do.

You can't get to Liz without talking to a hundred other people, so you text **u ok? come hang out over here so you don't have to listen to Aunt Eileen for another hour!**

You and Liz slept in the same bed last night. The two of you will leave your dresses on the floor of her bedroom and jump into the ocean later, sit around on the screen porch in your wet swimsuits, fall asleep in the same bed together again without showering. Liz mouths, *I'm good*, across the room before Hailey shoves a phone screen in your face and hugs you again.

Liz

Sonia is home from Florida early for the funeral. She's listening to Uncle Pete over at the kitchen island, literally stuck, because someone opened the refrigerator door and she can't move around it. You and Sonia will sneak into your room to play Cloud Campaign II later while everyone is still here, picking up where you left off, pausing for you to tell her about your night with Gabe, but you won't see her a lot the rest of the summer. She'll pick up all the shifts no one else wants at the Tilt-A-Whirl to make up for all that time at her grandma's, and hook up with one of the guys who runs the bumper boats for a couple weeks. But the two of you will finally beat Cloud Campaign II by October; it will take a whole weekend.

After your mom comes inside, she sits on a barstool. She's gesturing with one hand and cradling a glass of red wine with the other. She takes off her blazer and lets her hair down from the taut low bun, and she looks very tired but comfortable, flanked by Aunt Melissa like a sentry.

Two hours into this thing, you want everyone to leave, but Carl and his wife, Diane, are standing next to you, presenting a plate of salami, cheese, and olives wrapped in plastic, and Diane is losing her shit. Diane is melting down and crying so much she shreds up her tissue, and Carl introduces her as he presents the salami ("This is Diane. We brought an antipasto. For the family. Condolences. Very sad.").

You've never met Diane before, and you don't know exactly how Carl knew that your dad died. (He said something between the salami presentation and the Diane explanation, but Carl mumbles a little.)

But really what is up with Diane, what do you say to Diane, why is Carl not comforting Diane or whisking Diane away, why is Diane your thing now?

When you try to figure out whether Carl has told Gabe your dad is dead, it comes out, "Do you want some dip?"

Gabe has been texting you, and you've been telling him you're sick. He keeps sending get-well-soon GIFs. Diane is calming down, focusing on removing the plastic wrap from a second salami and rearranging the cheese, stealing crackers from a plate she didn't bring, doing a few signs of the cross that end with kissing her thumb, which is not how your family does it, and squeezing your aunt's hand from across the food table and saying, "Condolences. Very sad."

Diane moves through this room of strangers with such brazen

emotion; her gestures, her hair-sprayed updo, her gray-and-black-geometric-patterned blouse, her purse, everything about her is bigger than your family's versions. Your relatives are sitting on the edges of the kitchen chairs, making neat stacks with the paper plates, talking in hushed voices, darting away one at a time to snatch empty cups from every surface whether people are done with them or not; but there's Diane, heaping a plate with food and crying again when she comes back to stand near you and Carl.

"Your dad, he was a good guy, didn't know him well but knew him," Carl says. "You got a job waiting for you next year if you want to take the rest of the summer off."

"Oh, I definitely want to come back this week," you say. You were supposed to consider it for a minute. It's still a little while until Labor Day, and the idea of whole days with nowhere to be makes you uneasy. "Can I come back?"

Carl will probably tell Gabe your dad is dead, and Gabe will be very confused, or very mad that you didn't tell him your dad was about to die. Who knows with Carl, though.

"More dip?" you ask Carl again.

Finish the scripted, public performance before the long, private improvisation with the slamming of the screen door when the last person leaves.

Evy

Olivia hands you an ice water garnished with a cucumber. She steers you away from your other texting, nail-biting, sloth-watching friends. She's spent half an hour in polite conversation with your grandma, who gave her a Panera gift card with six dollars on it and said, "Evy likes the soup there." Olivia's motions are deliberate. When she doesn't know what to do, she doesn't guess, she asks.

She sits down next to you, angles her back toward the rest of the room. Your other friends all signed a card with a picture of a bridge on the front, but Olivia slips you her own card, on thick cream-colored cardstock with a blue and gray watercolor design on the front and no cheesy prewritten message. The whole inside will be filled with her handwriting, the same tight cursive she covers journal pages with at the end of class if there's extra time, and when you read it later, you'll call her and talk until late.

CHAPTER TWENTY

Margot

Go straight to bed, Margot's college friend Tracy texted her from San Francisco. Tracy's mom had scheduled hip surgery this week, and Tracy had to be there to help her. She couldn't get away for the funeral, but she'd already sent Margot a ticket to SFO for October. **I'm ok, in bed with a book**, Margot texted back, a lie. But the zipper on her dress was stuck, so instead of dimming the lights and slipping into her pajamas she left the bright overhead light on and lay on top of the bed in her dress and scrolled and scrolled through the years-old posts on Brian's Facebook page: the worst way to spend the last hours of this long good-bye.

She blurred past the last year and slipped into a sickening daze when she should have been forty-five minutes into an Ambien-induced sleep. This was not Nora's magic, subversive journey through time in *The Girl with the Long Shadow*, to gain insight and wisdom, but a self-inflicted sabotage of any hope she would end this day in anything but a state of wide-awake despair.

She clicked on a new tab and wrote a post for the GBM Wives:

I've been on Facebook, which was designed by soulless coders who only understand the compulsive properties of human na-

ture. I'm just floating along through this algorithm I've leaned into, ladies.

Look, here he is in a group shot with a beer in his hand, I'm leaning into that, and here we finished a 5K together, that one got a lot of likes, which are good, you want as many of those as you can get. Then you can also lean into looking at other people's pictures, like the ones from last week, four perfectly nice people at Disney World, two old college friends doing CrossFit, well they're unfriended now, whoops that was Brian's account I was signed into, will they think he is a ghost now, a ghost who wastes time unfriending people on Facebook?

She was numbed out by the volume of words and years that streamed by in minutes, clicking through too fast to feel anything. She fell asleep this way, eventually, with the light on and her dress on and the laptop open.

She thought her GBM Wives post was funny and wry when she wrote it, but when she read it the next morning, she recognized an acerbic anger in it that she knew would settle in permanently if she didn't resist it. When she read it with coffee instead of cabernet, she saw a sarcastic disengagement that she defaulted to, because to be honest, it sometimes worked.

Unfriending and ranting and scrolling for hours served her in the moment, to distract and deliver cheap nostalgia, to sidestep what she really needed to do next; and while she knew it would be easy to do this every day, she also knew that it would never give her or the girls what they really needed.

It took her three hours and four deleted drafts to type her next post, and every attempt felt awkward and incomplete. She couldn't articulate a single thought without worrying more that she wasn't getting them all down at once.

She remembered the first day after the hurricane that she saw all their destroyed houses, and how she'd packed up one box of books, a tote bag of the girls' clothes, and one photo album from a shelf in their own bungalow. She'd stepped over their splintered screen door to slide the stuff into their car. Brian had grabbed a drill and a checkbook. They'd looked at their ridiculous, random pile of possessions in the backseat as they drove back over the bridge. When it was too much, you had to choose one thing, anything, to start with.

Margot wrote:

> *Brian's parts of our stories contradicted mine or made them real. I already don't trust myself to tell them all.*
>
> *I always start the story of our first daughter's birth by saying how it lasted twelve hours, but Brian would say, "Kid had her umbilical cord wrapped around her like a parachute harness when she came out! Margot was a champ, she was so loopy on the drugs afterward she asked everyone their favorite cocktails while they stitched her up."*
>
> *I always say, "Yeah, Evy came pretty quick, though," and that was Brian's cue to say, "Margot had a five-minute super-contraction on the couch that pushed the baby almost all the way out. I saw the kid's head and we had one wild drive to the hospital before Evy decided to deliver herself about a minute after we got off the elevator!"*
>
> *It's like we traded off riding shotgun, pointing out the land-marks the other person missed, detouring, taking a better route.*

What happened now, to the broken cadence of their how-we-met trivia, to the wry asides to their how-we-met-again monologue? Was she supposed to interrupt *herself* now and play both parts, or avoid introducing anyone new to the back catalogue of family stories?

He had been the one who called the town to get them to leave the tennis court lights on, so she could stay out there another hour. But she was staying out late whacking a tennis ball to no one two years after the hurricane because he had hurt her. She could try to write her next post about that.

Margot scooped up the dress she'd worn to the funeral off the chair. She'd finally figured out a way to peel it off without unzipping it, yanking it straight up over her head and pulling in one elbow at a time. Crumpled under her Spanx and wedged into the seam of the chair cushion, she found one of Brian's old Post-its, with the word *ember* scribbled on it.

Ember was the last glow in the dark after the riot of flames. Ember didn't demand you do anything else but sit with it and watch until it was gone. Ember still emitted warmth for an hour.

Ember said, *Don't leave me alone*. In the embers you stay and huddle closer together as the heat sinks into the ground. When ember went away it wasn't all at once, but gradual, until it was safe to sleep or to leave.

CHAPTER TWENTY-ONE

Liz

"Carl made everyone sign this card Diane made? Or maybe it's more of a book?" It was midmorning on Sumner Avenue, two days after her dad's funeral. Gabe handed Liz a huge handmade card held together by ribbons and silver twine, with hot-glued bead-encrusted clouds, a brown felt cross, and a pocket with a prayer card and a laminated Psalm 23 inside on the front. He shrugged, helpless at its ridiculousness, but required to deliver it.

While the other employees signed the card (*So sorry* –CJ and *Really sorry* –Nicole), Gabe said, Carl had brought him into his office, shoved him into a chair, and said, "She still your girlfriend? What kind of piece of shit doesn't at least show up to—"

"I'm sorry," Liz said, interrupting him. She pressed her face against his shirt, and she forced two big sobs back into her body before she pulled away and wiped her face with a beach towel. "I just wanted a different kind of summer."

"Hey," he said. He pulled her back toward him. "I know." She thought, *Hey, don't say you know. Hey, have you ever had to really take care of someone? Hey, what have you already lost?*

She wouldn't understand for a long time the unsubtle signals people would give to show you what they had already lost: the girls who would excuse themselves at weddings during the toasts, the mothers who would post colored ribbons on social media around the same time each year, the brothers who would organize huge 5K teams for a particular cause or a cure with the fervor and coordination of army generals.

She rearranged the display umbrellas, then took a deep breath before she tried to go ahead with her plan: offer a quick apology, and then break up with him. Be the one to do it so he wouldn't have to be the jerk who dumps the girl with the surprise dead dad. Recite her practiced lines. "Uh, anyway, I had a really really great time with you this summer but it's probably, you know, for the best if we don't . . . see each other? Anymore."

She wanted to escape to the backlit boardwalk with him for a little longer, to have a few more nights in their alternate reality. But she also wanted to choose what he knew about her and who she was when she was with him, and that was impossible now. She definitely did not want to endure some awkward slow fade from him. So she told what she thought was one last lie and waited for him to say, *Hey, no, but okay, if that's what you really want then sure.*

Before this summer, lies did not come easy to Liz. She always blurted out hurried confessions: *I wrote that field trip permission slip myself and signed my mom's name.* It had always felt better to face the small punishment than to feel the hollowing out of her stomach whenever she lied.

But she felt no shame for this preemptive breakup, or for the weeks of keeping her dying dad from him. What kind of bullshit rule required you to reveal the worst thing that had recently happened to you? What kind of guy wouldn't be grateful for the chance to skip spending the end of summer watching a girl ugly-crying on the sky ride?

Adults got to go to dive bars and cheat on each other in booze-fueled one-night stands, and what did teenage girls get, anyway? What were they required to give? He wasn't entitled to her whole it's-rough-all-over-Ponyboy story if it felt so much better for her not to give it to him. If they kept hanging out, then she had to.

"Wait, was that just you trying to dump me?" Gabe asked. "Were you gonna give a quick half-assed speech and then hope I went away?"

What was happening here? This was not the plan. She would say it again, a different way, the way she did when customers said the umbrellas were too expensive or they wanted a refund.

"Well, I am, I *am* sorry," she said. "Not half-assed. Actually sorry. For lying, and everything. But yeah, that was, I mean what I'm *saying* is, that you know it *is* probably better if we stop seeing each other. You know, so it's not weird."

She counted out the cash in her fanny pack and checked her watch, even though she knew what time it was because there was a giant clock behind his head.

"I'm a dollar short," she said. "Can you tell Carl I'm a dollar short? When you see him? I would, but you're gonna go right by his office."

He looked at her with his head cocked to the side, like he was about to say something but changed his mind. But he didn't leave yet. Why?

Did she need to say this three ways? Four? It was over because she said it was over. There were other things she could say that would be mean enough to *make* him accept the terms of her little speech: *You can just go find another underage girl to fuck. I wouldn't want to bother you with anything besides getting drunk and talking about your band and, like, the one single philosophy class you attended before you dropped out of the third-worst state school in Jersey.*

But instead she said, "I have to get back to work." When he slung his backpack over his shoulder and walked up the ramp to the board-walk, he didn't look back. She dragged another umbrella across the beach.

An hour later, the ocean was at high tide, churning up seaweed and clamshells across the beach, dumping a little girl in a ruffled pink swimsuit onto the shore to rub the salt out of her eyes and then go careening right back in. In the humid wind, the sunblock and sweat stung Liz's eyes.

"You got ice cream here?" a guy in a jogging suit and backward baseball cap asked her. She pointed to the sign without saying a word: SUN & SHADE UMBRELLA RENTALS in big yellow letters. "You're a cute one," he said, still standing there like he expected either an ice cream cone to materialize or for her to say, "Thanks, let's go get a room at the Topsider."

She planted twelve more umbrellas. Three different customers in-sisted on planting their own, even though she told them she was sup-posed to. The easiest thing on their egos was to let them do it, then come back and say you were adjusting it for wind and do it right.

It was good to be so busy, good to be alone between customers and reciting her lines about prices and deposits when they showed up. Evy and Margot were both working today too, Margot on E&E stuff, and Evy at Sal's. Liz glanced down at the group text thread with her mom and sister, but it was empty today. There was nothing to say to each other in the next seven hours of their work dipping apples in caramel, dragging umbrellas around, and sending emails, was there?

She ate the bag of cheese cubes and flower-shaped fruit left over from the post-funeral buffet and peed in the ocean while holding her fanny pack of cash above her head between customers. Carl finally came by to give her a real bathroom break and brought her a St. Chris-topher medal, which she shoved in the front pocket of her backpack.

She never stopped moving, and so the idea of her dad saying *Go get 'em, kid!* at the last curve of the track with his hands up like Rocky, and the idea of her dad driving with the windows open saying *We're going on a mission* to make the ordinary upkeep of all the E&E houses seem so important, never found even a second to slip through. Even when it got slow, she shoved the trash into bags to make room for more trash tomorrow so she wouldn't think of Uncle Pete, alone on the deck after the funeral doing a cheers with his beer into the air to no one.

Margot

She chose a cream-colored shift dress and a bright scarf to wear to the meeting with her realtor friend Deborah Ellsworth. Deborah had sold them plenty of E&E houses over the years, and connected them with Carol and her Victorian back when they were starting out, and now she would help Margot sell every last one of those houses.

Margot reapplied red lipstick after she finished her LaCroix. Deborah wore a golf shirt and shorts. She had sunburned cheeks and short white-gray hair, and she was not sentimental.

Let Deborah Ellsworth listen to buyers criticize the paint colors or kitchen layouts so they could get a better deal; let Deborah break the news that there was no way Margot was fixing anything broken in these E&E houses before she sold them.

Margot's left hand still felt unbalanced. She traced a dry smooth ring of skin where her wedding band and emerald engagement ring had been. She knew if she didn't take them off today, then she would wear them much longer than she wanted to. It was the same with this appointment with Deborah; it didn't *have* to be today, and it absolutely *had* to be today.

While Deborah Ellsworth excused herself to gather some documents, Margot browsed real estate listings in Galesta, Pennsylvania, on her phone, a place she'd discovered when she Googled "best small towns in America." It sounded like the next best thing to shoving yourself through the TV screen to live inside an idyllic movie set. A few Hallmark movies had actually been filmed there.

I think this is the one, she posted to the GBM Wives, along with a link. The house was a Craftsman style with a wide front porch, a neat square of grass in the front yard, and a bright-red door. She imagined it in the fall, when children in Elsa and Captain America costumes would meet Margot on the porch. She would sit on the swing and sip hot cider, handing out candy. In the winter, snow would settle into white drifts, her breath would freeze into clouds, and the air would smell like pine and soil. Every spring: that sudden relief and joy she remembered from living somewhere landlocked in college, when March finally blew gusty across the farms and the crocuses burst through the brown, cold earth, when the April mud teemed with its slowly warming life emerging from the thaw, when the rivers rose after the snowmelt and washed away the final hunks of ice along their banks.

Galesta had a small high school and grocery store, a cobblestone Main Street with coffee shops and candle shops whose doors jingled with little bells when you walked in. There was a small college nearby, and its website listed plays, music, and lectures open to the community. It was five hours west, far enough from Seaside, and pictures of the annual Pumpkin Festival and parade were full of grinning strangers.

In Galesta, she and the girls could make fires, they could go to the football games on Friday night and to the café where the waitress would know their order by heart. Margot could buy white bedspreads and white dishes. She could substitute-teach until she was ready to apply for a full-time position, showing up every day to a room full of new faces, following the handwritten directions left by their real teacher, and adapting to whatever subject and grade level she was assigned to. Something new every day.

Yes, they would miss that softening air when you drove over the bridge into Seaside, but they would feel a new lightening in their hearts when they crossed a state line.

Margot peeked in to see Deborah halfway through copying a stack of papers, and she opened her own laptop. After the link to the house, Margot wrote to the GBM Wives:

> *I will say to my daughters, I know this is so sudden, but couldn't it also be beautiful?*
>
> *Evy could be voted homecoming queen and ride through town in a red pickup truck. Liz could get a job at the diner on weekends, join the track team again and run along the river.*
>
> *I want to reclaim a version of myself when I believed I was making a series of choices I had a say in, when I was sure that I was in charge of the path I was plotting.*
>
> *If I stay in Seaside, I will lose the tiny grain of myself buried under the layers of the life I built with Brian, I WILL lose this window of time and space opening a little between this anesthetized aftermath and the approaching pain—I know it's coming.*
>
> *I took off my ring today.*
>
> *If not right away, then when? I'm leaving tomorrow to buy this house.*

Deborah returned to the office with a calendar, with a list of comps, with many documents and ideas about how to make them both a bunch of money. Margot half-listened, nodding along, until Deborah said, "I'm excited to sell that Victorian property!"

Margot imagined the shiny-Audi-driving bankers who had rented it signing the mortgage between their other meetings, imagined the house empty on the weekends when those bankers were somewhere else. She imagined them forgetting to water the red geraniums.

Margot said, "Let's talk about those C and J Street properties, Deb."

CHAPTER TWENTY-TWO

Liz

The wind switched to cooler blasts from off the Atlantic. A faraway storm could move in and pick up speed; a static bright-blue sky could turn black in a minute and throw down bolts of lightning before you could take shelter.

I'm writing a Scrabblemary45 post myself, Liz texted Evy, between customers at Sun and Shade. They'd both read Margot's latest plan to road-trip alone to some backwoods town with a cutesy quilt store and buy a house tomorrow, followed by her text to them: **Going to see Aunt Melissa in NYC for a visit tomorrow!**

go ahead, Evy texted Liz, **I'm done with her.**

Scrabblemary or mom?

The typing dots appeared and disappeared, and so did Evy, while Liz helped another customer. When she came back, Liz typed in the Wives' thread: *Hey, maybe you might want to think about some kind of compromise, and definitely talk to the girls before you go all the way out there. . . . Are you ok?*

that does not sound like Scrabblemary45 at all, btw, Evy texted. **but it doesn't matter. here, fuck it, I'm gonna do one like that now too. Evy posted in the forum:** *STAY IN SEASIDE!!!!!!!*

this is dumb, I'm calling her, Liz texted.

Evy texted, **yeah, she's got her lines all ready for you, she's got the Post-its in the self-help book scripts . . . if she says COULDN'T IT BE BEAUTIFUL, you tell her I said she can move to the moon if she wants, I'm staying here.**

Wind gusted in off the ocean, and a flimsy umbrella someone else had planted all wrong went flying, flipping in a whirl of red and white down the beach until it hit a little boy hard enough to knock him down. The kid started crying, and his dad scooped him up and wrapped him in a towel. The canopy of gray clouds shifted; though the air felt charged and on the verge of something the rest of the afternoon, it never did storm that day.

Liz called her mom twice, but she didn't pick up.

Evy

Sure you're ready for a whole shift at Sal's? Olivia texted. **Seems kinda soon.**

After she'd read Olivia's card, they'd talked on the phone that night, and Evy had told her about the last drive she took with her dad to the inlet, and about how her mom listened to some lady on the internet in Arizona who said Margot wouldn't be sad anymore if she changed her zip code, and Olivia told Evy about the time her mom had a panic attack and the paramedics were there when she got home from class.

??no?? Evy texted. **but also maybe the dumbass customers who ask if we sell salad at a candy store will distract me??? from this eat pray love garbage trip my mom is taking to buy a house TOMOR-ROW . . .**

Hailey arrived to work then. She pulled out a plastic bottle of orange-tinged juice, chugged from it, and then handed it to Evy.

"Quick, before Irene comes back," Hailey said. The last time Evy had taken whatever was handed to her was the night with the lucky juice, when she'd barely managed to stay in the buzzed-but-not-drunk zone. The effects had worn off enough before Olivia arrived, and Evy liked how it felt being herself around her, and had decided to try that more, to do the spinning-oblivion-drinking thing less. But Hailey was waving her hands around, hurrying Evy to take a sip, and Evy's head was still cluttered and confused from her mom's suddenly more-real plans, and then, while Olivia texted **what????** Evy was chugging down the first burning sips.

"That's strong," Evy said, so Hailey poured in some simple syrup from the storage room and solved everything and the next sip went down like melted candy. Irene was arguing with the UPS guy out by his truck; then she was back and staring at them like she knew something was up, but she sighed and went back to doing payroll.

Hailey was hungover anyway, after another night at Cameron's pool, and she said Evy *had* to come next time no matter what, though it mattered *what.*

What was a few days of watching movies with Margot and watching the hospital bed get hauled away, *what* was eating the last of the IDCs in the fridge, *what* was why she hadn't been at Cameron's pool last night and probably shouldn't be at Sal's yet except her mom and sister weren't home anyway and Olivia was busy today, so it was probably better than being alone.

"Who was there?" Evy asked, as they passed the barely-orange-juice bottle back and forth, and Hailey named everyone, including Olivia. "We follow each other again."

Irene was on the phone, then Irene was unloading the boxes she had been fighting about with the UPS guy. That distracting buzz built inside Evy, and the lollipop colors of the shop blurred and all the customers were so funny, and somehow they got the little gummy bear bags tied up with bows and made them talk dirty to each other before they went in each bag (*bye-bye little guys!*) though each one took a while, and they *bleep-blorped* the register buttons and grinned at other customers, not rude or anything, but they put whatever in their bags and said everything weighed six ounces to simplify things, price-wise, so the people were really getting a deal, no wonder they were smiling back!

"I'm going to smoke and get singles for the register. Dumb idiot at the bank gave me a buncha fives," Irene said. "If the caramel apples aren't done when I get back in an hour, I'm telling Sal about this nonsense."

The second she left they turned off the doo-wop music and put on a dance party playlist, and Hailey turned up the bass so loud the glass counter vibrated. They danced around and stocked half the candy they were supposed to, they made beards and mustaches out of the cotton candy and did more dirty-mouth stuff with the lollipops and gummy worms.

It seemed like only ten minutes had passed, but Hailey said, *fuck, the apples*, and they only had fifteen minutes to cut them up and dip them in caramel and nuts, and Hailey whined she was tired and could Evy pulease do them, and they argued and wasted another five minutes until Evy gave in.

Evy's buzz was wearing off enough to make her remember she hadn't eaten anything except candy today, and she started in on the big bin of apples anyway, an awkward one-woman assembly line, slicing, slicing, caramel, nuts, nuts, slicing, big apple, small slice, sliver slice, hunk, caramel.

Her hand slipped.

She saw the blood on the cutting board before she felt the throbbing, sudden rush of pain or saw the gash across her finger. She screamed, then yelled, "Hailey!" and held her hand against her pink uniform shirt as the blood soaked through and spread. "Hailey!" she yelled again.

"What the fuck is wrong with you, what did you do?" Hailey asked, staring at the blood with a half-filled box of fudge in her hand, flailing her hands around and dropping the squares on the floor, frozen in place, staring at the apples and Evy. "Ew!"

Evy ran to the sink and the freezing water turned pink, and she retched when she saw how deeply the knife had sliced her. "Call my mom, and fuck, call Irene, I guess, do you have her number? Hailey?"

Hailey was hunched over, puking into the trash can, and then the wad of napkins she threw at Evy fluttered to the floor. Evy pressed her finger against her shirt again, dialed her phone with her other hand but couldn't hold it steady and dropped it, feeling light-headed, and then Irene walked in and rushed toward her, saying, "Oh, honey, what did you do?" grabbing a clean cloth and tying it tight around Evy's finger, telling Hailey she was on her own for a while, and guiding Evy into the front seat of her smoky-smelling Corolla.

"Try not to pass out," she said, rolling down the windows. "This was Hailey's idea, wasn't it? I knew I shouldn't have let you come back to work yet. Jesus."

Evy retched again when Irene took a turn too fast, and Irene said sorry and turned on the country station. "You're not on anything else, are ya?" she asked, and Evy shook her head and sank down into her seat, staring down at the drops of blood on her Vans and the empty Wawa cups on Irene's floor. The pain pulsed, she looked away from the red-soaked rag, she closed her eyes, and still the throbbing came in waves, and the motion of the car and the pain merged. It was worse when they stopped, and every nerve ending in that gash screamed and burned. The blood bloomed into the lap of her shorts and Irene's seat, and Irene managed to call Margot on Evy's phone to tell her to meet them at the hospital.

Pain hijacked every signal in Evy's body, and she only wanted a single thing the whole rest of her life: to be on the other side of this, to find a way to turn the hurt down even one degree.

Irene dumped her alone at the ER entrance and tried to find parking, and Evy stood in front of the triage nurse and bled and cried, and then someone in scrubs was leading her through a maze of curtains and little rooms and cubicles and computers, and then she was holding out her hand and getting pinched and Irene was back, and she was looking up to a bright light then and *I'm so sorry* echoed in her own head, and she must have said it out loud a lot too, because all the adults, Irene, and the nurse, said back to her *it's gonna be okay*. They waited and waited in the curtain-room, and then the doctor was pulling on her hand, and she felt pressure and the light went even brighter.

Margot arrived in a white dress and a scarf and glared at Evy and Irene and the doctor and the nurse and said, "How did this happen?" and Evy said, "Mom, I'm so sorry Hailey brought this um this vodka and I drank it at work and then I did the apples and—" She winced, and turned away from the stitches the bright light the rubber gloves, and she said, sobbing, "I'm so sorry because there are like real sick people here and the doctors should be helping them I'm so so sorry."

The doctor sewed more stitches, and Margot stepped away from Evy and said in a tired monotone, "Evy. Did you say you sliced your finger open because you were *drunk*, at *work*, at the *candy store?*"

The nurse caught Irene's eye and then looked down again at the doctor stitching Evy's finger. The light was so bright, and the pain settled and spread, but one of the drugs must have helped because the edges of it dulled. Evy's sobs had worn her out in a whole other way from the pain and panic, and they slowed down while she caught her breath.

"I don't want to go," was all she could get out, and the doctor and nurse looked confused and someone said, "It will be just a few more minutes," and her mom stared at the blood and searched Evy's squinting, wincing face for a second and then said, "Irene, I think we can take it from here."

Evy saw three drops of blood on the wrinkled white fabric of her mom's dress. They finished stitching, and the bandage on her hand was so tight, it felt like it was a hundred pounds, one part of the apparatus of her body, all slowed-down and clumsy.

Her mom guided her into the passenger seat of the van and leaned across to buckle the seat belt. When she put her hands on the steering wheel, Evy noticed her ring was gone. The gas tank was full. There were a Diet Coke and a bag of M&M's in the console already, her favorite road-trip snacks.

They drove home in silence, with Evy's hand resting on the console, wrapped in its layers of gauze and bandages, the pink Sal's uniform shirt still caked with her own dried blood, Margot's white dress flecked with red.

"When your boss called, she only told me there was an accident and to meet her at the hospital and then hung up," Margot said, once they were home, staring down at Evy's bandaged hand. "I am so sorry I let you go to work today—you seemed ready. Come on, let's go inside."

She helped Evy peel off her dirty shirt and shower with her hand held outside the curtain, and she helped dry her off and pull on her softest pajamas.

Evy spent the afternoon in a leaden sleep in her bright, hot bedroom. She woke up with her head still feeling foggy to find that Margot had straightened everything while she slept: her clothes were folded and put away, her empty cups had been cleared, her books returned from their facedown piles to their places on the shelf. She'd set a jar of tiger lilies on Evy's dresser. It smelled like lemon Pledge. On her nightstand, Margot had stacked papers, and Evy's last report card was on top: a bunch of B's, one C, and one A+, in Economics 101. It was probably the painkillers that let her test the edges of memory so soon, that clouded the image of red-black blood and the sharp blade that had sliced her open and allowed another memory to play like a grainy old movie all the way through instead.

"I'm taking a study hall, all my friends are in study hall," Evy had insisted to Brian. It was last September, and she needed him to sign a form so she could drop her elective. "I'm not staying in that music class they put me in, everyone there wears matching tie-dye T-shirts from their marching band competitions and gives each other shoulder massages."

Brian had read every word of the form and pulled up the course catalogue online before he said, "Then you're taking economics. And here's why." He used to teach econ, and he launched right into his pitch. "Those apps you scroll through all the time? You think they're cool? Well, they were funded with startup money, they sell your data, which has value and you give it away for free. You want to learn about that?"

He would only be himself for another few weeks.

"Dad, are you gonna, like, do a rap about econ now to show how cool it is?" Evy rolled her eyes.

"The phone itself: made in China. You ever wonder why, you ever wonder who assembles it, or what a marvel of a supply chain and man-ufacturing and human capital gets all those tiny parts together? We live near a beach, and people pay thousands of dollars to stay here for one week—one week! Why? Supply and demand. You're taking econ and you're gonna love it."

"If I'm failing by midterm, my counselor will *make* me drop it. She will literally call you and tell you she is making me drop it."

"You're not dropping it," he said, filling out the part of the form for a class change to Economics 101.

Evy had snatched it away and said, "Cool, thanks, I'm not gonna hate it or fail it at all, I love this for us."

Later, he'd brought popcorn to her room and his old hardcover copy of *Freakonomics*, full of Post-its and margin notes, and she ate the popcorn and threw the book under her bed. *I love this for us*, he'd written on a note stuck to the front of the book. Signing that form was the last normal-parent decision he ever made for Evy.

Another few weeks into the semester, Brian's patience had faded, his impulses taking over and telling him to charge ahead into crowds, or yell at strangers.

Evy did like how economics wasn't free-floating symbols and variables, but real stories of wealth or ruin. She liked the case studies about companies coming back from bankruptcy, the simulations on the power of compound interest, and the stock market game Mr. Vasquez got so pumped up about that his face turned red. She asked better questions about inflation than the senior boys and did an extra-credit poster on interest rates. She looked up elasticity and diminishing marginal utility and emailed Mr. Vasquez questions about the Wikipedia articles she found on them, and he took her aside and said she should sign up for AP next year.

A few times after Brian got sick, Evy had tried to tell him about the class and how well she was doing, but it always triggered a mangled monologue; she couldn't ask him anymore about things he used to understand. He thought he sounded like a TED Talk, but he was more like the Jabberwocky, and it felt both cruel and punishing to listen to him.

The market was just like people, because it was controlled by people, and people were volatile and predictable, people were brands, people were safe bets or junk bonds, people went bankrupt a month after they had a million dollars, and if you could see the patterns of how people would behave around money, then you could be rich.

When Evy finally moved from her room to the couch, Margot had cleared the house of all the browning flowers, the cards, the baskets of cookies covered in cellophane. Margot made Evy a smoothie and beat her by fifty points in Scrabble, then sat with her on the sofa and turned on *The Office*.

Hailey never texted to check on Evy, but when Evy told Olivia what had happened, she texted **I'm coming over**, and the shadow of the slow-fading pain, the image of Brian's handwritten *I love this for us*, the diminishing haze of afternoon sleep, and the idea of Olivia sitting next to her soon all coalesced and found Evy at once.

Liz

Half an hour before closing time, Gabe texted Liz:

> **Hey, can I walk you home today?**

She never texted him back, but he showed up anyway at 4:59 as she was throwing the last umbrella into the storage box.

"You're not supposed to close early," she said. Liz had arrived for her first shift at Sun and Shade last summer, eager to impress Carl. "You're on time. That's good," Carl had said that first day, opening up an umbrella and digging it into the sand. The umbrellas Carl rented were sturdy. Big, yellow, moldy, rusty, splintery. But sturdy.

She had opened one herself, driving it down as far as she could, gauging the wind's direction, while Carl watched. He pulled the umbrella out, and said to start over. On her second try, she struggled—it seemed impossible to get it to go any deeper. Carl demonstrated again. You didn't have to be big or strong to do it right, he said, it was all in how you focused your strength, how you tilted it against the wind. She got it right, finally, on the third try.

"Okay, boss," Gabe said.

She let him walk her to her door, but didn't invite him in.

Evy

Evy's painkillers were wearing off enough for her to joke about her accident, which she called the apple-murder scene, and to talk shit about Hailey, before she and Olivia settled in for Netflix on the couch.

Margot puttered around in the kitchen, talking loud to someone on the phone, or hovering nearby, asking Olivia if she was taking the SATs this fall and suggesting Evy sign up early too. When Liz got home, her eyes darted around, from Evy's stitched-up hand to Olivia, cross-legged on the couch, then again to Evy's injury. "What happened?"

"I'll tell you about it later," Evy said, without looking away from the TV.

When Evy's unbandaged hand slid into hers, Olivia bit her lip and Evy thought she almost, almost felt her pull it away. But then Olivia moved even closer on the couch and tightened her grip.

Liz

Let me take you to a show tonight Gabe texted. The sharp smell of rotten lilies still lingered inside the house, even though the flowers were gone. If she woke up tomorrow and Margot was gone too, that meant she was actually buying a house somewhere else.

She didn't want to crash Evy and Olivia's Netflix session. The door to her dad's room was closed, his CD binder still on the shelf in hers. Liz's cross-country coach had texted her again to tell her the first day of practice was coming up.

She texted Gabe: **ok let's go**, and half an hour later they were on their way to Asbury Park to see The Machine Is Red, a show she and Sonia had tried to buy tickets for months ago when the site had crashed. Gabe said he knew a guy who got him tickets, or maybe he'd spent too much and bought some marked-up ones but didn't want to admit it.

Before the show, the room went black, then filled with beams of light and the singer's big, ethereal voice. Gabe pulled Liz into the middle of the crowd, close enough to feel the sweat and breath of two hundred other bodies.

On the drive home, they played the slower, live versions of The Machine Is Red songs, and he finally told her what he'd already lost—what his brother *did*, what he *used to do,* who he *had been* before he died, all in the right tenses: the past, the past progressive, the past perfect.

At a concert, you could look around at all the strangers and think: *We love this band, yes, we're the same, in this one particular way. We're so glad we're here in this dark room that we will scream with joy and sing along to the songs we know by heart, and this is the one place in the whole world right now where you can sing with the people who wrote these songs.* What magic.

When someone tells you what they've lost? Yes, you're the same, in this one particular way. You occupy the same dark room, but you both hate it here. Gabe named the kinds of strangers his brother had been: addict, liar, thief.

Liz said the worst for her, worse than who her dad turned into, was what her dad had turned *her* into when he was sick: impatient, embarrassed, absent.

CHAPTER TWENTY-THREE

Margot

Early the next morning, Margot left for Galesta. On this drive, she did not want the horror of podcast murder stories. She did not want the nostalgia of Springsteen. She wanted music to get her out of her head: bright pop, big sing-along choruses, lyrics she and Tracy used to sing while they flung their sparkly party clothes into piles on the bed, and all this summer's pop songs she'd only heard snippets of before she switched the radio back to NPR. As the interstate exits streamed by, she wanted to listen to Mariah Carey hold a high note and some Gen Z singer she'd never heard of sing about staying up all night.

She accelerated past semis and took the curves in Pennsylvania fast before stopping to get gas. She would check in with the girls when she was farther from Seaside—she was still too close, hardly a hundred miles away, and that was not enough. She settled into a meditative state of recycled air and highway fumes and music. A few hundred miles west, the leaden emptiness let up a little. She would make it to Galesta by the afternoon.

Evy

When they woke up, Margot was already gone. Liz called her twice, but she didn't answer. Irene had given Evy some days off after her accident, so Liz took Carl up on his offer and took the day off too.

"Should I try again?" Liz asked Evy, her hand hovering over the green CALL button.

"Go for it," Evy said. "Ask her to FaceTime you from Times Square." She showed Liz the Starbucks app they shared. Margot had spent $5.73 on coffee at a Pennsylvania rest stop ten minutes ago.

Liz put her phone away. Evy didn't think a phone call was the way to make their mom hear them—Evy didn't believe, after all the months reading the most honest version of Margot's voice in the GBM Wives forum, that her daughters could convince her of anything.

Evy scrolled through the Wives' posts one more time. Margot's last one said she wasn't seeing any Galesta houses until tomorrow. She wouldn't arrive in the terrible new town until the afternoon. They each tried to write more Scrabblemary45 posts, traded them, and agreed they were garbage. When Liz got up to refill her coffee, she came back wearing her bikini and their dad's old Tilley hat, and she was slathering herself with sunblock. Then she was shoving stuff from the fridge and some beach towels into a bag.

They walked to the quiet beach they'd been to every summer day as kids, where they had built sandcastle civilizations with moats to protect them. Liz pulled out a jug of iced tea and a bag of cherries, and they passed them back and forth, sucking out the pits from the sour fruit, spitting them out, and burying them in the sand. They played Never Have I Ever, and Evy told Liz all about driving around New Jersey with Brian, but left out the part about getting pulled over. Her sister didn't recite all the bad things that could have happened, or tell her how stupid she was for breaking the rules again. She said she'd teach Evy to parallel park if she hadn't figured that out yet on her own.

As Margot moved west, farther away from the Atlantic and from them with each mile, they faced their chairs toward the ocean.

Margot

The bed-and-breakfast was situated among the other hundred-year-old homes, along a street with perennial flowerbeds in alternating reds and yellows. There was a park with a baseball diamond nearby, and a canopy of evenly spaced trees. The B&B owner, a sturdy woman named JoAnn, asked how many keys Margot wanted.

"It's just me," Margot said. She unpacked and let her eyes refocus after the hypnosis of the interstate. The room had lace curtains and antique furniture, porcelain cherub-children on every surface. The late-afternoon light filtered through the curtains into a warm white kaleidoscope pattern on the quilt.

She soaked in scalding water in the bathtub, then sprayed herself down with the cold shower, and when she caught her tired eyes in the mirror she felt the acute absence she'd been holding off with all that motion.

She knew exactly what Brian would have done next if he were here with her, hundreds of miles from home: run five miles around the perimeter of the town, found the mayor walking her dog and asked her about their tourism economy, and discovered a dive bar to take them to after dinner. He would have asked the bartender if he'd grown up here or ended up here, or found another traveler finishing a burger and discovered some coincidence that connected them.

Margot was as adept at connection as Brian had been, and as curious about how hard or lucky or strange someone else's life was. But he had always been the one to make that first foray across the space between strangers.

She emerged from her fussy room with wet hair, two minutes early for the evening wine and cheese hour. JoAnn poured Margot a glass of cabernet, then disappeared into the kitchen, and another guest appeared at the cheese table and asked Margot whether she knew if the crackers were gluten-free. The woman explained what gluten did to her digestive system.

"Um, I'm not sure if they have gluten," Margot said. How was she supposed to know anything about the crackers? What kind of person told you about her stomach before she told you her name? "Sorry about your, uh, allergy?"

"It's more of an intolerance."

"Right, sure," Margot said, as if she understood the difference, then slipped outside to the porch swing. A minute later that gluten-intolerant woman followed her. "They found me something I could actually *eat*," she said, holding out a pile of crackers on a plate to show Margot.

"Oh, *good*," Margot said. She felt a guilty tug in her gut for sounding snarky and slipping away, so she asked where the woman was from and what had brought her to Galesta. The woman nibbled her crackers. She answered *Iowa* and *crafts* and did not elaborate on where in Iowa or which particular crafts before popping up from her seat and saying she should go get more of *her* crackers.

Annoying old ladies like this were exactly the kind of people Brian could get talking, and maybe this Iowan–craft-hunting-gluten-intolerant woman was more interesting than Margot was willing to find out. Well, fine. If she'd once been a circus performer or a getaway car driver, that was wonderful, but she was also rude. Margot's radar for other people's strangeness was more sensitive, her bar for who she was willing to expend her stores of social energy on higher than Brian's had been.

For so long, she would miss him in these moments, meeting strangers. But slowly, by talking about the weather with one corner-dwelling oddball at a time, by dragging herself to the dance floor for one wedding "Shout" sequence after another, by pivoting away whenever it became clear someone was a name-dropper, mansplainer, or MLM devotee, she would start to feel that her quieter way of deciding what kinds of strangers deserved her attention wasn't wrong: it was just hers.

A long time after that night in Galesta, Margot would be at a fancy Chicago bar by herself. She would ask a wild-haired woman wearing chunky glasses the same what-brings-you-here questions she'd asked the gluten lady at the B&B, but by then she would have a better sense of herself and which new people might be *her* people, which cues, from what they were drinking to how often they looked at their phone or out at the skyline, were likely to indicate they were thinking about the world the way she did.

"I'm speaking at a conference tomorrow," the wild-haired woman would say. "Actually, I'm giving the keynote speech. I've escaped here from the conference people." And Margot's eyes would widen as she imagined this woman with darker hair and no glasses. And her vague recognition would become sudden near-certainty that she knew who this wild-haired woman was. But she would ask one more question to be sure.

"What's the speech going to be on?" Margot would ask.

"Oh, it's called 'Atomic Particles and Love,'" the woman would say. "It's a big pretentious literary conference, but they're paying me an ungodly amount of money, so cheers!" The wild-haired woman would raise her glass of wine and offer to buy them another round.

Margot had stared at this woman's black-and-white author photo inside the book jacket of *The Girl with the Long Shadow*, and now in this hotel bar she would get to explain what the book had gotten her through. She would get to thank the author for building a world she could escape to over and over.

And as they drank their second glasses of wine together, the author would lean in to ask Margot blunt and intimate questions that led them to Brian and what it had been like to be with him, questions that would make Margot remember how the time he was not himself had changed her. Margot would explain how dissociative and demeaning it had been for her to face him day after day, and how watching her daughters endure it and feeling herself retreat from them still sickened her.

She would be nervous at first that she was sharing too much, but then again, she knew the worlds the author had imagined so clearly. Was hearing someone's sad story any more intimate than knowing the depths of their imagination? Talking to the author, Margot's fear of saying too much would fall away just as the rest of the world had always fallen away whenever she read *The Girl with the Long Shadow*. Margot would confess to all the moments, in the author's book and in her own life, that had broken her most.

It was the kind of coincidence no one would believe without some evidence, but there would be none. The only record of their meeting would be Margot's memory, and a few passages in the author's next book, a darker and more disturbing descent into a world of specters and ghosts, of mistrust and epic journeys, where no one was themselves for very long.

Evy

They swam for hours in the warm late-August ocean. They bought bomb pops from the ice cream truck and read every word of the *In*

Touch magazines Margot had brought them from the rental houses. They wrapped up in towels when the wind shifted and watched families schlepp their carts of beach gear away, but Evy and Liz stayed late because they had nowhere to be. Margot texted **Checking in! museum was great, heading to a bistro with Aunt Melissa!**

"Well, you know, maybe by 'bistro' "—Evy made air-quotes—"she meant *interstate Burger King*."

"And by Aunt Melissa, she meant *truck drivers*," Liz said.

Then Evy grabbed her phone and dialed Margot before she lost her nerve, but it went straight to voicemail. Evy said, "Heeeyyyy, Mom, just, um, calling to say I hope you're having a *great time*, and you know I was just thinking about all the life lessons you've taught us, you and Dad did a great job not screwing us up. I think. So keep up the good work, k? Bye."

Liz stared at her, and Evy could tell she wasn't blinking even behind her sunglasses.

"Wow, that was a journey, Ev. What *was* that?" Liz asked.

"I . . . don't know," Evy said, already scripting a possible more careful, Instagram-therapist-bullet-point-plagiarizing, truth-bombing version of whatever that random mess was. Olivia's sister had made her see a real therapist, and Olivia had told Evy about *boundaries*, and *processing*. "I'm bad at voicemails to selfish, unstable women who want to ruin my life, okay, *Elizabeth*?"

Back home, they emerged from their post-beach showers with fresh clothes and shampooed hair. They applied aloe to the streaks of sunburn.

Olivia texted Evy: **ugh, in the weeds with this project . . . I need a pep talk!!** When Margot took off, Evy had thought the only small upside was that she could invite Olivia over for two days straight. She'd imagined lying out with their towels close together at the beach, then listening to their playlist in her bed while the room got dark. But when she found out Olivia's schedule was full of work shifts and coding homework, she hadn't tried to convince her to skip or miss her deadline; instead she'd sent her a bunch of encouraging GIFs. At least Liz's umbrella guy was also busy, with some band thing in Brooklyn, so Evy and Liz drank Margot's nicest cabernet on the screen porch together and talked about love, instead of about leaving. Then they talked about ways to stay, brainstorming plans B, C, and D, a series of speculations about emancipated minors, train routes, and benevolent relatives.

Would Margot be lonely? Wasn't that what she deserved?

"I do have one more idea," Evy said. It was not elaborate or complicated; it was not another new identity or a middle-of-the-night drive across state lines to beg her to stay. Evy said she was sure it would only piss Margot off and push her further into her new-town fugue state, but Liz agreed they had to do it anyway.

Margot

"How long have you owned this place?" Margot asked JoAnn, who'd swooped in to save her from the gluten woman.

"Oh, I inherited it when I was in my twenties," JoAnn said. Her husband had wanted to sell it, but she'd refused. He left her, and she stayed, raising her children here while she ran the B&B.

She'd hosted a presidential candidate once, and several world-famous quilters. Her kids had moved to Philadelphia the first chance they got. JoAnn excused herself to set out more cheese. Margot listened to a voicemail from Evy and noticed a hint of suspicion beneath her usual sarcasm. She listened again and thought she'd try to call her later, after she'd settled in a little more. She sent her a **love you ev** text.

On her way to Main Street for dinner, Margot watched a little league team file into their dugout, heard an ice cream truck's bright, tinny music, and stepped around a lawnmower throwing off thick, chopped-up clippings. It had been so long since trees, grass, settled-in brick houses, and the distant scent of fertilizer surrounded her; Seaside was all stones and sand, seagull caws and salt air. There was comfort in this landlocked place.

Sitting alone in a candlelit restaurant, she was friendly to her waiter. The couple at the next table argued over a kitchen remodel, but she did not interrupt them with her expertise. She'd brought a novel with her from the B&B, but it had so many characters it needed a map on the first page to tell you who they all were. She set it aside.

That night she slept in the center of the firm mattress, forgetting where she was when she awoke wanting a glass of water. In the morning, she took another bath in the claw-foot tub, let it cool to tepid. She skipped breakfast with JoAnn and made coffee in the French press, and then set off to buy a new house.

Coneflowers bloomed in front of the wide white front porch. The inside of the Craftsman house had been gutted and reimagined from its original 1920s design, and the bright, open living room was furnished with a sectional and leather chairs. Margot scanned the spines of the books on the built-in shelves, imagining how she would arrange her own. She ran the water in the farmhouse sink and looked at the shaded patio out back.

The bedrooms were staged with gray duvets and soft blankets, and the bathrooms gleamed, empty of the plastic bottles and hairbrushes that would take over in real life. She opened all the kitchen drawers and gaped at the bright, bare refrigerator and the cavernous pantry.

We can't just leave now, she knew the girls would say when she told them they were moving, but by then it would already be decided, she could show them pictures of this perfect place; it wouldn't be an abstract idea they could convince her was a seismic, insane change. She could show them the Pinterest boards she'd already made for the family room, and some ideas for color schemes she envisioned for their bedrooms (though they could decorate however they wanted!); she could offer to put a hot tub in the backyard; she could show them the bookstore and the outdoor theater, the secondhand shop they would both love, the diner. Once she'd bought this house, she could say, *It's done,* firm but certain; she could promise them it would be okay once they were all settled here.

"What do you think?" her real estate agent asked. "Do you need more time?"

She had never let herself imagine anything good in Seaside after Brian died. Before she left this house, Margot needed to touch more of it: the buttery upholstery on the sofa, the maplewood mantel above the fireplace, and the pewter sculptures on the shelves. She lingered in its smells of wood polish, brand-new carpet, and fresh-cut lilies in a vase in the dining room. She pictured herself settling into the armchair near the fireplace with the local newspaper, making a roast and chopping vegetables in the kitchen, drinking coffee on the patio. She already felt at ease here in a way she knew she never would again in Seaside.

"I'm ready now," she said to the realtor. She told her the offer she wanted to make, and walked back past the empty baseball field, the fresh-cut lawns, across the cobblestone main street back to the B&B. Her phone buzzed: the Galesta agent texting to ask for some mortgage documents. When she opened her email to find them, she discovered two messages from Evy. The subject lines said *READ NOW–FIRST* and *READ NOW–SECOND.*

The first email was one line from the girls: *Please read all of these before you decide anything about leaving???—Evy and Liz,* and a document titled margotbrian.txt. She sat on the edge of the bed, staring at the first lines of the emails for a full minute while her memory caught up to what was on the screen: so many layered identities, so many decisions, such a different version of love.

How had she forgotten that the gold data CD was wedged in with Brian's music? Her stomach clenched and her head throbbed. As she read and scrolled, she was in too many places at once: her cinder-block dorm room, a café in Spain, her parents' house on their slow bing-bonging dial-up internet. She was at the inlet and at the Buccaneer and in their bungalow for the first time.

The emails were such a small window on her life, an imperfect record of that time; but when she read them they awakened the disparate, connected, swallowed-up versions of her that had retreated and gone silent for so long, all the Margots between that lonely, lovesick girl in the computer lab and the woman sitting in this fussy, doily-covered bedroom.

They told her what they knew and what they wanted now and what they had understood about the world and their place in it. All of the Margots crowded around her atop the thin quilt: the snarky, skinny widow and the hopeful college girl; the jaded real estate investor; the postpartum new mother; the lying, road-tripping mom of teenagers; the depleted, confused caretaker; the betrayed, lonely, loyal wife; the embarrassed anonymous lady at the grocery store with a strange man wandering down the pickle aisle; the uncertain, untested teacher; the open-hearted and confused Catholic; the disappointed, distant daughter. They all whispered their sides of a long story, assuring her that the time she was in right now, brutal and lonely as it felt, was only one part of it.

In the emails she found a version of herself in the throes of long-distance love, aching for a signal from Brian to tell her he was still there. *I think Sundays feel kind of homesick everywhere.* She found a version of herself falling in love and finding Brian again that didn't belong only to her, but to her daughters now. But they'd stolen this look at a past Margot that she hadn't chosen to share with them.

Her real estate agent in Galesta called, but she didn't pick up. The *READ NOW–SECOND* subject line stared back at her, but her heart was beating too fast; she paced around the bed, guessing what could possibly be in there. Some slideshow of family pictures they'd unearthed? One of those online DNA test kits that said Margot had some gene mutation about to take her down too? It could be anything.

She went to the bathroom and gulped a glass of tap water. JoAnn had refilled the organic, sandalwood-scented shampoos and stacked fresh logo-embroidered towels, had wiped everything down while Margot was gone. It was hard work, making things nice for people.

Margot opened the second email. At the top of this one, Evy had written:

> *It was just these two—all the other moms were real, I think. I'm sorry. But also you're in the middle of a 500-mile-away lie, you're reading a bunch of posts you already read and cared about when you thought they were from strangers. But we're still right here, right where we were when we wrote them to begin with. So can we stay here? In Seaside?*

Evy had cut and pasted all Margot's most recent exchanges with the GBM Wives, highlighting the Scrabblemary45 and Pamplemousse7 posts. Margot felt the wave of recognition that came when you saw behind the set on a stage, all the wires and strings, the hatches in the floor, the flimsy plywood side of a whole neighborhood where for hours you'd really believed the characters lived.

She'd always felt uneasy with the performative way kids her daughters' age were required to live every moment online, and how comfortable they were with it. But THIS, waltzing in and masquerading as the most important friendships she'd had this year? It felt beyond uneasy, it felt—at first glance—manipulative and violating. Reading and scrolling again, pausing at the questions she should have known were not anonymous, she thought, God, they got so much in these invented women *right* that she hadn't even noticed the details that didn't add up. *If you ask, your daughters might be able to help you.*

She had never asked.

Yes, she'd given clichéd answers when they asked *what next,* and yes, she'd retreated. But she'd held it together, because she had to. She had protected them, provided for them, paid attention to them, and intentionally allowed them space to screw up and get their hearts broken and keep secrets from her, even though she would have preferred they stay home every night with a bowl of ice cream on the couch.

Maybe they would blame her, always see her best-she-could-do attempts at persevering as too weak or distant or cold. Maybe they would forgive her. Could they ever understand how hard she had tried?

She closed the curtains, making little shadows of all JoAnn's tchotchkes, and slid under the quilt. When she shut her eyes, she saw the hundreds of miles of asphalt between her and home, she saw the empty rooms of the house Brian had built her, she saw her girls in the glow of a screen, looking for her.

Margot called her Galesta real estate agent back. "They didn't accept your offer. They don't want to counter," the agent said, sounding unsurprised. No, Margot said, she didn't want to see any other houses tomorrow.

Margot knew better than to offer so far below the asking price. Her offer was a lowball, even though she had the money to pay more, now that a few of the Seaside bungalows would sell soon. She had needed to stand in that beautiful house, spend a night in this town, and say a not nearly big enough number to really understand why she couldn't move here.

So much for imagination, for escape, for *self-care*, as the Casserole Bitches would say. She had sabotaged the next chapter of the story she'd crafted this year all on her own, even before her girls had tried to.

She shoved her clothes into her suitcase and cleared away her toiletries from the bathroom counter. She hovered her finger over Evy's name on her phone, but paused. She needed to put miles of interstate distance between what the girls had sent her and whatever she said out loud to them next, or risk some stream-of-consciousness rant she could never take back.

Margot stripped the bed for JoAnn and folded the quilt on top of the bare mattress. She consolidated the bits of trash into one bag and tied it, rinsed out her water glass, opened the curtains, and set the room key on top of a doily.

She started the car and turned the radio volume all the way down. She texted the girls **We will stay in Seaside**, then turned on the app that would message them saying she was driving if they tried to write back. She pulled into the left lane and did ninety miles an hour, feeling her steering wheel shake in her hands, feeling the surge of all that reckless speed press her seat belt against her chest, moisten her palms with sweat when she came up on another car's tail. She wove around semis and took the curves too fast. Even through the surge of adrenaline, the same numb aura that she'd felt after every too-much moment this year descended. It offered protection from pain, but narrowed the spectrum of what she could feel at all. She didn't know if it would ever lift.

She eased down to seventy-five and then dialed Brian's number the second she finally had two bars of cell service. His voice said, "Hey, you've reached Brian at E&E, leave a message!"

That voice had changed this year, taken on a more clipped, impatient tone; that voice had become hollow and exaggerated, become a voice she dreaded. She almost hung up after his familiar, easy *hey*, but she held on for the beep, then barely got out a few raw-throated words to him, to no one, shouting over the highway noise, "Help me, just—HELP me," before she hung up and went into a long dark tunnel through a mountain.

When she emerged, she noticed a billboard for the Mountainair Lodge, a Poconos resort they'd been to one fall weekend when the girls were little. She also noticed she was nearly out of gas. She pulled off at a rest stop, where there was a display of brochures for the Mountainair Lodge again, collages of grinning children tubing on a river. She had four missed calls from Evy and Liz, and her email inbox was full of questions from Deborah Ellsworth about selling the Seaside houses.

It had been Brian's idea to go to the Poconos that fall weekend, when rates were discounted; it was one of the only times they were the tourists, gorging on breakfast buffet waffles, buying whatever gift shop junk they wanted, calling housekeeping for extra towels and tiny shampoos, signing up for an afternoon kayak rental. At the time, they were still in the last stages of rebuilding their properties from Sandy, and it was the perfect escape.

A rest-stop Starbucks made her more jittery than alert; four hours from now seemed too soon to be driving back over that bridge to Seaside. The Mountainair Lodge was twenty minutes away. There were hours of daylight still left.

She called and made a reservation, a little unnerved at how her voice could sound so professional and friendly with the woman at the front desk. Then she sent a few texts and arranged for Uncle Pete to bring the girls to meet her. Finally, Margot texted the girls: **We need to go somewhere else for a few days. There is so much more to say.**

Chapter Twenty-Four

Evy

Uncle Pete dropped them off in the Poconos, stopping to get a soda in the resort lobby and give Margot a hug. Then he waved good-bye, heading back to Philadelphia to catch a flight. Margot was wearing a Galesta Real Estate visor, a tie-dyed Mountainair Lodge T-shirt, a lanyard and key card around her neck, and a neon wristband to prove she was allowed to use the waterslide if she wanted to. If she was trying to dress like enough of a dork to make Evy briefly forget everything she'd said to the GBM Wives and not to them, it was working, a little.

"They gave you a visor, even though you didn't buy a house?" Evy asked. Uncle Pete had offered a confused, short version of what Margot had told him about Galesta and getting them here.

"I got you some to match," Margot said, handing the girls their own visors, sliding them onto their foreheads and fixing their hair underneath them.

There is so much more to say. Yeah, there was. Neon visors and a cheap run-down resort weren't gonna make Evy forget what it felt like when Margot lied to their faces and faded instead of facing them with all the real talk she saved for internet strangers.

Margot's **We will stay in Seaside** was so fresh, Evy didn't trust it. What if she turned right back around after a few days here and went back to Galesta? Evy was trying to be less impulsive after the vodka-apple-murder-scene thing, after Olivia and her had talked about *mindfulness*; as long as they were staying in Seaside, she was willing to try waiting, a few hours or a month, or until whenever she could talk to her mom without swearing at her, which she knew would not be *mindful.*

Anyway, there Margot was in that dumb shirt like, when in Rome, a.k.a. the Mountainair Lodge. There were ways to say *I'm sorry* with a gesture and a silly gift, there were ways to say you were not ready, there were ways to ask someone for space without ever saying it outright, but, Jesus, that shirt was saying it all LOUD.

Liz

Liz and Evy wore their visors for all forty selfies they took in their room. They rolled around on the yellow plaid bedspreads, pulled the green curtains around themselves like dresses, and posed in front of the duck oil paintings making duck faces, being silly and fake-serious and making Margot laugh with her reading glasses perched on her nose. They edited in some sparkles and unicorn horns to their selfies and texted them to each other.

It was as if Margot had pulled the emergency brake by bringing them all here. Soon they would have it out, over and over, flinging all their hurt at each other, hurling sharp fragments at each other: *you never—you have no idea—I needed—I just wanted.*

The fault lines had formed. There would be rifts and small tremors forever. But there would be quiet, still stretches in between. The relief was still only a few hours old.

Liz could have stood in the middle of their nonsmoking, patio-view room and insisted on here and now to have it out, to holler, *Hey, you left us, you lied to us, oh you were sad? So what, so were we, and we were alone.* But it felt so much better to give in to the inertia of this in-between. She'd missed having fun with her mom so much she could cry in this ugly room if she thought about it too much.

They didn't post the photos they took; it was no one's business to judge which stage of grief this tacky seventies-tastic resort was. The Mountainair Lodge was none of them. They didn't have to bargain with or accept or deny anything until noon checkout two days from now at the earliest.

"Where are the heart Jacuzzis they showed on the billboard?" Liz asked. The last time they'd been here, she was eleven, still young enough to make friends by swimming up to them at the pool and saying, "Hi, my name is Lizzie, what's yours?" Eleven was the in-between age when you were old enough to ask if you could try shrimp cocktail off the grown-up menu in the restaurant for the first time, but could still order a kids' hot fudge sundae with sprinkles for dessert. On that trip, Evy ate only chicken nuggets and played mermaids in the pool, hovering longer than Liz had in that space where you could still play imagination games.

"I saw online they have a room with a ten-foot-tall champagne flute bubble bath, maybe they can switch us to one of those," Evy said. She and Liz took one more photo, in the yellow-tiled bathroom with the scary-looking heating coils on the wall.

"Oh god, do you girls remember they put us in one of those heart-Jacuzzi rooms on that trip here when you two were little, because the family side of the resort was full?" Margot said. "There were mirrors everywhere, Evy, you were always making faces in them."

Evy called the front desk, but there were no champagne flute rooms available. She spent the rest of the trip guessing which other guests were staying in them, whispering, "Champagne people," at the exact moment to make Liz giggle as they passed couples holding hands in the lobby.

The Mountainair Lodge was surrounded by jutting rocks and skittering little forest animals they didn't have in Seaside; it was nice to wade into the cold lake water and to be out of breath while your body adjusted to the elevation.

The activities kiosk offered horseback rides, a zip line, and a rafting trip. Her dad would have signed them up for all three. Margot held her pen above the zip line sign-up, ready to make a reservation for the next day's session, then flipped to the next page of evening indoor activities instead.

They took third place in the trivia night and won more gift shop swag, then played gin rummy on their patio. They turned on their fake fireplace and tuned in the only available radio station, all eighties power ballads. The sun set through the trees. They ate vending machine goldfish crackers, and Evy said, "Remember when we were here before, and Dad and me got that broken pedal boat that only went around in circles?"

Liz picked up where she left off: "Remember when he got hypnotized onstage?" Evy scooped up all the cards because she'd won that round.

Margot shuffled the cards and said, "Liz, you were so scared to go off the diving board, and then all of a sudden we couldn't get you to *stop* diving. Evy, do you remember how Dad convinced you the little door in the hotel hallway was connected to an elf world?"

Before diving into the pool alone, Liz had watched twenty kids angle their bodies so they sliced the water's surface instead of slapping it; she'd timed herself holding her breath underwater in the shallow end, so she knew she could do it in the deep end. There was nothing sudden about how she got brave.

Evy

The second day, Liz went for a hike on her own while Evy and Margot found a secondhand store in town. Evy tried on a dress and opened the fitting room curtain to see what Margot thought of it.

"Reminds me of that one Olivia wore, when she was over the other day," Margot said, letting silence settle in for several seconds, a trick Evy had noticed she used when she had something important she wanted to talk about, though she hadn't used it much in the last year. Ms. Thrall had used the same trick, when no one answered a hard question about the reading right away.

"I need help with this zipper," Evy said, and turned her back toward Margot so she could pull it down. Margot held her hands on Evy's shoulders, both of them facing the fitting room mirror. She had some new Mountainair Lodge gift shop sunglasses perched on top of her head, and Evy was barefoot in this flowery old dress.

"I like Olivia," Margot said. "I think she's mature and smart, and—I think she gets you, Ev." Evy remembered her and Olivia's hands, knitted together, holding on. Margot held her hands on Evy's shoulders for a while longer before she let the fitting room curtain fall closed so Evy could try on the other clothes. "Which probably means you'll stop dating her and find someone I hate," Margot said.

It bothered her how closely her mom was paying attention to Olivia because there was so much her mom hadn't noticed about Evy this year. Margot still had no idea Evy had driven past semis on the Jersey

Turnpike going seventy-five, or that she could say, "Ten dollars, regular," to the guy pumping gas like she'd been doing it forever.

Evy, alone in the fitting room, let the dress fall to the floor. Also, *dating?* Margot might as well say *going steady*, or, in a British accent, *Mr. Farnsworth shall accompany you to the ball in his carriage*, it sounded so old-fashioned and formal.

"At least, that's what I did when I was your age," Margot went on, "before I met your dad—well, you kind of know more about that part now, huh?"

Evy pulled the next outfit off the hangers, a pair of dark high-waisted jeans and a silky purple top. She slid her feet into some platform heels and added a rhinestone necklace. She stood up straighter and popped her hip to pose in the mirror before she opened the curtain. She loved how this outfit felt casual and glam at the same time, how the cut of the jeans and the heels made her legs look super long.

"I like this look," Evy said, then opened the curtain to show Margot and do a little spin. Margot folded her arms across her chest, considering.

"It looks great, but you have to hand-wash that top, not throw it in with all your other clothes," she said. How did she not see that the right thing to say when someone spins around in an outfit like that is, *Get it!*

Back in the front of the store, Evy picked out old postcards from a five-for-a-dollar bin, of places she'd never been. Strangers had scribbled notes on the back: *Wish you were here*.

Olivia had sent Evy a new playlist of ten songs for the trip, bands who sang and stomped and hollered about love, whose lyrics were so loaded but turned suddenly bright. She memorized them all and hummed the bridges while she walked alone through the woods.

They all went down to the hot tub, where the smoke from the fire pit drifted over them and hung in the damp air. They stayed in until their skin was pink and wrinkled, and wore their hair up in wet buns for dinner. The music in the lounge that night was a piano player doing all Billy Joel cover songs they sang along with. Evy won three straight games of gin rummy before they went to sleep, before they woke up early to drive back down the mountain, feeling their ears pop as they descended.

When they got back home, Margot posted again in the GBM Wives forum:

It's so silly, the things I'm proud of from the last few days, but here goes: I spent an afternoon alone and made conversation with the bartender, and I read three chapters of a new novel without losing my place. I talked to my daughter about something important without interrupting it myself, in all the ways I do that sometimes.

I didn't bring up anything I said here with them. I'll try, soon. It's hard to know where to start, but I know where doesn't matter as much as the starting.

For a little stretch of interstate, when the girls played Taylor Swift songs and we were freshly caffeinated, and we had just passed some semis and had the next miles of road to ourselves, I was very nearly happy. It was still a wanting what I couldn't have happy, a happy competing with the same nasty, nagging voices that never leave. It came and went, but I held on to it for a few miles at least. It's not a kind of happiness I know very well yet. It's a heavy happiness.

But I'm not going to turn it away.

I think that trip might be my first new, good memory since Brian died: the girls jumping into a volleyball game, all of us at this silly trivia night, the clear sky and stars.

Evy responded for the last time as Scrabblemary45, for the first time knowing she had nothing to hide:

It was a really great idea to take that trip. Did you know there is also a town called Seaside a short drive from Seattle? A lot of Seattle people seem to love it. That's a funny coincidence.

Anyway, you wouldn't think just a few days away would be any big deal, but it can really help, I think. It's ok you needed to go to that terrible faraway town to figure some things out, since you didn't stay there.

I'm sure the girls are relieved, but don't do anything crazy if they're not themselves for a while. It will take a long time.

The things you said you were proud of aren't silly at all. They're really important. I'm glad you felt happy, even if it was a kind of happiness you're not used to.

Chapter Twenty-Five

Liz

Liz followed along behind Gabe and his friends on the boardwalk, breathing through her mouth so she wouldn't have to smell their cigarette smoke. They talked about Brooklyn nonstop, naming band after band and bar after bar she didn't know, leaving her out of the conversation or talking over her when she tried to join in. He'd been up there for a few days, and they'd come back here with him.

They made fun of a family in matching Old Navy flag shirts ordering cheesesteaks, and of the cover band playing Journey songs at Spicy's. They didn't converse with each other so much as they declared things and made statements about what they individually knew or liked and what other people were stupid for liking.

Liz thought it was especially annoying that even though they seemed really into knowing about the most obscure music, they all dressed alike, in dirty thin black T-shirts and jeans even though it was ninety degrees and they must have been sweating.

She kept waiting for her Gabe to show up, the Gabe who had surfed with her all day, kissed her neck, and taken her to see her favorite band, the Gabe who had walked her home and who loved this town.

But that guy who had been looking at her like she was brave and cool, that guy who'd smiled back at her in the photo booth like he might love her was nowhere to be found, no matter how much she stared at him and willed him to wake up in there.

Gabe hadn't seemed like himself since he'd gone up to the city for those few days. He'd drunk-dialed her from outside some bar in Brooklyn and said something about how his brother had taught him how to play the guitar chords to "Everlong," before he hung up.

Since returning to Seaside from Brooklyn, he'd been talking constantly about his band and where they were going to play in the fall, and his and Liz's only other time together at his aunt's rental house was different too.

Gabe's friends were one-uppers: everyone seemed to need to know about some out-there music festival, some new food truck, some mutual acquaintance who was on the edge of making it big with their coffee roasting business or their app. As the night went on, Gabe picked up their rhythm and threw his own thoughts out there, dismissing some things and insisting on others she had never thought he cared about at all.

Liz was bored, but she stayed because she wanted to see exactly how long he could play this part, and because she had nowhere else to be. When Liz told the group they'd been to see The Machine Is Red, two of the guys rolled their eyes and said they were okay five years ago, and Gabe said nothing. Over pizza, they called Seaside *trash* more than once. They laughed about it, as if they had license to say that because their buddy was from a town five miles away and had invited them here.

It wasn't the first time Liz had heard people say that, and she knew why. Sometimes 4 a.m. brawls spilled from the clubs on the Boulevard onto the street. In the winter, the motels cut their rates and filled with people who needed a cheap place to stay, instead of partiers. People on the Seaside Heights boardwalk didn't wear expensive tiny-whale-patterned shorts and two-hundred-dollar swimsuits like they did in the fancier beach towns.

I mean, who would ever come here?

For a second, she saw her town the way they must see it, the way a lot of people who didn't love it must see it. If the guys had seemed fancy or wealthy and usually only hung out in villas or on yachts, she could have understood their disdain. But they were the kinds of people who could just as easily have thought Seaside was cool, the way they arbitrarily decided certain cheap beers were now cool.

She waited for Gabe to get his head out of his ass, for him to look those guys in the eyes and say, *Hey, you just have to get to know it. Hey, it's not like that. Hey, you know Liz is from here.*

But she got impatient. She couldn't wait around all night.

"So where are *you* guys from?" Liz asked, interrupting one of them for the first time. They looked at her as if they had just then noticed she was there. "Like, I know you live in *Brooklyn* now, but, you know, originally?"

They named three towns, two she'd heard of, one she hadn't.

"Oh, cool," she said, standing up and pushing her chair away. "I gotta go."

When Gabe didn't show up for work the next day, she typed a text: **You were kind of a jerk last night**, and deleted it. She typed: **Your friends are assholes**, deleted it, **It's not cool to ignore someone when you bring them to meet your friends**, deleted that too, and got back to work, feeling like he'd made her into a sucker, like she was no wiser about what was real and who she should trust than the people who put their money down at those boardwalk games for a dollar and hoped for the best, only to watch it be swept into a hole.

At work, she checked her phone constantly, feeling the phantom buzz in her hand, waiting. She wanted him to send a text promising he wouldn't ruin everything now, that he'd keep showing up, that they could go to another concert and get pulled into the crowd, that they could stay out another night or two and joke about what jerks his friends were.

That text never came, and Gabe never showed up at work. He was hungover in his borrowed house in Seaside, or he had left town already. He wasn't thinking about her as much as she was thinking about him. He cared so little for his job that he would leave his last paycheck without even bothering to pick it up.

He wanted to leave this little trash town and the silly girl he'd met here and hung out with a few times and go to Molly-fueled all-night warehouse raves or hook up with women who lived in tiny apartments with bars on the windows.

She had asked too much of him. She'd made up the rules to suit her and assumed he was playing along to the same ones. She shouldn't have let him walk her home, or take her to that show.

She should have known better: he was as-advertised, one of a million exact factory models she'd thought for a minute had been custom-made for her, and she'd convinced herself he was different, special, and better. She should have understood there was no such thing. She should have understood how people would always change into unrecognizable versions of themselves right in front of you.

She walked herself home from work, stripped off her Sun and

Shade uniform, and dug through her drawers to find what she knew she needed now.

She laced up her running shoes, put on her headphones, and queued up her favorite album by The Machine Is Red. She let the screen door slam behind her, and for the first time in months, she started to run. She felt her phone finally buzz with a text from Gabe and stopped to read it. Then she kept going.

She ran up her street and across Central Avenue to the quiet miles of boardwalk in Seaside Park. She dodged the people leaving the beach late, then opened up her stride in an empty stretch, settling into the comforting rhythm of breath and rubber on wood as the wind shifted, a salt-cool balm she breathed in.

Her body felt unfamiliar at first, heavier and stiffer, but also uncomfortable in her old running clothes, filling out the shorts more so they rode up. She was tired even one mile in, though she felt other muscles carrying her that hadn't before: her back and shoulders, her arms, driving forward and back when her legs fatigued.

The beauty of the familiar route let her forget a lot. She could have closed her eyes and still seen the green gazebos, the mounds of dune grass, the Victorian where the renters were out on the porch with their gin and tonics. But her eyes were open, seeing it all with a grateful ease. This route was a remedy, a solution, an infusion of faith. The act of pounding her feet along the boards was a defiant meditation and a refusal to be ignored or hurt.

After a mile, her body remembered and relaxed. She sweated out some toxic mix of salt and accumulated heat that left her skin slick and her shirt damp. Her legs found a more fluid turnover, her hips opened up, her lungs let in an extra measure of breath. She didn't look at how fast she was going, and she didn't care. At the end of the boardwalk, she kept going, down the ramp and toward the state park, that long, empty stretch of road that went all the way to the inlet.

This fall she would finish midpack in some cross-country races, then spend the winter working through paced quarters, bleacher sprints, and hill workouts, relearning to run every one of the eight straightaways and curves of the 1600 smart and strong. Then in the spring she would hit her negative splits, flying past her rivals, breaking the school record, and placing in the state meet.

She would accept the small statue they gave her of a golden-winged foot, engraved with her name, and set it on a shelf between her dried-up school dance corsages and her yearbooks. She would run even faster for a few years, then slower; she would bring her running shoes with her everywhere, exploring the perimeters of so many new towns and cities.

It was almost dark by the time Liz emerged from the state park and turned toward the bay for the final stretch toward home, sore and thirsty. She paused her music and listened to the rubber of her running shoes on asphalt, and to her heart, for the last mile. She walked the last block and read her messages from Gabe again, one long block of text at a time.

He was not an oblivious idiot; he knew he'd been a dick to her, and he knew his friends were the worst. But he was already back in Brooklyn, or said that's where he was. And while he devoted three texts to guessing correctly what had made her mad, he stopped short of a simple apology and blamed her for leaving, for making a big deal out of nothing.

She knew she hadn't done anything wrong, and that it wasn't her job to try to convince him of that. Let the next girl do that, the next girl like her he would find in a crowded room, drinking bitter gin and lemonade from a plastic cup, or at the next job where some other girl was his boss and better at making lattes or waiting tables than him.

She hit DELETE everywhere she had his name stored and BLOCK anywhere he might find her, before she lost her nerve.

CHAPTER TWENTY-SIX

Margot

Margot dragged her big rubber mallet out and centered the FOR SALE sign in the front yard, pounded it down so it was straight and even, and stood there as the hush descended on her town. It was Labor Day, and she had listed almost all the other E&E houses now and had new offers on several. Deborah Ellsworth had not involved Margot in one discussion of leaky faucets or unwanted refrigerators.

The ends of other seasons in Seaside are gradual, uncertain transitions. Fall gives way to winter with the slow graying of the sky and the sharpening of the wind off the ocean. Winter ends and spring begins with sheets of rain blowing in a brown wall across the bay and weeks of stubborn cold refusing to let go. Summer begins slowly, one ninety-degree day at a time, one still-freezing dive into the breakers at a time, one sunburn at a time, as the weekend crowds swell through Fourth of July.

But summer's end is sudden. By late afternoon on Labor Day, there is a consuming quiet, an overwhelming feeling of having stayed a few minutes too long at a party, a certainty that there are more serious things happening elsewhere, like a shift from carnival music to a song in a minor key.

She could not live anymore in the house her husband had built to cure her homesickness. She could not stay in this house he'd transformed from its rotting, abandoned state into something beautiful so she would notice, the way Gatsby had tried to do for Daisy. She could not stay in this house where he'd died, not from a bullet to the brain but from something rogue and sick inside it.

She walked a few blocks to the Victorian. The last renters had left early, and she took her time changing the sheets and wiping their fingerprints off all the surfaces, bleaching the bathtubs and running the towels through the laundry.

She would bring the girls here tonight to sleep. She would take a guest bedroom for herself and leave the fancy suite for the girls to spread out in; they had been sleeping in the same room every night like they did when they were little. She would use her suitcase as a dresser and keep the FOR SALE sign propped against the side of the house for when she needed it again. Liz would leave for college next fall, and Evy in two years, and they would stay here in the Victorian at least until then. She would hand over the box of Brian's things she'd collected for them, before she donated or stored the rest: his soft, faded concert tour and 5K T-shirts, his stack of highlighted AP Economics teaching notes, a few of the Post-its she'd found when she was packing up, two small E&E signs she'd framed for them.

Until her girls left Seaside, she would face east toward the ocean as the sun set across the bay three blocks west. She would sip a single gin and tonic instead of red wine on that big front porch, and when her girls came home each day they would push open the big, heavy front door with its beveled glass instead of their old screen door.

Evy

"You did a good job with this one," Olivia said. Evy held up her hand to show her how she'd rewrapped it in a fresh, neon-pink bandage. The stitches underneath kept opening up; the gash was still scabbing and healing, but slowly.

Evy and Olivia stopped at Sal's, where Irene gave them some gummy bears that had melted and reformed that she couldn't sell. She was smoking inside the store now and said she was heading to Florida after Labor Day to stay with Kenny. He'd paid her back the money he owed and had a boat now.

They stopped to say hi to Cameron, who was wading around wrangling the bumper boats, and got free fries at the hot dog stand from Cameron's older brother, but he was out of ketchup. By Labor Day, everywhere on the boardwalk was out of something. All the businesses would stay open through the warm September weekends while the owners tried to serve whatever they had left in the freezers.

"When should I take it off?" Evy asked, holding up her bandaged hand. They walked down to the beach to sit on the sand and passed the gummies back and forth.

"Let me see," Olivia said. She traced the skin on Evy's wrist and pressed down gently to see if it hurt. Evy stole a look as Olivia concentrated. She felt a tightening between her hips and a little catch in her throat as Olivia let up on the pressure.

"I think it will be okay soon," Evy said. Olivia's breath smelled like candy when she kissed her.

The weeks between Labor Day and the beginning of October are a best-kept secret: warm and calm, bright and empty. Evy loved to spend long afternoons alone on the beach, to fall asleep with the windows open to the silent island. The constant salted wind would bring the fall, but not quite yet.

Liz

Labor Day was Liz's last day at Sun and Shade. She took a good long look at the cloudless sky and the choppy ocean, and that something-missing feeling descended, familiar and right on schedule like every year. By four, she wrapped herself in a sweatshirt and towel, and by five the beach was deserted and the wind had switched again and the late-summer sun goldened every shadow.

There was plenty of time between customers to finish her AP Lit summer reading, *1984*. The farther she got into that book, the more it seemed like a cruel joke to assign it to rising seniors to read on their own. Shouldn't the adults be checking in, assuring them dystopia was all hyperbole and it would never *really* happen that way? She forged ahead, speed-reading through the darkest scenes and making notes in the margins.

When Liz closed the lock at her Sun and Shade stand for the last time, Carl shook her hand and gave her a paycheck with a few extra bills for staying the whole season, and then she was alone.

Her dad had always celebrated Labor Day with a full-throated yelp and a dive into the ocean exactly five minutes after the lifeguards left the beach: his personal ritual to mark the start of locals' summer.

Liz's version of her dad's tradition started with a selfie and #localssummer post instead of a yelp, before she dove into the warm ocean. She sank down and held her breath, feeling the slight undertow pull her away from the shore, giving in to it without panic. She knew better: fighting that invisible force was a good way to drown.

Her #localssummer post was public, and when she got out, she already had forty likes and three comments, including one from Gabe's band account. She'd blocked his personal accounts but had forgotten about the band ones. She scrolled through their recent posts: pictures of them onstage in an anonymous dark bar and some blurry action shots of them packing up a van. The recent photos answered the question of *what* Gabe was doing now, and his camera-grin showed *how* he appeared to be doing: fine.

The *like* showed he was still looking for her, circumventing the barriers she'd put up, and maybe he still wanted her, or at least wanted her to know he was looking for her, thinking about her enough to like a picture of what she was doing two minutes after she'd posted it. She could return the interest, *like* his last band selfie post back. Or she could ignore him.

She wanted for a minute to forget the way Gabe had disappointed her, to indulge in the idea of escaping beyond the boardwalk and imagine meeting him, forgiving him, visiting him in Brooklyn. Part of her wanted to pick up where they'd left off, before she had glared at him with the hope that he would say the right, honest thing, before he'd made a string of text-bubble excuses she'd read wishing they said something else.

She could ask about the band, or tell him how slow Sun and Shade had been that day and how much Carl had given her for a bonus. She could figure out a way to call him out on his sudden exit but leave the door open for him to say he hadn't meant it to go that way.

But she listened to the voice that protected her from giving in to impulse and from wanting attention, the voice that said no to the instant rush that talking to him would deliver. That voice had become stronger as the summer waned, as she logged a few more miles alone before she showed up stiff and sore for the first summer cross-country practice, as she wrote her notes in the margins of *1984*, and as she spent time with her mom and sister.

What did it say about Gabe that he would try to find her after she'd made it difficult to be found, and why did he feel like he deserved to *like* anything about her life and the pictures she took as she lived it?

If it had been any other day, she was almost sure she would have responded in some way to Gabe's little overture, believed that his interest and pursuit and wanting, again, was enough.

But on Labor Day, everything is stripped down. On Labor Day, it's easier to be honest. She set her phone down and dove back into the ocean, sinking below a small wave and staying underwater as long as she could, until her chest burned. When she rubbed the salt out of her eyes, the lights on the pier were already on, as they would be for the next few weekends until they all went dark for winter.

Liz walked home listening to her dad's favorite sad songs about nightswimming and closing time, noticing each house where the E&E Rental sign had been pulled up out of the ground, replaced by Deborah Ellsworth's face and FOR SALE or SOLD underneath.

She would shower off the salt and sweat from today, and she would drink the last of the cold, bitter, sun-brewed iced tea before Margot poured it down the drain. She would go back to school with her skin still tan. She would remember this as a summer of unnameable sadness, but also as a summer she was proud to have moved through with a nascent, uncertain wisdom she felt swelling inside her.

Gabe had given her both a new model of confidence and a reason to remain cautious the next time, and the next time. She wondered what would have happened, if they had not both waited so long to tell each other what they had lost.

She would be grateful for Gabe as a distraction, but embarrassed by how much she'd ceded control, believed he was special. She would remember how the nights with him recharged her and gave her permission to take risks and find joy, and how that had been exactly what she needed. She would feel other pulls toward people who tasted like bitter gin, who texted her **hey**, who wouldn't disappoint her. She would be able to sleep again, soon, without the mind-racing that kept her up sometimes now until dawn, without the hours of sick, lonely wakefulness that refused to recede.

The end of summer would always be a charged, on-the-verge-of-something time of year, no matter where she was when it happened. The earlier, blazing-red September sunsets, the perfect late-summer tomato with salt, the stores full of fresh notebooks would always signal a change she was never quite ready for, a time to ask for more of what she needed and get rid of what she'd outgrown.

Brian

E&E, I tried to write your names but the rest of the letters got lost, turned to strange scribbles. So I tried again, and again. *Embark, empathy, emissary.*

When you find more notes, inside boxes and books, fold them into your palms, slip them into your pockets. *Empower, embrace, empire.* They're evidence of trying.

One day you'll meet people who are as bored as you are by the inconsiderate in-crowd at some party, people who will tell you where they're from and ask you the same question. You'll know more about what broke their hearts and what brought them there after one drink than you know about most people after years and years.

You'll say to them that you were once from an old-fashioned carnival, a town near the inlet where you could hear the roller coasters rattling, where the ocean tempered the air all year round.

You will always be from every beach destination from Santa Cruz to Nantucket, and you'll recognize the hustlers in every tourist town.

You were from the love stories we told you, the ones you found, and the ones you'll never know, the one-sided thoughtlessness and the unresolved secrets.

You won't be from anywhere right after your mother leaves Seaside, though you'll each live on separate campuses somewhere between your old town and her new one, in a ten-by-twelve room with other girls who have never heard of your hometown. For four years, you will move in small radii, crisscrossing green quads, drinking beer from plastic cups, working campus jobs scrubbing cafeteria trays or shelving library books, arguing about how the world should be on the cold stone steps of hundred-year-old buildings. For those four years, you will feel alternating ease and hesitance with who you let come close to you.

Your mother will be from a new place: a landlocked town where farmland expands beyond its borders, deep green then brown and desolate when November descends. You'll never stay there longer than a few days at a time. You will have dinner on a Main Street with her and the new man who loves her, where they will spend the meal discussing house repairs and what to order for dessert. The man won't remind you to change the oil before you back out of their driveway and head east again together; you'll remember that on your own.

Then you will be from your own homesick exchanges with the people who first broke your hearts. You will be from the early morning light in a hotel room.

You will be from your sister's hand in yours during the aisle-walking and first-dancing at weddings. You will feel at home the second you see each other's faces in the crowd in more airports than you can count.

Where you are from is everything: an empire and an ending, a temporary joy and a permanent resilience. Where you were from doesn't exist anymore, and you'll wonder forever if it ever really did.

ACKNOWLEDGMENTS

Thank you to my incredible agent Elisabeth Weed, a better ally, advocate, and editor than I could ever in my wildest dreams have hoped for; to Hallie Schaeffer, DJ Kim, and everyone at The Book Group. And many thanks to my editor, Kara Watson, for your understanding and love for this family and for Seaside, for your insightful edits, intuition, and enthusiasm. I am so grateful I got to work on this book, this year, with both of you.

To the team at Scribner and Simon & Schuster: Emily Polson, Nan Graham, Joal Hetherington, Laura Wise, Jaya Miceli, Leora Bernstein, Roz Lippel, Paula Amendolara, Denise Domeck, and Wendy Sheanin. Your weekend and train-ride and nighttime hours reading and for making a space for this story are so appreciated. Thank you to Stuart Smith, Annie Craig, Elizabeth Hubbard, Tristan Offit, and Wendy Blum. Many thanks to Clare Maurer and Ashley Gilliam.

For their generous, kind, early support of this book, I am so grateful to Lydia Kiesling, Rachel Beanland, and Claire Lombardo. Thank you to Jenny Meyer and to Michelle Weiner.

Thank you to Rufi Thorpe and Catapult for the course "The Novel: Chapter 1," and to the talented group of writers I met in that class: Andrea Arnold, Meg Duell, Norah Brzyski, and Veronica Gorodetskaya. Megan Angelo, thank you for being such an open-hearted guide.

Acknowledgments

I'm grateful to the faculty and staff at the Warren Wilson MFA Program for Writers, especially Dean Bakopoulos, Liam Callanan, David Haynes, Adria Bernardi, CJ Hribal, and Alix Ohlin. Thank you to Ellen Bryant Voigt, Deb Allbery, Alissa Whelan, and Amy Grimm. What a gift to spend time in such a rigorous but unpretentious place, what perfect training for writing long after you've earned your walking stick.

Thank you to Michelle Collins Anderson, Elisabeth Hamilton, and Virginia Borges, for your honesty, encouragement, and community, from the North Carolina mountains to faraway-city friendships.

This book wouldn't exist without the Tin House Summer Workshop, especially Claire Vaye Watkins who gave us permission to get the lay of the land, or without the talented and tough writers I met there: Caro Fautsch, Alexa Dodd, Caitlin Palmer, Anna Held, and Isle McElroy.

I hope for every writer to find a group as thoughtful, kind, and encouraging as Nicole VanderLinden, Corey Campbell, and Gloria Carver. Thank you to everyone at the Iowa Summer Writing Festival; there is no more welcoming, generative, and inspiring place for a new writer.

Thank you to Jami Attenberg, for creating the #1000wordsofsummer community, where I found friends, inspiration, and accountability to push me over the finish line, and to the Coralville, Iowa City, and New York Public libraries for being the best places to work and eavesdrop. Thank you to Prairie Lights and Sidekick Coffee and Books, the best local indies.

Many thanks to Natalie Cannon for your nuanced edits, and to Rachel Mans McKenny, Liv Stratman, and Rachel Yoder, for reaching out to offer support in such a strange time. I'm grateful to John Runde, Sheila Flynn, Emily Bonneau, Kristin Cordova, and Alexis Gutierrez for your early reads, feedback, and friendship. Thank you

Acknowledgments

to Katie Rossmann, Stephanie Radke, Kat Durst, Sarah Sperling, Meg Willett, Jenny Czwornog, Michelle Davenport, Joe Runde, Victoria Ronan, and Adrienne Wasserman, for sharing your wins and worries and listening to mine.

Thank you to the Cooney and Sweeney families, for trusting me to traipse around New York City with your kids, and to Mary Wilcynski, Kara Asmussen, and Tracy-Lyn Habig for giving me the chance to teach the coolest kids in Iowa and California.

I'm grateful to Kathleen Mueller and Janet Pitman, my Ms. Thralls, and to Megan McCafferty for the Jersey inspiration.

Thank you to Kim Magowan, Aaron Burch, and Alyssa Songsiridej for publishing stories that grew into my favorite chapters, and to the whole online lit-mag community for your risk-taking and eye for the weird, boundary-breaking, fun stuff.

Geoff and Liz Ball, thank you for showing me the best version of young love at a boardwalk job, and many thanks to the staff at Marty's Doghouse, especially Patrick Smith and Michael Carr.

Thank you to the dedicated team at Penn Medicine for the incredible care they took of my dad from 2001 to 2004 during his own battle with a glioblastoma multiforme tumor, and to their families. So many characters have tiny parts in this book, but so many people played huge roles in caring for my dad, especially the Carr, Gavin, Walsh, Fisher, and Westhoven families. Joan Cavanaugh is so missed and loved.

For sharing your stories, thank you to the people who know the loss-before-loss of a GBM: Tracy Milcendeau, Emilie Fowlkes, and the Fitzgibbon family. And to anyone who has been through this particular, heartbreaking kind of loss. You were on my mind writing every page.

I'm so grateful for all the teachers at Preucil Preschool and the Iowa City Public Schools who cared for and taught my children, in person and online, through the constant pivots of pandemic teaching. You are incredible. Thank you to Ruth and Kathleen Runde, for giving my girls all your love and giving me time to finish one more chapter.

To Tricia Martin, my best friend, first reader, and sharer of imagination and the unimaginable. To my mom, for navigating both the magic and the tragic with resilience, strength, humor, and love.

Thank you to Dan Runde, whose college emails are lost in the internet ether somewhere, but they must have been good. May every writer's partner say, "You have to do it," as fast and with as much certainty as you. Thank you for your extroverted confidence, and for your all-in-early kind of love I'm grateful for every day. And to Jane and Alice, thank you for your questions, your curiosity, and your chaos-muse-energy, and for being brave and patient (most of the time) through such a hard time for the whole world.

Thank you, and a whoosh wherever you are, to anyone who ever loved Marty.

BOOK
CLUB
FAVORITES

READER'S
GUIDE

THE
SHORE

Katie Runde

This reading group guide for The Shore includes an introduction, discussion questions, and ideas for enhancing your book club. The suggested questions are intended to help your reading group find new and interesting angles and topics for your discussion. We hope that these ideas will enrich your conversation and increase your enjoyment of the book.

INTRODUCTION

Meet the Dunne family, year-round residents of Seaside, New Jersey, who run a vacation house rental business for the tourists that come and go every year. Between last summer and this one, Brian developed a brain tumor that has transformed him into a stranger to his wife, Margot, and their teen daughters, Liz and Evy. Each of the women fight to maintain a sense of normalcy as they adjust to new caretaking responsibilities and the anticipatory grief of a long good-bye. Liz seeks distraction in a flirtatious relationship with Gabe, a coworker at her boardwalk job who doesn't know her family's situation and is only in town for the summer. Evy secretly adopts the persona of a middle-aged mom in an online support group, where she learns some of her own mother's deepest secrets—all in between shifts at Sal's Sweets and falling in love with her best friend, Olivia. Meanwhile, Margot juggles running the family business, remembering when she first met Brian, and planning a new future for her and the girls somewhere far away from the hometown that shaped her.

A heartbreaking story infused with moments of spiky humor, *The Shore* explores first loves and family secrets, grief and growing up, and the ways we find comfort while coping with unimaginable loss.

TOPICS & QUESTIONS
FOR DISCUSSION

1. We meet the Dunnes after Brian's brain tumor has already changed him into a different person than the husband and father Margot, Liz, and Evy knew. How has his diagnosis also changed each of them? How do they deal with the uncertainty of not knowing when the end will come? What changes when Dr. Zimorodi tells them, with more certainty, "by the end of summer" (page 72)?

2. Discuss the use of social media in the novel—from Evy and Liz curating their Instagram profiles and checking up on their friends and crushes to Margot finding support in an online forum and going through Brian's old Facebook posts. How does social media function as an outlet for the characters? What positive and negative effects does it have?

3. What do you think of Evy's decision to invent a new identity on GBM Wives forum? Discuss her reaction to learning privileged information about her parents on the forum. How does this compare to Liz's reaction to stumbling upon Brian and Margot's college emails?

4. Writing as Pamplemousse7 about losing someone to a glioblastoma multiforme tumor, Evy asks the GBM wives: "It's worth it, isn't it, to buy a few more months even if he isn't himself, even if he can only see in tunnels and splotches? . . . If it's a person parading around who looks like your husband but who's acting like an agitated stranger you wouldn't want to sit next to on a bus? If it means taking care of a person who is not a person you know? Even then?" (page 14). How does each woman in the Dunne family deal with this existential question? What final moments with Brian lighten, if however briefly, the pain of losing him?

5. Discuss the relationship between Liz and Evy. While they each have their own lives—jobs, friends, romances, and ways of coping—how do they come together to support each other and their family over the course of the summer?

6. "Coexisting with a stranger was not possible without imagining escape" (pages 22 to 23), thinks Margot as she dreams about selling off E&E Rentals and starting fresh. Why do you think she is so eager to move away? What do you think of her choice to hide this decision from her daughters? Why do they feel differently about the prospect of leaving Seaside?

7. "Distraction is medicine," thinks Liz on page 48. Have you found this to be true? How does the girls' way of finding distraction and escape in Seaside differ from Margot's? What moments of humor and levity from the book help balance the heaviness of the plot?

8   As Evy and Liz chase after their own "firsts," they worry: "Is it okay if I do this even though we're in this shitty holding pattern?

Is it okay that this is all happening at the same time, am I a horrible person for wanting these things right now?" (page 175). What would you say to a friend or sibling in this situation?

9. "There were so many ways to break someone's heart and leave them when they needed you," muses Margot on page 139. Discuss previous betrayals in their marriage. Do you think that kind of "emotional affair" is "no better or worse" than a physical one (page 169)? How did they come to a place of forgiveness?

10. Why doesn't Liz tell Gabe about Brian's state? Discuss the rocky ending of their relationship. How do you think she'll remember him? How do you feel about your first love?

11. Discuss the idea of anticipatory grief—what the author describes as "loss-before-loss" (page 289). How do each of the Dunnes begin processing their grief while still caring for the person they will lose? What role does memory and nostalgia play in this process?

12. Part III opens with a shift into the second-person point of view. How did this shift impact your experience reading that chapter?

13. The tension between Margot and her daughters reaches a tipping point while she is in Galesta. How do they address their conflict? Do any parts of their mother-daughter dynamic remind you of your relationship with your own mother?

14. Discuss the idea of double lives in the novel—Liz hiding the truth about her father from Gabe, Evy creating a fake identity online, Margot hiding a major secret from her daughters, and

each of them saving face in their professional lives despite what's happening at home. Do you think we are different people in different situations?

15. How do the glimpses of Brian's perspective shape your opinion of his character?

16. How will being from Seaside shape the course of Liz and Evy's lives? How has where you're from shaped your life?

ENHANCE YOUR
BOOK CLUB

1. Do some online window shopping for vacation rentals on the Jersey Shore. See if you can find any family-run businesses that remind you of E&E Rentals.

2. Make a playlist of songs and artists mentioned in *The Shore* for your book club meeting. Are any of them nostalgic favorites of yours? What memories do you associate with them?

3. Look up and discuss the poems mentioned in the book: "One Art" by Elizabeth Bishop and "The Raincoat" by Ada Limón. How do they resonate with the themes of *The Shore*?

4. Read *The Fortnight in September* by R. C. Sherriff, a 1931 novel about a family's annual vacation in a seaside town, where they stay in a family-run rental. What parallel themes or echoes do you notice between this book and *The Shore*? What ideas about families, growing up, endings, and life in a seaside tourist town resonate over time?